I am reminded today of the futility of earthly wealth. "Your gold and silver is cankered; and the rust of them shall be a witness against you, and shall eat your flesh as it were fire. Ye have heaped treasure together for the last days." James 5:3 I pray for the souls of those who use the gift of gold to perpetuate slavery.

Prudence Willard
September 1863

Secrets of Wayfarers Inn

Family Secrets
River of Life
All that Remains
Greater than Gold
A Flame in the Night
Never the Twain Shall Meet
The Innkeepers' Conundrum
At Face Value
Moonlit Shadows
Picture This
Forget-Me-Nots
All the Inn's a Stage
Stolen Goodbyes
Red, White, and True
The Secret Ingredient
Submerged Surprises

Submerged Surprises

OCIEANNA FLEISS

Guideposts
New York

Published by Guideposts Books & Inspirational Media
110 William Street
New York, NY 10038
Guideposts.org

This is a work of fiction. Marietta, Ohio, actually exists, and some characters may be based on actual residents whose identities have been fictionalized to protect their privacy. Apart from the actual people, events, and locales that figure into the fiction narrative, all other names, characters, businesses, and events are the creation of the author's imagination or are used fictitiously.

Every attempt has been made to credit the sources of copyrighted material used in this book. If any such acknowledgment has been inadvertently omitted or miscredited, receipt of such information would be appreciated.

Cover and interior design by Müllerhaus
Cover illustration by Greg Copeland, represented by Deborah Wolfe, LTD.
Typeset by Aptara, Inc.

Printed and bound in the United States of America
10 9 8 7 6 5 4 3

Submerged Surprises

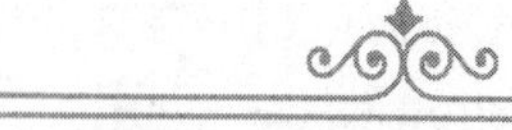

Chapter One

Camp Putnam, Marietta, Ohio
September 22, 1863

"How much farther, Mama?" Prudence Willard's little boy, Moses, asked as she walked with him toward Camp Putnam. It had been a difficult few days, and Prudence fought tears as she pondered her morning. She had held two newly orphaned children as they cried for their mother. She finally comforted them by telling the one Bible story they longed to hear—how Moses freed the Israelites. Prudence made sure to explain that only with God's help was Moses able to free them. Charles and Sarah, merely three and four years old, had lost their mother just a few days earlier. She had fled a brutal life in which her children were going to be taken from her. Even though she knew the Underground Railroad had to cease its work because of the war, she could not bear to lose her children. She had somehow found a former conductor who had led her to the Ohio River crossing, and then signaled Prudence.

Prudence had been happy to help those souls in such danger, but the mother had grown sickly. The river crossing was too much for her. How Prudence and her helpers had fought to save her. And yet, it was God's will to take her.

Now Prudence was left with two toddlers and no formal Underground Railroad. She had already spread the word that two small children, escaped and on the run, needed a family to spirit them the rest of the way. She trusted that abolitionists would help. *Father, preserve our work*, she prayed. *And find a way to the Promised Land for these little ones.* In the meantime, they stayed in the secret room, being carefully cared for by Elizabeth and herself.

These thoughts made her clasp her own Moses's hand tighter as he toddled along beside her.

"Almost there," she answered her son. In Prudence's free hand she carried a large basket of supplies for the soldiers based at Camp Putnam. Although Prudence's Quaker faith taught her to embrace peace, not war, her compassion still burned for the hardships the soldiers endured. Most were single young men. Others were slightly older with families left behind. A few had family in the camp in small cabins. The war called for all to come, regardless of personal obligations.

Prudence thanked God for the sacrifice the men made for the cause of freeing those so unjustly enslaved, and she thanked Him also for the families' sacrifices. Providing provisions was but a small gesture. She was happy to do it.

She and Moses reached the camp and strode toward the one-room schoolhouse where the camp's children as well as children from the town studied. The teacher stood outside ringing the bell, signaling local families that school was out. A rush of children scampered from the school, carrying lunch pails and releasing the energy they had been storing for the last few hours.

Prudence smiled at the children as they passed.

"Mama?" Moses glanced up at her. "I go to school?"

Prudence knelt. "Thee is still too young. And it is our tradition to train thee at home. We will see what thy papa says."

This pacified Moses well enough, and his attention turned to one of the soldiers who was hammering siding onto the outside of the school. Cynthia Knight, the teacher Prudence was going to distribute the supplies with, stood next to him. Her blond curly hair spilled from her bun in spots. She must have had a busy day with the children.

"I say hello?" Moses asked.

"Of course."

Moses ran ahead, with Prudence following. Before she got very far, a stocky man who had worked with her on the Underground Railroad sidled next to her, almost without her noticing. His face and demeanor seemed calm, but his eyes reflected urgency. She'd seen this look a thousand times working with those who wanted to help the fugitives—forced calm in the midst of danger. Something was wrong. In what seemed like a blink, he slipped a note into her hand then melted back into the busy camp.

Prudence's heart thumped in her chest. Why had he broken protocol? To even approach her in public was forbidden. There could be no connection between conductors, even now.

The note was written on thick paper, folded only in half, and fit perfectly in her palm. Discreetly, with one hand, she unfolded it and read the words.

Urgent. Fox here in henhouse tonight. All called to smoke it out.

If Prudence's heart raced before, now it dropped to her boots. *Fox* meant a spy, a southern spy. *Henhouse* was a general term meaning "among us." The hens being those they helped rescue. The word "here" seemed out of place. It must mean in Camp Putnam. A spy was in Camp Putnam who was putting those they helped at risk. She longed to know the details. How would they be exposed? Where did they get this information? When did the spy arrive? What was the plan? But like so many other things in this work, the less she knew the safer for everyone. The best she could do was to simply watch for clues and pray.

Prudence returned to following Moses's path toward the teacher and the soldier. She smiled at the kind reception he received, despite the concern now weighing on her.

Reaching them, Prudence waited silently as the soldier joked with Moses.

"Which letter of the alphabet has the most water?" The soldier removed his blue kepi hat and shook out his dusty brown hair, seeming to enjoy letting it air out, before returning the hat to his head.

Moses, suddenly shy, slid next to Prudence and held her hand.

The soldier's dark brown eyes twinkled. "Let's start saying the alphabet together, and you'll know." He squatted in front of Moses. "A..."

Moses let go of Prudence's hand and took a step toward him. "B..."

The soldier raised his eyebrows and gave Moses a significant look as together they said, "C..."

Moses's eyes grew wide, and then he clapped his hands. "Sea!" he crowed. "That's water!"

"That's right!" The man straightened and tipped his hat to Prudence. "How do you do, ma'am."

Cynthia stepped forward. "This is Corporal Austin Jensen. He's been helping with repairs to our makeshift school. I truly believe it was thrown together with the scraps they found about the camp."

"You're probably right," the corporal said. "Amazing they took any time away from training whatsoever to build it."

Cynthia nodded. "You are right. And yet, I am grateful for the school and to you for your help."

Austin Jensen's gaze rested on Cynthia's blue eyes a mite long, Prudence thought, before he spoke. "You're very welcome." He patted the plank he had nailed. "She should be secure for now. Let me know if there's anything else you need. I'll stop by when I can."

"That's very kind of you," Cynthia said.

Austin nodded toward her and Prudence again, then left.

"He seems nice," Prudence said as they watched him wander back to his duties.

Was that pink glowing on Cynthia's cheeks? "He is very nice," she said, and then her affectionate look was replaced by her usual businesslike cordiality. "Are you ready to deliver the supplies?" She glanced at the basket Prudence still held, then to a similar one next to the door of the schoolhouse.

"I am," Prudence answered as they walked to the entrance. "Shall we begin with the Millers?"

"Yes." Cynthia picked up the basket. "If you think by delivering to them and their eight children first our load will be considerably lightened, I'm in total agreement."

Prudence chuckled. "It is what I was thinking as well." She held Moses's hand, and together the three began their rounds throughout the camp.

Before they had gotten very far, Cynthia halted her steps. "I forgot something."

"Do we need to go back?" Prudence asked.

"I'm supposed to bring three *McGuffey Readers* to the Millers. They only have one primary level for all eight children."

"That will not do," Prudence said. "It is a mercy any of them have learned to read."

"Indeed."

"I shall get them for thee!" Moses took off running back to the school.

"Moses!" Prudence called after him. "Thee does not know where the *McGuffey Readers* are!" She smiled at

Cynthia. "Nor does he know what they are." She chuckled. "I had better go after him. Where are the books? I will fetch them."

"There is a stack of three on my desk."

Prudence hurried after Moses, catching up to him at the door to the school.

"I find the 'guffey, Mama." He opened the door.

Prudence took his hand. "Thee is a quick runner, young one. Slow down, now. We must respect the schoolroom."

"Yes, ma'am."

They paced the dirt floor among the wooden desks, tables, and chairs lined up to form a classroom. Prudence admired Cynthia for her orderliness. The alphabet, in uppercase, lowercase, and cursive, was written on the blackboard. A math problem in a child's handwriting was below that. And above them both, at the top of the blackboard, were the words, *"For God so loved the world, that he gave his only begotten Son, that whosoever believeth in him should not perish, but have everlasting life." St. John 3:16.* The children must have been practicing their writing using the scripture verse.

Prudence refocused her attention on getting the readers. She glanced at the desk and, just as Cynthia had said, they were there.

"I see?" Moses asked.

Prudence held out one of the readers for him to look at. "Does thee recognize this?" She pointed to the alphabet written on the first page.

"A," he said, pointing. "B..."

"Right. And here is the Lord's Prayer. Thee will learn that too someday." She closed the book. "Now, come. We must return to Cynthia."

"Look at this!" Moses had moved to the blackboard and was running his fingers behind it. "There's a hole."

"Moses." Prudence went after him. "What did I tell thee? We must respect other people's property." As she spoke, an object fell from behind the blackboard and hit the ground with a thud. Prudence picked it up. It was a wooden disc. The disc had the alphabet etched in uppercase on an outer ring and in lowercase on an inner ring. The outer ring moved in a circular motion. Her stomach clenched. She knew what this was. In the center of the middle ring was etched the letters, CSA.

"Confederate States of America," she mumbled.

This was a Confederate cipher. The kind spies used. Why was it in Cynthia Knight's schoolroom?

"So you can see"—LuAnn peered at the small audience crowded into Marietta Historical Society's wood-paneled meeting room—"Wayfarers Inn's rich Underground Railroad history serves to fascinate, illuminate, and inspire even the most modern minds." This was the last in her three-part lecture series on the history of Marietta. She'd walked through early settlements, the War for Independence with the famous visits of George Washington and Lafayette, Marietta's expansion after the war, and its abolitionist roots. She ended with the Underground Railroad history. She thought her inn's unique history would be fitting. She'd told her friends and co-owners, Tess Wallace and Janice Eastman, she was saving the best for last. They'd readily agreed.

Even now, Tess's smiling face in the audience displayed her ever-present support as she filmed the lecture on her phone. Janice was back at the inn. It was her turn to keep things running. She'd watch the video later.

"Any questions?" LuAnn scanned the room, her gaze landing on the other member of her support system, Brad Grimes. Their friendship had grown over the last year. She depended on him almost as much as she did Tess and Janice. How grateful she was for his presence in her life. In the instant she glanced at him, he turned to his phone, which apparently had vibrated. A frown spread over his face for a moment before his reassuring smile returned.

Looking around, she recognized most of the faces as locals, but one young woman sitting next to their friend Margaret Ashworth, the historical society's director, looked unfamiliar. Throughout the lecture, she'd been very attentive, especially for a young person, even taking notes. Most of the historical society folk were of an older generation.

After taking a couple of questions, LuAnn paused, waiting for others. Toward the back, a hand went up, belonging to a woman with straight brown hair who had been looking at her notes most of the lecture. She now lifted her chin, and a gleam shone from her eyes that sent a happy thrill of recognition to LuAnn's heart. "Ashley?"

The woman nodded and then smiled with a hint of mischievousness. "Miss Sherrill, I was wondering, you mentioned the Underground Railroad history of Wayfarers Inn. Are you available to discuss this in more depth?"

LuAnn tilted her head toward her former student, chuckling inwardly at her mock formality. "Yes, I'm happy to share the inn's rich history. Feel free to contact me, and I'll be happy to set something up."

"Thank you very much. I certainly will do that." Ashley smiled.

"I look forward to it." LuAnn picked up her pencil and notebook. "If there are no more questions, I'll close with this quote from the famous Underground Railroad conductor, Harriet Tubman. 'Every great dream begins with a dreamer. Always remember, you have within you the strength, the patience, and the passion to reach for the stars to change the world.' Thank you."

The crowd clapped as LuAnn moved to the side table where Margaret had displayed several books about Marietta's history as well as some travel guides—none of them hers. LuAnn sighed. She'd always wanted to write a book. It would be amazing to have her own book sitting among the others on the table. Hers would be a novel, of course. Her love for Marietta comingled for a moment with the book dream, birthing a new thought. A novel with the setting in Marietta? Her heart raced at the idea. But writing a novel was a long-ago fantasy. She brushed the thought aside.

Tess approached, but LuAnn's gaze snagged on Brad, who lingered by the door trying to catch her attention. He tilted his head apologetically and pointed toward the door. He had to go. Disappointment touched her heart, but he mimicked a phone, reassuring her that he'd call. She knew he would.

Tess waited, apparently noticing LuAnn's attention toward Brad. "Aw, he has to go?"

"Yeah. He'll call me later though," LuAnn answered with a grin.

"You could tell that from a look?" Tess asked.

"And a few hand motions." She leaned into Tess's hug. "I'm glad you made it."

"You did great. You're a natural at this stuff."

"Thanks. Once a teacher, always a teacher, I guess."

"That's right."

At that moment, Ashley orbited LuAnn and Tess, and LuAnn stepped forward. "Ashley?" She pulled her into a hug. "I can't believe you're here. Sneaky of you raising your hand at the last minute like that."

Ashley grinned. "I thought it would be fun to surprise you."

From LuAnn's memory of Ashley sitting in her history and English classes, she guessed Ashley to be in her late thirties or early forties. They had kept in touch now and then via email and social media, but she hadn't seen her in person for years. "You look amazing."

"Hi, I'm—" Tess started.

"Oh my! I forgot to introduce you." LuAnn pointed toward Tess. "This is my friend and business partner, Tess."

Tess shook Ashley's hand. "It's nice to meet you."

"What brings you to Marietta?" LuAnn continued. "I would have thought this would be the busy time of year for a Princeton history professor."

Ashley nodded. "It normally is, but I'm on a sabbatical right now."

"That's awesome," Tess said. "How long did they give you?"

"Would you believe a whole year?" she said. "I'm planning to finish my third book—among other things."

"Wow. Three books. Good for you." LuAnn smiled. "You always were my star student."

"You inspired me." Ashley tilted her head. "You really did."

Words LuAnn's teacher heart loved to hear. "Thank you for saying so." She eyed her prestigious friend. "So, what's the other thing you're throwing yourself into?"

Ashley's lips curved in an excited smile. "Apparently there's a historic site here called the Castle."

"We know about that place. It was built in the 1850s. Isn't that right?"

"That's the one. They're doing some rehabilitation of the brickwork and the outside grounds. While they're doing that"—she rubbed her palms together—"the inside is all mine."

"What do you mean?" LuAnn asked.

"The museum board hired me to go through the rooms and rewrite the historic plaques. I get to fact-check, rework the wording, and also dig up any more historic nuggets about the place. They're also having me do full profiles on the owners and even write a script for a short documentary they're going to show visitors."

All the history talk made LuAnn's pulse race. "Sounds like a lot of fun."

"A lot of work," Tess put in.

"Both," Ashley agreed. "But I'm up for it. It'll be a nice change from the classroom."

"I can understand that," LuAnn said.

"Where are you staying?" Tess asked.

LuAnn peered at her friend. "I would have noticed your name in the reservation book. Don't tell me you came to Marietta and aren't staying at our inn."

Ashley cringed. "I'm afraid I procrastinated, and when I checked, you were booked up. I figured it would give me a chance to surprise you, but I admit, I was a little disappointed. I've heard such amazing things about it."

LuAnn eyed Tess. "Do we have any openings?"

"I do think we're pretty booked up, but..." Tess's eyes twinkled. "The Johnsons in Apples and Cinnamon are checking out tomorrow instead of Thursday. So..."

"So you have an opening?" Ashley asked.

"Sounds like tomorrow we will," LuAnn answered. "Come by around noon or so. We'll get you checked in, and you and I can have lunch. Sound good?"

"Absolutely. I better head out into your gorgeous late-summer afternoon. I want to stop by the Castle before it gets too late."

After Ashley departed, Margaret stepped up. The young woman LuAnn had noticed stood next to her.

"Well," Margaret said, "I don't want to interrupt, but I wanted to introduce you to my niece. She's my great-niece, actually." Her wrinkled hand pointed toward the younger woman. "Dahlia. This is LuAnn Sherrill and Tess Wallace."

Margaret's niece tucked her wavy brown hair behind her ears as she stepped forward. "Hi." She smiled warmly. "I'm so glad to meet you. My aunt has told me all about you."

LuAnn eyed Tess questioningly. She didn't realize Margaret knew "all about them."

Dahlia seemed to perceive LuAnn's doubt, and she giggled nervously. "I'm sorry. I don't mean 'everything.' I'm just a big history nut, and she said you both own the inn. I'm so fascinated by its history." She pushed her dark-rimmed glasses up. "I admit. I'm an aspiring writer. I'd love to write a novel about your inn." She glanced at her hands. "I don't know. It's a dream, I guess. But history seems to be alive in this town."

LuAnn smiled more stiffly than she meant to. "That's... a great idea."

"You should come by sometime," Tess offered. "We can give you a tour."

"Thanks."

Thinking the conversation was winding down, LuAnn edged away, but Margaret stopped her. "I have something else to tell you." Her eyes gleamed as she focused on LuAnn, then she shifted a glace toward Tess. "You might even like this."

LuAnn grinned at Tess, acknowledging the slight. "What is it?"

"Well." Without finishing, she began a slow march toward the stairs, accompanied by Dahlia.

LuAnn and Tess followed obediently.

They reached the musty downstairs room criss-crossed with 1940s-looking metal shelves, perfectly ordered. Labeled plastic containers filled the shelves, and one sat on a small round table. Margaret grabbed her afghan from her desk chair in the corner and wrapped it around her shoulders. "It's always so chilly in this room, no matter how warm it is outside." She then returned to the table, pulled out a chair, and sat. Her gaze urged the others to join her.

As LuAnn sat down, she noticed the label on the plastic container. It said, "*Marietta Times* 1863 Sept-Oct." Old clippings about Marietta? What had Margaret found?

Margaret opened the container and removed a worn manila folder labeled "Sept. 2." Cautiously, she lifted a clipping from the file and held it up.

"Gold Coins Lost in Marietta," the headline read.

LuAnn inspected the browned paper with its black courier script. "Gold coins?" She tilted her head toward Margaret. "Someone lost gold coins here?"

Margaret nodded, so LuAnn started to read.

Sources have confirmed that while the citizenry slept in Marietta, a Confederate delivery of gold coins was routed. At printing, the coins have not yet been found...

"I may not be a history buff," Tess said, "but this is pretty cool."

"It is." LuAnn's pulse sped. "It makes me want to go on a treasure hunt." She grabbed her phone from her pocket, thinking she'd take a photo, maybe post it on the Marietta history-lover's webpage she'd recently discovered.

After LuAnn took the picture, Margaret put the clipping back into its home in the folder while LuAnn slipped her phone back in her pocket. "Can I come back and study it more carefully?" she asked. "I'm very interested."

"Of course," Margaret said. "It's getting late though."

"Four o'clock is not late, Aunt Maggie." Dahlia smiled at Margaret, who didn't seem to hear her.

LuAnn and Tess followed Margaret and Dahlia as they wandered upstairs. A wave of exhaustion hit LuAnn. She enjoyed speaking engagements like this, but she was feeling tired tonight. She took in a breath for strength, then turned to Tess.

"Let's get you home." Tess patted her shoulder. "I have a feeling Janice will have an early dinner waiting—or at least something delicious to fill our stomachs."

The thought of a delicacy made by their third business partner and friend brought a smile to LuAnn. "Nothing would be better." She grabbed her jacket, books, and lecture notes from the table where she'd left them and followed Tess out the door.

As they walked home, LuAnn posted a short note to her Marietta history-lovers group about the article Margaret had shown them and included the picture. Her friends who followed the site would love it—and possibly have information about it. If not the coins, at least more about the time period. Who knew what she could discover?

An hour later, the Inn Crowd sat in their fourth-floor kitchen, sipping their after-dinner iced tea.

"That was the perfect meal, Janice," LuAnn said. "That green goddess salad. And the beef panini. It was just delicious."

Janice folded her napkin and laid it on her plate, her eyes sparkling. "I thought it would be fitting. It's still warm, but I can feel fall in the air."

Tess nodded. "Me too. That and with school starting—Lizzie has the triplets in preschool. Can you believe it?"

Janice stood and collected the plates. "And my Larry's in first grade! Time flies by."

"All those years we were in the throes of teaching this time of year. Right, Janice?" LuAnn sighed. "Seems like forever ago."

"Yeah." Janice peered out the window. "Do you miss it?"

LuAnn wrinkled her brow. "Not really."

Janice turned back to her, laughing. "Me neither. It was so much work."

"You two." Tess shook her head.

"Do you miss teaching at the community college?"

Tess pinched her lips together. "Not really. Running the inn is much more fun."

"It truly is," LuAnn agreed.

The three finished the dishes and headed to the sofa and chairs in their common room. "Oh, by the way, how's the planning for the Taste of Marietta?" LuAnn asked. "That's this Saturday, right? I've been so preoccupied with these lectures—I'm afraid I haven't been much help."

Janice nodded. "Yeah. Winnie ordered the ingredients from Marcus today. I'm glad we're doing it. I always enjoy those events where you pay five dollars and get a sample of the different restaurants. I've tried things I never thought I would at those things." She chuckled.

"I remember," LuAnn put in. "You actually tried alligator that one time." She joined in the laughter.

"And you said it tasted like chicken," Tess added.

Janice's eyes widened. "It really did!"

"Anyway." Tess returned the conversation to the topic at hand. "We should talk about who's going to take care of the inn while that's going on."

"Sounds good."

After finishing her evening chores, LuAnn settled into her apartment. She fell asleep wondering why Brad never called.

The next morning, LuAnn glanced at her phone. Still no call from Brad. Strange. He was usually so reliable. What could be going on?

After dressing, she joined Tess and Janice in the common room, and they went down the staircase to help Winnie with the guest breakfast. The inn was full, so she knew it was all hands on deck this morning.

About midway through the café service, LuAnn's phone rang. She glanced at it. Not Brad. It was a number she didn't recognize. She stepped behind the large antique desk, which had been a bar when the bottom floor of the inn was a saloon, and answered.

"Hi, Miss Sherrill," a young woman's voice started. She sounded worried, almost frantic. "I'm sorry to bother you—"

"Who is this?" LuAnn asked.

"It's Dahlia. Oh, Miss Sherrill. I thought you would want to know—"

"Dahlia. Call me LuAnn."

"My aunt is gone."

"Margaret's gone?" LuAnn responded. "What do you mean?"

"I think…I think she was kidnapped."

Chapter Two

Kidnapped?" LuAnn said the word louder than she meant to, and Tess and Janice looked up from the tables they were bussing, their eyes filled with questions.

"I don't know." Dahlia's voice was frantic. "She went to her room last night like normal. When I woke up, she wasn't there. She usually wakes me up. We have breakfast together, and we go to the historical society. At least that's what we've been doing since I got here. Last night she said she'd see me in the morning. I assumed we'd fallen into a routine."

"And she's not at the historical society either?" LuAnn asked.

"No. I've tried calling her cell phone, but she's not answering."

"Did you call the police?"

"Yes, but they say I have to wait twenty-four hours before they'll consider her missing. Isn't that stupid? I know my aunt wouldn't just leave without telling me."

"Okay, Dahlia." LuAnn took a breath. "Listen, you sit tight. I'll be there as soon as I can, okay?" She hung up.

"Details," Janice pleaded.

"There's not much to tell. When Dahlia woke up, Margaret was gone. She's not at the historical society."

Tess shook her head. "She's a creature of habit. You can tell that from how she organizes that place. She wouldn't leave without giving precise instructions about how to carry on without her."

"Something's definitely wrong," LuAnn agreed. "Her poor niece is beside herself."

The three glanced at each other. LuAnn knew they were assessing who should accompany her to meet Dahlia. The café still had an hour to go before they stopped serving breakfast.

"I hate to leave before closing time," LuAnn finally said.

"Don't worry about it." Janice smiled. "I think I should stay and help Winnie in the kitchen. Robin can handle serving the tables. We'll be fine." She glanced at Tess.

"Should I come with you?" Tess's forehead creased.

"You know," LuAnn said, "there's so much to do here. I'll go solo this time. Maybe I'll see if Brad can meet me there."

Janice clapped. "Yes, that's it. I hate to have you go alone, but Brad will come to the rescue."

"Perfect," Tess agreed.

Twenty minutes later, LuAnn returned to the historical society. She'd left a message for Brad and half expected him to be waiting for her in the parking lot, but he wasn't.

She stepped across the driveway to the concrete steps leading to the door. A few bits of trash blown in overnight littered the steps. Margaret would have swept those away first thing. A pang grabbed LuAnn's heart. The decision-making process along with the rush of getting there had overshadowed the fact that her friend was missing. The thought of Margaret being held somewhere against her will sent a lump to her throat. Had she gotten lost? She was so sharp. It seemed impossible. She could be hurt. Had she fallen? Broken her hip? Or collapsed? LuAnn would ask Dahlia about her health. She had always thought Margaret seemed spritely, feisty even.

Entering the building, LuAnn's shoulders relaxed into the warmth contrasted with the morning's chill. The door opening must have alerted Dahlia to her presence, because she jogged up the stairs.

"I'm so glad you're here." She gave LuAnn a hug.

"Of course. I'm sorry my friends couldn't make it. Mornings are hectic at the inn." She squeezed Dahlia's arm. "How are you doing?"

Dahlia slouched. "I feel so bad. I should have been watching out for her…" She took in a breath. "My imagination is racing. Where could she be?"

"Do you think she came here this morning?" LuAnn glanced around the foyer of the building.

"I don't think so. We always came here together. I mean, I haven't been here that long, but that's what our pattern was."

"Okay." LuAnn pulled her notebook and a pen from her purse. "She spent most of her time downstairs, right? Organizing, taking notes, studying?"

Dahlia nodded. "She couldn't get enough of this stuff. You'd think she'd get bored with it after all these years, but she never has. She loves this town and its history. At least that's what she told me."

LuAnn tilted her head. "What do you mean?"

"Until I found her a week ago, we hadn't talked my whole life, so everything I know about her is just from what she's told me." Her lip quivered. "I finally found her, and now...she's lost."

LuAnn patted her shoulder. "I'm sorry. She's a special lady. When we find her, you'll have lots of time to find that out for yourself."

"Thank you. I'm so glad you're here."

They headed down the stairs to Margaret's office. It didn't feel right. It wasn't empty and cold like she expected it would be in the first traces of morning. "How long have you been here?"

"I came by earlier to see if she was here. Then I went back home, checked around town, and got back here just a few minutes before you did." She shrugged. "I looked downstairs again, thinking maybe she made it back, and I'd find her at her desk. But she wasn't here. You can see, the room looks like it always does. Nothing on the table, the desk perfectly orderly. No signs of life at all."

LuAnn moved to Margaret's 1950s-looking black chair. Scanning the desk, she noticed a tear-off calendar, "This Day in History." The date read September 19. "Today's date," she mumbled, then glanced at Dahlia. "You're sure she wasn't here this morning?"

"I don't think so. Why?"

"The calendar is on today's date. Did you tear it off?"

Dahlia shook her head. "No. I'd never touch anything on her desk. She keeps it just the way she wants it. I don't think anyone would dare mess with it."

LuAnn thought it odd that the date had been torn off. It seemed to point to Margaret being there that morning. She smiled at Dahlia and pulled out a chair from the table where they had sat last night. She was going to ask her about her history with Margaret. Why had they not kept in touch all those years? Why had she searched for her aunt?

Then she noticed something else. "Dahlia, did you move the box that Margaret had on the table last night?"

Dahlia looked at her, blinking. "No, I didn't touch it."

"Well, it's not there now, and I know when we left last night, it was still on the table." Before she could say anything more, a door opening upstairs caught their attention.

"LuAnn?"

LuAnn unleashed a breath. It was Brad's voice. "Down here," she called.

In a moment, Brad's presence filled the room. His eyes seemed distracted as he gazed at her. "I'm sorry. I just got your message."

"It's okay. I was getting a little worried..."

Brad smiled in apology. "I am sorry. I just..." He glanced at Dahlia and smiled. "And who is this?"

"Oh dear, I'm not doing very well with introductions lately." LuAnn chuckled. "This is Dahlia. Margaret's niece."

Brad reached out a hand. "I didn't know Margaret had a niece."

Dahlia nodded. "I hadn't seen her for a long time... I mean, ever. I'm not surprised she hasn't mentioned me, or my mom."

"It's nice to meet you," Brad answered, then turned toward LuAnn, who was still pondering Dahlia's words. Before she could query more deeply, Brad spoke again. "I got your message. Margaret's missing?"

LuAnn nodded.

"I'm so sorry," he said to Dahlia. "I would have come earlier but..."

LuAnn had never seen such a frazzled look on her friend's face. She ached for him, and she didn't even know what was wrong. She turned to Dahlia. "Can you excuse us a minute?"

She and Brad walked to the edge of the room. "Brad, what's going on? I don't mean to pry, but I'm starting to get worried. You're acting so—"

"I know. I'm sorry. Nothing like this has ever happened to me."

"Margaret!" A man's voice echoed down the stairs, footsteps following. "You here? There are cars out front."

LuAnn was startled away from Brad, and they both stepped back to the open space just as a tall, heavyset man in his mid-forties, she guessed, walked through the door holding a box of pastries from Jeremiah's.

"Roy," Dahlia said.

The man stepped into the room. "What're you all doing here? Where's Margaret?" He set the box down on the table. "I was going to help her go through some of these boxes. We've been working together to get things labeled and organized."

LuAnn reached out her hand. "I'm LuAnn," she said.

"Oh, I know you. You did that lecture last night. Pretty good job. I'm not from these parts, so you may be right about the history. I wouldn't know."

LuAnn wasn't sure how to take that, so she ignored his comment. "You're a friend of Margaret's?"

"You could say that." His gray eyebrows narrowed over squinty, yet kind-looking, eyes. "Why? What's going on?"

"She's missing," Dahlia answered, her voice more panicked than it had been. "She wasn't here when I came this morning—"

"She's not at home?" Roy asked.

Dahlia shook her head.

"Not like her to not let anyone know." His eyes showed concern as he looked at Dahlia.

Brad's phone vibrated. He glanced at it, then edged toward the door. "I'm sorry," he said to LuAnn. "I have to go. We'll talk later, okay?"

LuAnn's chest tightened, but she smiled. "Okay." She listened as his footsteps climbed the stairs and the door closed, then returned her focus to Margaret's disappearance. "You're a longtime friend of Margaret?" she asked Roy.

"No." Roy glanced again at Dahlia. "I've only lived here for about six months."

"And you've been helping her organize these boxes." LuAnn pointed to the table. "Last night Margaret showed us a box that held articles from the *Marietta Times* dated September to October 1863. This morning the box is gone." She swept her arm toward the shelves. "Do you know what box I'm talking about? Is it back on the shelf?"

Roy nodded slowly. "Yes, I know what box you're talking about." He went to the shelves and walked up and down the rows, running his finger along the boxes stacked on them. "That box has a blue label, which indicates it holds newspaper articles." He finished looking at the labels on all the boxes and pointed to an empty spot on the shelf. "That particular one should be right here."

"It might be a good deduction that whoever took Margaret also took the box," said LuAnn. She jotted a note to herself in her notebook. "So..." she ventured, looking up at Roy again. "How did you become friends with Margaret?"

He patted the table. "This place. I love history, and being from the Pacific Northwest, well, other than Lewis and Clark, we don't have much to do with the birth of this nation—not like here. I can't get enough of the early settlers, the Revolutionary War, the Underground Railroad." He glanced at the bins on the shelves. "Sweet Miss Margaret enjoyed sharing her knowledge with me, I think."

"Sweet Miss Margaret?" LuAnn asked.

"That's what I call her."

"So are you two...?" She raised her eyebrows.

He chuckled. "Oh no. Just friends." He picked up the pastry box and set it back down. "A sweet lady, though. Anything I can do to help find her, I will." He frowned. "She could be anywhere. Hurt or..."

Dahlia's eyes moistened.

"I'm sure she's fine." LuAnn tried to comfort them with confidence. "I need to get back to the inn and talk this over with my friends. They're good at figuring stuff out." She eyed Dahlia. "Why don't you go back to Margaret's place, in case she comes home?"

"Okay," she said, but her face looked doubtful.

"I'll call you in a bit," LuAnn said. "We'll have a plan by then, okay?" Then she glanced at Roy. "Will you stay here? She may come back. I know it's not like her to leave abruptly like this, but we don't know for sure anything is wrong. She may have gotten distracted at a store or simply had car problems and had to wait for a lift...We just don't know."

Roy nodded. "That makes good sense. I'll let you both know if I hear from her." The three of them shared contact information, and then he threw LuAnn a serious look. "Keep me updated, okay?"

"I will. I promise."

LuAnn climbed the stairs. When she stepped outside, her phone buzzed. A text from Brad had come through. She took in a breath. Not knowing what was going on with him was causing her shoulders to tense. She clicked on the text.

I'm sorry I left like that. I wanted to talk to you about this in person. I know you must be curious.

Before she could finish reading, Dahlia ran out the door, calling her name. "LuAnn! Something's wrong with Roy. He collapsed!"

Chapter Three

By the time LuAnn returned inside the building, Roy had hoisted himself to a chair, and the pastry box was open on the table.

"I'm sorry I scared you." His voice sounded weak. "A little dizzy is all. I haven't eaten breakfast. I was going to eat with Margaret, but...well...." He took a bite from a half-eaten scone. "I'm feeling much better now."

LuAnn inhaled, relieved.

"You looked pretty bad," Dahlia said as she moved toward him.

Roy's kind eyes paused on her for a moment. "I'm fine. Really."

"Okay," LuAnn said. "You're sure?"

Roy nodded.

"Then I'm going to head out. But let me know if you need anything, okay?" She peered at both of them. "I'll be in touch soon."

As she climbed the stairs for the second time, she heard footsteps behind her. She turned and saw Dahlia following her. She got to the last step and moved into the hallway, waiting for Dahlia to catch up.

Dahlia motioned to LuAnn to move away from the stairs. She kept her voice low. "I wanted to let you know. I was asking Roy again about Aunt Margaret, if he'd seen her this morning or heard from her. He acted like he was going to answer, and that's when he 'fainted.'" She used air quotes, obviously not too sure Roy was on the up-and-up.

"Do you think he was faking it because he didn't want to answer your question?" LuAnn said.

"I'm just saying it was pretty convenient, that's all." Dahlia raised her hands, palms up. "He's a pretty big guy. He wants us to believe if he misses breakfast, he faints?"

LuAnn thought about this. Roy seemed like a kind, compassionate man, but was he telling the truth about why he collapsed? Dahlia had a point—he was a pretty stocky gentleman. It was hard to imagine him falling down from lack of nourishment. Then again, if he was hypoglycemic or had diabetes, she supposed it was possible. She definitely lacked medical expertise about such things. Perhaps she'd research the topic. Another thing to talk to her friends about.

As she walked home, her mind again focused on that text from Brad. What could be so wrong? She fished out her phone again and continued reading where she'd stopped.

A customer is threatening to sue me.

Her heart dipped to her ankles. "Oh Brad," she whispered. "Oh no."

Her mind swirling with even more questions about Brad's situation, she walked through the inn's front door. Robin was wiping down the tables in the café, and her friends' voices floated from the kitchen.

"Hey," LuAnn said as she entered the kitchen.

Tess and Janice paused doing dishes and greeted her with smiles.

"You're back." Janice wiped her hands on her green Wayfarers apron.

"What did you find out?" Tess asked from the sink. "Is it true that Margaret's missing?"

LuAnn didn't know where to start. She moved up next to Janice, who was drying a skillet. Grabbing a dishrag, she half-heartedly wiped the island.

"You okay?" Janice asked.

LuAnn tilted her head. "Yeah, I am." She took in a breath, deciding what to tell them first. "Well, I got a text from Brad."

Tess turned toward them again. "What's he up to today? Did he meet you at the historical society?"

"He did, but..." LuAnn sighed. "He seemed distracted and then left quickly."

"That's not like him," Janice commented. "Is something wrong?"

LuAnn folded the dishrag and unfolded it. "He sent a text saying he's being threatened with a lawsuit."

"A lawsuit?" Tess turned full around this time. "Our Brad? Why on earth would someone sue him?"

"He didn't elaborate," LuAnn answered. "I don't know any more than that. He's been... I don't know."

"Engaging in radio silence?" Janice offered.

"Yeah. I'm sure he's just busy and preoccupied, but I'm getting a little worried."

"Of course." Janice's eyes exuded compassion. "It's a scary thing to be sued. I'm sure you want to be there for him."

"I do. But I can't keep pestering him." She tossed the dishrag in the bin. "That wouldn't be much help."

Tess rinsed off the last coffee cup and put it in the dishwasher. "I think you have to wait till he's ready to talk."

"You can pray for him while you're waiting," Janice offered. "We all will."

Sharing this burden with her friends lightened the heaviness she'd been carrying. And she knew their advice was sound. Wait and pray. So many struggles in life came down to those two things. "We have to talk about Margaret. I'm worried about her too."

"Let's sit outside." Tess glanced out the window. "I just love the turning of the leaves."

"Me too." Janice poured them each coffee in their favorite mugs, and they headed to the patio.

"It smells so good out here," LuAnn said as she brushed a few stray leaves from her chair.

"It does." Tess set her coffee down.

"So tell us." Janice frowned. "You're sure Margaret's missing?"

LuAnn glanced at her phone to check the time. "It's ten thirty. Unless there's some other explanation, I sure think she would have at least gotten in touch with someone by now."

"Yeah, one would think," Tess said. "Did you get any more information at the historical society?"

"I found a few strange things," LuAnn responded. "First, her niece, Dahlia."

"She seemed nice," Tess put in. "We met her last night."

"I didn't know Margaret had a niece," Janice said.

LuAnn tapped her pencil on her notebook. "I didn't either. I guess they haven't been in touch in years. Anyway, Dahlia said she was sure Margaret hadn't been to the historical society this morning, but she was there earlier. I'm sure of it."

"Why?" Janice asked.

"Well, for one thing, it was warm."

Tess nodded. "So someone must have turned on the heat. Margaret's always cold. I bet that's the first thing she does when she gets there."

"At least one of the first things," LuAnn said. "Also, you know that afghan she would drape over her shoulders?"

"Of course," Janice answered. "Except for the hottest summer days, she wears it all year round. She said it holds sentimental value." She stared toward the sky as if thinking. "Do you remember why it was significant?"

"I think she said her sister crocheted it when they were children," Tess answered. "It reminded Margaret of her sister."

"Yesterday, when we all left after my lecture, she hung it on the back of her chair in the basement."

"I've seen her do that too," Janice added.

"It wasn't there this morning."

"So…" Tess's eyes brightened. "She must have put it on this morning, and then—"

"I think she took it with her—wherever she is," LuAnn finished.

"That seems odd," Janice said. "If she left of her own free will, she would have hung it on the back of the chair like always. If she was forced to leave, why would the kidnapper let her take her afghan?"

"Maybe whoever took her—if someone did take her—was in too much of a hurry to have her remove the afghan," Tess suggested.

"I think the afghan being gone makes it pretty clear that she didn't leave on her own," LuAnn said.

"So that means…" Janice's shoulders drooped. "I hate to even think it, but she must have been kidnapped. Don't you think?"

"It seems that way," Tess said.

"Another strange thing happened," LuAnn continued.

Janice sighed. "What else?"

"Last night—remember, Tess?—she had left one of the archive boxes on the table."

"Yep. She showed us the newspaper clipping about the gold coins—"

"What?" Janice perked up. "What gold coins?"

"Apparently, during the Civil War, some gold coins went missing in Marietta. According to the article, they weren't found, even after the war ended," LuAnn explained.

"Wow. Are they still out there somewhere?" Janice asked.

Tess took a sip of coffee. "I think that's what Margaret was implying, although she didn't exactly say."

"I think that's what she was telling us," LuAnn agreed.

Janice's eyes widened. "That's so cool. A treasure hunt."

LuAnn exhaled. "I was really excited too. I'm afraid I posted about it on my history-lovers' web page." She set her pen and notebook on her lap. "I wonder if whoever kidnapped Margaret and took the box saw my post."

"You think so?" Tess leaned in. "I suppose that could be."

"It would make sense, wouldn't it?" Janice ventured. "They saw your post, got it in their head to find the coins, went to the historical society, found the box, and..."

"But why kidnap Margaret?" LuAnn asked. "What good would that do? She would have happily given them any information they asked for."

"Right," Tess said, then all three sat quietly.

"It's a mystery," Janice finally said.

"One that we simply must solve." LuAnn wrote *Figure out motive* in her notebook.

"So, what do we do next?" Janice asked.

"I need to call Dahlia and Roy," LuAnn said.

Tess's forehead creased. "Roy?"

"I forgot to tell you about him. He's Margaret's new friend. He's been volunteering at the historical society, and he seems to really care about her. He's almost as worried as Dahlia."

"The more people who care about you the better, I suppose," Janice said.

"Yeah," LuAnn agreed. "He seems like a very nice man. Smart too. Interested in history."

The warm autumn breeze moved a strand of hair into LuAnn's eyes, and she brushed it aside. "I am concerned about one thing though. He collapsed, apparently. I had left, and Dahlia came running after me, saying he had passed out when she asked him if he'd seen Margaret this morning. She thought that was suspicious. He said he was dizzy because he hadn't gotten enough to eat. He's a pretty stocky guy. Does that happen?"

"I think it could..." Tess ventured. "But I'm not sure."

"I'll stop by Stuart's clinic and ask him sometime this afternoon," LuAnn said. "I'm curious."

"Good plan," Janice agreed. "He'll be able to help. Tell him to call his ma once in a while, will you?" She sighed. "So you'll call Dahlia and this Roy. Then...?"

"I have lunch with Ashley at noon," LuAnn said. "She said she's doing work on Marietta's history. Maybe she knows something about the coins."

"Sounds like we have a plan to get started," Tess said. "Hopefully we'll find Margaret soon." She shifted in her chair. "We should get back inside."

As the three women stood, Taylor came out. "Someone's here to check in."

LuAnn glanced at her friends, then to her watch. "It's too early for it to be Ashley."

They grabbed their mugs and walked inside. Standing at the desk was Dahlia, a notebook in one hand and a suitcase in the other.

The three women approached her.

"Dahlia." LuAnn smiled. "What are you doing here?"

Dahlia's eyebrows arched. "I'm sorry. I got a little creeped out at my aunt's place. Without her there, it feels, I don't know, wrong." She shuddered. "Besides that, what if the kidnapper comes back?"

Janice stepped forward. "I'm Janice. You must be Margaret's niece. I'm so sorry."

Dahlia's lip quivered. "Thanks. I was hoping maybe I could stay here."

LuAnn glanced at her friends, whose faces communicated what she already knew. They didn't have any free rooms. "Dahlia, I'm so sorry. We're all booked up." She sighed. "I wish…"

"Lu." Janice nodded, indicating she wanted a word.

LuAnn glanced at Dahlia. "Just a minute. Okay?"

LuAnn, Tess, and Janice stepped back a few feet.

"I feel for her," Janice whispered.

"I do too," Tess said. "But…"

LuAnn knew what Janice was thinking. "Should we let her stay on our couch?"

"If we knew her better, I would say yes, of course," Tess said. "But, I hate to say it, we don't know anything about her. She's been estranged from Margaret for a long time. They just got back in touch a week ago, wasn't it?"

"I understand what you're saying." LuAnn rubbed her arms. "We should be careful."

Janice frowned. "But she's Margaret's niece. She's a scared young woman. Shouldn't we help our friend's niece if we have a chance? Wouldn't we want someone to do the same for us?"

Tess looked at LuAnn. "You've talked to Dahlia more than any of us. What's your take on her?"

"I haven't had enough time to make a judgment call, but she seems nice. I share your concern about the estrangement she and Margaret had for so long, and to be honest, my intuition says we should be careful until we know more about that."

"So..." Janice said.

"I think we should let her stay." LuAnn smiled. "Like Janice said, Margaret's our friend. We have to help her out in any way we can."

Tess took in a breath and nodded. "Okay. I'll trust your judgment. You know I want to help, I just—"

"Someone has to voice concerns." Janice grinned.

"That would be me." Tess rolled her eyes.

They moved back to Dahlia.

"Come on." LuAnn picked up her bag. "I'll show you where you can stay. It's not the best..."

"I thought you were booked." Dahlia adjusted her backpack.

"We are," LuAnn said. As she led Dahlia up the stairs, her two friends went back to their chores. "We'd like to extend an offer for you stay with us, as our guest."

A grateful smile spread over Dahlia's face. "Thank you."

Reaching the fourth floor and their common living room, LuAnn set Dahlia's bag down next to the sofa. "I'm afraid you'll be sleeping in here." She patted the sofa. "It's actually pretty comfy."

Dahlia plopped down on it. "It feels great. This is so kind of you. Thank you."

LuAnn sat next to her. "No problem. We love Margaret." LuAnn thought she noticed a shadow cross Dahlia's face when she said Margaret's name. She must be worried about her aunt.

"I do too," Dahlia said after a pause. "I mean, I don't know her very well, to be honest. I was just getting to know her, and now..."

"I'm sure she'll be okay."

"I hope so. I had more I wanted to talk to her about."

"Oh?"

Dahlia dug in her backpack and removed a thick spiral-bound notebook with clouds on the cover. "I have lots of notes about the town of Marietta. I want my book to be for teens. Maybe have some time travel as well. Wouldn't that be cool? Someone from the Civil War shows up at the inn?"

LuAnn actually appreciated the idea, not that it was something she would write. She had her own ideas. "I like it."

Dahlia grinned. "That's so awesome coming from you. My aunt told me you were an English teacher. I really love to write, but I don't know if I'm any good at it." She held her notebook to her chest. "You don't think you could help me with my book, do you?"

LuAnn wasn't sure what Dahlia was asking, exactly. "What do you have in mind?"

Dahlia twirled her pen between her fingers. "I could show you what I have, and you could give me a few suggestions. Something like that. I won't take much of your time."

Sort of like teaching English again, LuAnn thought. She'd left that world behind her, but she still loved writing and literature. "Well...sure," she finally said. "It might be fun."

"Oh, thank you!" Dahlia opened her notebook.

LuAnn gave her a gracious smile. "I can't right now though—"

Dahlia quickly closed her notebook. "Of course, uh..."

"Maybe Friday morning, say ten fifteen?"

"Perfect."

LuAnn stood. "In the meantime, make yourself at home here, okay?"

"I will."

As LuAnn grabbed her purse and jacket from her room and headed downstairs, she received a text from Ashley. *Running late. Could we meet at the Castle? I'll treat lunch.*

Sure, LuAnn wrote back then continued down the stairs, shoving her arms into the sleeves of her jacket. As she put her hands in her jacket's big pockets, she felt a thin, rectangular object. "What is this?" she mumbled.

Janice was at the front desk. "What is what?" she asked.

LuAnn eyed the brown, aged object. "A book?"

"It certainly looks old," Tess said as she walked toward them, coming into the lobby.

LuAnn ran her hands over the plain, coarse hardback. No title showed on the outside, so she opened it. "Oh my!"

"What is it?" Janice asked.

"A *McGuffey Reader* from 1859," LuAnn answered. "How did that get in my pocket?"

September 22, 1863

A sick ache formed in Prudence's stomach. Could Cynthia be the spy? It was a perfect cover. Who would suspect an upstanding schoolteacher? Prudence put the cipher in her pocket,. placed the *McGuffy Readers* in the basket, and took Moses's hand.

What would she do? Should she simply confront Cynthia? Ask her about it? That seemed dangerous. If she was the spy, how would she react? If not, would it make Prudence look suspicious? Would her role in the Underground Railroad be compromised somehow? These questions swirled through her mind as she walked toward the Millers' dwelling.

"You found them," Cynthia said as Prudence and Moses reached her waiting outside the Millers'. "I thought I'd wait for you. I didn't want to steal all the fun."

Moses ran off to play with the Miller children. Prudence's arm was aching from carrying the large basket. As she set it down, the items inside settled, causing a *McGuffey Reader* to spill out onto the ground. When she bent over to pick it up, the cipher fell out of her pocket and landed on the ground. She quickly picked it up, but it was too late. Cynthia had seen it. Her eyes sharpened for a second before she resumed a relaxed look.

"Oh," she said with a smile. "You found that. Isn't it interesting?" She pointed to the letters. "We use it to practice spelling." She reached for it, but Prudence held on to it.

Prudence's pulse galloped. She looked around. Thankfully a regiment of soldiers marched in formation not ten feet away. Another small group stood outside the mess hall that was next door to the Millers'. And Prudence could hear Mr. Miller's voice inside the house. If she confronted Cynthia about being a spy, she would not be able to do anything to hurt Prudence or Moses, nor could she run away. All Prudence would have to do was shout, "Spy!" and the whole camp would converge on them.

"I know what this is," Prudence said in her quietest voice—a voice she had used often when conducting her secret work. "Thee had better explain this." She held up the cipher. "Or I will turn thee over right now."

Chapter Four

It does look old," Tess commented.

"Yeah." LuAnn gingerly fingered the pages. "It seems fragile." She lifted it to her nose. "Smells old."

"You are such a bibliophile," Tess said. "Do you always smell your books?"

LuAnn chuckled. "Of course I do. Don't you? How else do you know if it's good?" She grinned. "That and the smoothness of the pages."

Janice gently took it from LuAnn's hands and sniffed it herself. "It does smell old."

"See, I told you." LuAnn continued to eye the book as Tess took a turn smelling it.

Tess turned it over and looked at the back. "Where did it come from?"

LuAnn reached her hand into her pocket, hoping to find a clue that would show how it got there—but nothing else was there. "It was in my jacket pocket." A chill came over her.

"Your pocket?" Janice asked. "How did it get there?"

"Someone must have put it there at some point," LuAnn pondered.

"You didn't notice till this morning?" Tess asked.

"No, but I don't always look in my pockets. Plus, it was warm yesterday afternoon, so I didn't wear my coat home. I just carried it. With the other books I was carrying, I wouldn't have noticed the extra weight in the pocket."

"Hmm." Tess leaned on the desk. "So you did wear this coat to the lecture last night?"

"I did."

"So someone from there knew it was yours and put this in the pocket." Janice finished Tess's thought.

LuAnn glanced at her phone as Tess attempted to hand the book back to her, but she pressed it back. "Will you put it in the safe? I have to go if I'm going to stop at Stuart's on the way to meet Ashley."

"I thought she was coming here," Janice said.

"Change of plans. I'm meeting her at the Castle."

"Will she still be staying in Apples and Cinnamon?"

"As far as I know." LuAnn let out a breath as the thoughts that had been hovering near the surface of her mind pushed through once again. "I'm so worried about Margaret. I'm hoping Ashley will be able to shed light on those gold coins—even if it's a long shot."

"But worth a try," Tess said. "I'll put this in the safe." She eyed LuAnn. "We need to figure out why someone wanted you to have this when you get back."

"Definitely," Janice agreed.

LuAnn pulled into Marietta Family Practice feeling grateful that Stuart had a cancellation and was able to talk to her. Doctors were so busy these days. She supposed everyone was.

After being instructed by the receptionist, LuAnn followed the hallway to Stuart's office and knocked.

"Come in."

LuAnn opened the door and entered his clean and organized office. A picture of him with his sister Stacey, her son Larry, and Janice at the park hung on the wall. Also, a framed picture of his father sat on his desk. Stuart was on the phone, and he smiled and pointed to a chair in front of his desk. LuAnn settled into it and waited as he finished.

"Hi," Stuart said as he hung up. "I'm sorry about that. Ma texted that you were coming. What can I do for you?"

LuAnn leaned forward. "It may seem like a strange question, but I'm just wondering what would cause someone to pass out, suddenly. I googled it, but it's way too broad a subject to get any definitive answers."

He tilted his head. "There's vasovagal. Did the person—was it you?"

LuAnn shook her head.

"Did they see blood or a needle? Sometimes that will do it. It's called vasovagal syncope."

"I don't think he did. He says it was because he didn't eat breakfast. Is that possible? He's not a small man."

"His weight wouldn't make a difference if his blood sugar was low. So you're saying he actually passed out, not just got dizzy."

"I wasn't there, but I was told he was unconscious."

Stuart's eyes widened. "For how long?"

"Not very. By the time I arrived—after about a minute, if that—he had gotten himself back up on the chair."

"I see. Even for someone with hypoglycemia, just missing breakfast wouldn't normally cause a loss of consciousness. A person with diabetes who took too much insulin may pass out, but that's very serious, and they wouldn't just snap out of it, like you describe."

"What are some other reasons someone might pass out?" LuAnn was feeling more confused than she had before she got here.

"There are many reasons. Generally, the brain isn't getting enough oxygen. Other than hypoglycemia, it could be an underlying illness—heart disease, some types of cancer, anemia. I'm afraid I'm not much help. I'd need to examine the person, check his medical history." He picked up his pen.

"Thank you so much, Stuart." LuAnn stood.

"I'm sorry I wasn't more help." He stood also.

"No, you were. I have some things to think about now."

Maybe Roy had hypoglycemia, LuAnn thought as she walked to her car. But then, Stuart seemed skeptical that that alone would cause him to completely pass out. She'd have to talk to Roy again and see if she could get a clearer explanation.

Stuart's office was in a cluster of medical buildings, and across the street from where LuAnn stood, she spied Roy striding down the sidewalk. She couldn't see where he had come from.

"Roy!" she called.

He turned his head to find who called his name. Seeing LuAnn, he offered a welcoming smile, and she traipsed across the street. Once she reached him, she wasn't quite sure what to say.

"Hi," she said.

Roy cocked his head, his kind eyes tinged with a touch of confusion. "Hello, LuAnn. Did you find Margaret?"

Of course he'd assume that's what she wanted to talk about. "Oh, I'm sorry, no. And the police can't do anything until she's been missing for twenty-four hours."

"They should help find her anyway. Poor woman." For a moment it seemed as if his eyes glazed over, then he inhaled and returned his gaze toward LuAnn.

"I agree," LuAnn said. "So, I was just... I was wondering if you're okay. I was worried about your fainting episode this morning."

"That's so thoughtful of you." He glanced at his watch.

LuAnn also checked the time. She still had a few minutes before she had to meet Ashley.

"It's nice of you to worry about me, but you really don't need to." A gleam came over his face. "I'll be just fine."

The tone in his voice stirred compassion in LuAnn's heart. Something lingered beneath the surface of this man, but she wasn't sure what it was. "And you're sure you're okay?"

He eyed the ground. "I've got some things to take care of." He'd changed the subject, LuAnn thought, from physical ailments to something deeper. "I'm not afraid to admit I carry regrets." He shook his head. "They camp out on your shoulders, at times sojourning for so long, a person might not realize they're there, until..." He paused. "Anyway, that's why, if at all possible, a person oughta make things right." He sent her a crooked grin. "True?"

LuAnn nodded. "True."

His words had sent her mind on an unexpected journey. She wanted to ask more specifically about why he fainted. Was it really because he hadn't eaten breakfast? It didn't seem so, but he also didn't seem like the kind of man who would lie. Suddenly she didn't feel comfortable prying.

He glanced at his watch again. "I'm sorry. I've got to be going."

"Okay." LuAnn smiled. "Thanks for chatting. You've given me a lot to think about."

"I have?" He shrugged. "Well, if my ramblings meant something to you, I'm glad to hear it." He eyed her. "Please let me know if I can do anything to help find Margaret."

"Of course," LuAnn said.

He walked away, and as LuAnn paced to her car, she decided it was better she not press him about his health. For one thing, it was none of her business, but also, if he was a suspect in Margaret's kidnapping, she didn't want to alert him to her suspicion. Sometimes it was best to let the truth come out on its own. It always did, one way or another.

After leaving Roy and returning to her car, LuAnn drove down Fourth Street and parallel parked next to the Castle Museum. She relished the old building, which rose above the other structures on the bordering streets with its red bricks and high tower. She assumed a railroad mogul or high financier built it sometime in Marietta's history, but she'd never taken the tour. Even though she was the resident, Ashley would be the one to fill her in on this piece of Marietta history. How exciting to learn a new history nugget.

She hopped out of her car and walked along the wrought iron fence toward the brick path that led to the front door. Scaffolding hung all around the building, and tarps covered the windows. As she approached the pathway, she spotted Ashley sitting on a bench on the side of the walkway. When she spied LuAnn, she smiled and stood.

"Hey there," LuAnn said as they hugged.

"It's so good to see you." Was that a tremor in Ashley's voice? LuAnn didn't realize her friend had missed her so much.

Ashley seemed to shake off the burst of emotion. "So, for lunch I was thinking of a picnic." She glanced at the bright blue sky. "It's so nice out. I hate to be stuck inside."

"Eating outside sounds wonderful." LuAnn smiled. "And you'll get to see more of Marietta. Do you have any ideas what you'd like?"

"Actually." Ashley raised her eyebrows. "I noticed a park down by the river that looks lovely. So, I packed a picnic—well, that cute coffee shop, Jeremiah's, actually packed it for us."

"Riverfront Park is a perfect spot," LuAnn said. "And so is Jeremiah's. You are brilliant." She grinned.

Ashley returned the grin as they strolled down the sidewalk. "I liked your lecture last night. And such an organized historical society."

"About that," LuAnn started. "I'm afraid I have some horrible news."

Ashley frowned. "I can't imagine anything horrible happening in this lovely town. What is it?"

"Margaret, the curator from the historical society—" LuAnn's heart sank at the thought of what she was going to say. "Sh—she's disappeared."

"What do you mean, disappeared?" Ashley paused and eyed LuAnn.

"Her niece woke up this morning and couldn't find her anywhere. It's just terrible."

Ashley gasped. "Oh no. Poor woman. Are you sure she didn't take a last-minute trip out of town or something? I mean, she was there last night."

"She's a creature of habit. She doesn't do things on impulse." LuAnn smiled sadly at the thought of Margaret being spontaneous. "She also loves that historical society. She'd never leave it for any amount of time without making firm arrangements for it to be taken care of." They started walking again.

"I see."

They strode in silence a moment, Ashley seeming to be taking it in.

"We think it may have been a kidnapping," LuAnn finally said.

"What? Why do you think so?"

"A few things seemed out of place." They hung a left onto the street that headed down to Riverfront Park.

"Like what?"

"Well, we know she was at the historical society yesterday morning because the daily calendar showed yesterday's date, plus the heat had been turned on, and..." LuAnn paused as they crossed the street to the park and looked around, figuring out where to settle.

Finding a picnic table overlooking the river, they sat down. An old steamboat waited in the river for its next tour group to settle in, and kayakers floated along the peaceful river. Late summer into early autumn seemed like a perfect time to enjoy the river.

A man with a scruffy beard and wearing a white, unkempt uniform plodded toward them.

"You ladies want to take a tour of the river? Couldn't ask for better weather, and there won't be too many more chances this season."

LuAnn remembered seeing this man before. Tobias? Terrence? "Not today, thanks."

He shook his head. "You sure? For you lovely ladies, I'll only charge fifteen dollars."

"For us, huh?" She pointed to a sign next to the dock that said, TOURS $15.

The man grinned. "Well, it's worth every penny. You'll never get a better tour guide than old Thaddeus—that's me. I've lived on the river my whole life. I can tell you secrets you won't hear anywhere else."

LuAnn tilted her head. "Do you mean tall tales?"

"Oh no. Not a one. Everything I say is true." He grabbed her gaze. "It really is."

LuAnn wasn't sure whether to believe him or not. "I'm afraid we can't make it today. Another time though."

He took a step back and nodded. "I hope to see you again then." And off he went.

"You meet all sorts here in Marietta," LuAnn said as she watched him walk to another group of picnickers.

"I love it." Ashley laid a yellow tablecloth over the picnic table. "I can see why you and your friends settled here. I'm already finding it to be a special place."

LuAnn thought of all the adventures she, Tess, and Janice had encountered here. "It is. We love living here."

Ashley opened the Jeremiah's bag she'd been carrying and retrieved their lunches. "The waitress said the chicken salad sandwich is their most popular, so I went with that." She handed the wrapped sandwich to LuAnn.

"Perfect," LuAnn said. "My favorite." After they started eating, she re-opened the subject of Margaret's disappearance. "I was hoping you might have some insight that can help us, since you've been studying our fine town."

"I'll try."

"Last night, Margaret showed me a newspaper clipping describing a sack of gold coins lost in Marietta during the Civil War. They were never found, and she thinks they may still be here."

"Wow. Still here? This town has everything." Ashley swallowed a sip of her soda. "But what does this have to do with Margaret's disappearance?"

"I'm afraid I posted about it last night on the Marietta history lovers' online group I belong to. This morning both Margaret and the box with the article were missing from the museum. We think someone might be after the coins."

"You're wondering if I know anything about the coins?"

"I know it's a long shot."

Ashley frowned. "I'm really sorry, but the only thing I've researched so far has to do with the Castle. I didn't find anything about lost coins."

LuAnn sighed. "I thought I'd try."

"Yeah. I understand you want to find your friend. When someone you love is hurting, you'll do almost anything for them, right?"

LuAnn nodded as she took a bite of her sandwich. After swallowing, she continued. "That reminds me, I haven't asked about you. How do Paul and Dustin feel about you spending the fall semester here?"

Ashley brushed some crumbs off the table. "They're good, actually. Paul is teaching."

"He still teaches at Princeton with you?"

"He does. And Dustin is spending the fall semester studying sea life in the Florida Keys. It's a special program for high school seniors."

"That's so awesome. I can't believe he's a senior in high school."

"He's seventeen now."

"Wow."

The women finished their sandwiches and chips. When Ashley reached across the table to gather the trash, she tipped over her big duffel bag, and a book slid out.

"Oh." LuAnn grasped it before it tumbled to the ground. "What are you reading?" She looked at the cover, then opened the book and turned some pages. "Historical submarines. That's pretty neat."

Ashley reached for the book. "Yeah, it's interesting."

LuAnn turned another page. "Oh, I've heard of the *Turtle*. Sure, it was basically a wood-plank ball covered with steel plates and hand-powered propellers and gears—but still, for its time it was amazing."

"It was. I'm sorry. I should probably be heading back to work." With an apologetic grin, Ashley grasped the book. "I really have to go."

LuAnn closed it and handed it to her. "I'm sorry. I get a little carried away when it comes to history."

"I remember." Ashley grinned, then put the book back in her bag and stood. "I loved that about you. You made history fun. It's one reason why I went into it myself."

"Aw, that's sweet. I'm glad my enthusiasm did some good." LuAnn stood up. "I can't help but get excited about the stories of people who came before."

The two began walking back to the Castle.

"I totally get that."

"I'm sure glad to reconnect with you," LuAnn said as they reached the Castle.

"Me too." Ashley smiled. "And in person, not just over email."

"That's right." LuAnn pointed to where her car was parked. "I'm over here."

"My car's over there too. I need to grab something from it. I'll walk with you."

Getting to where she had parallel parked, LuAnn noticed no other cars on the street. She glanced at Ashley, who was turning all around with a confused look on her face.

"Ashley? I thought you said you were parked here."

"I'm pretty sure I was." Ashley gazed up and down the street, then walked toward the corner. "Maybe I parked over here."

LuAnn trotted to keep up with her. "Do you see it?"

"No." Ashley paced back to LuAnn. "This is so strange."

"Your car was stolen?"

"I think so. Wait! There it is!" Ashley yelled as a light blue Honda Accord sped down the street going east. "That's my car! Stop!"

Chapter Five

I can't believe that just happened." LuAnn gasped to catch her breath. "Did you see the driver?"

Ashley furrowed her brow. "Not really. Just a head. The sun cast him in shadows—or her, I guess."

"I caught a glimpse. It seemed to be a man. I think he was bald or balding. That's all I could see. You're right about the shadows."

"Not much to go on." Ashley shook her head.

"He stole your car right in front of our eyes in broad daylight," LuAnn said. "That took guts."

"Yeah." Ashley's lip trembled. "Why do things keep going wrong?"

LuAnn touched her arm. "What do you mean?"

Ashley bit her lip, seeming to force it to stop trembling. "Oh, I don't know. My...research has been difficult, and they're asking to see more progress. They're rushing to get the renovations on the exterior done before winter, and that's taking longer than they wanted, so I guess they're just pressuring me too," she said, her voice weak. "I'm sorry. It's just been a bit overwhelming."

"I understand. Renovations make everyone crazy." LuAnn smiled, hoping to lighten the moment. "If there's anything I can do to help..."

Ashley nodded. “I’ll let you know.”

They started walking back to LuAnn’s car.

“We should call the police,” LuAnn said. “I can text Officer Randy Lewis, if you like. We know him. He’s a good man.”

Ashley shook her head. “I’ll call. I have the information they’ll need.”

“I understand.” LuAnn dug in her purse for her keys. “If you need to borrow my car, let me know, okay?”

“Thank you,” Ashley said as they got to LuAnn’s car. “At least a lot of places in Marietta are within walking distance.”

“Yes. So, the inn is right across the river. A short walk. Will you be checking in today?”

“Oh, yes. I almost forgot about that.” She rubbed her shoulder. “I’ll come by later, okay?”

“Sure. Any time is fine. Apples and Cinnamon is ready for you.”

LuAnn gave her a hug, and the two parted.

Marcus, Winnie’s grandson who delivered their grocery orders, was passing through the inn’s back parking lot as LuAnn arrived. “See ya, LuAnn,” he said.

“See ya.” As LuAnn entered the inn, the fragrance of Winnie’s soup teased her senses. If she hadn’t just eaten a scrumptious sandwich from Jeremiah’s, she probably would have helped herself to a cup. Right now, she wanted to connect with Tess and Janice. She had some things to sort through with them.

Not finding them in the kitchen, she peeked into the office to find Tess sitting at the computer, working on the books.

"Hey," LuAnn said.

"You're back." Tess swiveled the chair toward her. "How'd it go?"

"It went okay." She glanced at the safe. She hadn't had a chance to look at that *McGuffey Reader* yet. She opened the safe door and retrieved the book. Maybe she and her friends could study it together and try to figure out why someone put it in her coat pocket. But first she wanted to tell them what happened on her outing this morning. "Where's Janice?"

"Upstairs, I think—"

"I'm here," Janice called from the hallway.

"Good." LuAnn set the book on the desk. "If you both have a minute, let's talk."

"Sounds good." Tess turned off the computer. "And I'm glad you got that book out. I've been curious to dig into it."

"Me too," Janice agreed as she moved into the office and closed the door. "What did you find out from Stuart? Could Roy have passed out from lack of breakfast?"

LuAnn shrugged. "Stuart said it could have happened, but even if he has hypoglycemia, passing out after missing one meal is unlikely."

"That's what we thought," Tess said. "So why would he mislead you?"

"I don't know, but he seems like a genuine guy. He may have his own reasons."

Janice furrowed her brow. "Yeah, not everything has to point to nefarious motives."

"I feel like we're not any closer to figuring this out." Tess's shoulders slumped.

"Me too," Janice agreed.

"And something else strange happened. Ashley's car was stolen. Practically right in front of us."

"You're serious?" Janice asked.

"I am. Isn't it terrible?"

"Where were you?" Tess asked.

"Right in front of the Castle," LuAnn answered. "When we got back from our lunch, her car was gone. Then we saw someone driving it down the street. Neither of us got a good look at the driver, but he seemed to be a bald man."

"Did you call Randy Lewis?" Tess asked.

LuAnn shook her head. "Ashley said she would call. She was pretty shaken."

"I can imagine," Janice said.

"I told her she could use my car if she needed it."

"That's a good idea," Tess agreed.

LuAnn took in a breath, then picked up the *McGuffey Reader* from the desktop. "So, did you two come up with any ideas as to why someone put this in my pocket?"

Tess glanced at Janice, who was shaking her head. "Nope."

LuAnn put on her glasses and opened to the title page. "*McGuffey's First Eclectic Reader.*" She glanced up. "So this is for kids in kindergarten or first grade." She turned the page, and together they looked at the Table of Contents. The next page had the alphabet listed in two vertical columns with both the capitals and the lowercase letters. She almost turned past that when something on the page caught her eye. "Do you see that?"

Tess adjusted her glasses. "There are marks next to some of the letters."

"Those little black marks?" Janice leaned in. "I see them."

LuAnn opened her notebook and took the pen from its place in the spine. "What letters have the mark?"

Tess ran her finger along the page. "*A, E, F, M,* and *R*."

Janice chuckled. "I thought this was going to be a clue, but that doesn't mean anything."

"Hold on." LuAnn's English teacher skills switched on. "Were the marks all in the capital letters column?"

"No," Tess answered.

"Read the capitals."

"*A, F,* and *M*," Tess said.

"Now the lowercase."

"*E* and *r*," Tess read. "Does this make sense to you?"

"What words are usually capitalized?" LuAnn asked.

Janice jumped in. "Proper nouns."

"Exactly."

"Or to begin a sentence," Tess added.

"Right." LuAnn tapped her pencil on the table. "What were the lowercase letters again?"

"*E* and *r*."

"So, let's go through and try the capital letters with the lowercase and see if anything makes sense," LuAnn suggested.

"*A-e-r*," Janice tried. "'Are' . . . oh! That's a word."

"Yep." LuAnn wrote *are* in her notebook. "Keep going."

"*F-e-r*...no." Tess gave it a try. "*F-r-e.* That doesn't work either."

LuAnn glanced at the page. "Wait a minute. There are two marks next to the lowercase *e*." Her pulse increased as she wrote, *Free* in her notebook.

Janice swallowed a breath. "It spells 'free'? You're so smart, Lu."

"But what about the *M*?" Tess asked.

LuAnn studied the letters in the reader, then returned her gaze to her notebook. Her heart really raced as an idea hit her. "What if I do this?" She wrote, *MA*.

They stared blankly, questioning.

"I don't get it," Janice admitted.

"Margaret..."

Tess perked up. "Ashworth!"

Janice clapped. "'*Free MA*' means *Free Margaret Ashworth*!" Then she sobered. "We have to let the police know about this right away."

"I'll call them right now," Tess said. She took her cell phone out of her apron pocket, and the other two listened as she spoke to someone at the station. When she hung up, she turned to them. "That was an Officer Bergen. He said Margaret's not a missing person yet, so there is no case. He also said he didn't think our finding what he called 'smudges' in an old book was going to help them at all."

"I guess that means we just keep looking on our own," LuAnn said.

Before they could talk more, the front door jingled. "I'll get it," LuAnn said as she closed the book.

"This is so incredible." Janice opened the safe.

LuAnn handed the book to her. "We should talk about this more. We haven't even searched the whole book."

"There could be more clues to her whereabouts," Tess agreed.

With her thoughts swirling, LuAnn left the office and approached the front desk where a man stood waiting. He looked to be athletic, maybe thirty.

LuAnn greeted him with a smile. "Can I help you?"

"I made a reservation this morning," he said. "Seth Jensen."

"I don't think we..." She opened the book. Seth Jensen was listed as having Apples and Cinnamon reserved. Above his name, Ashley's reservation was crossed out. Strange. Why would Ashley cancel?

LuAnn pointed to his name in the book. "Here you are. Your room is ready."

"Sounds good." Seth's crooked smile rose over his thin brown beard.

"What brings you to Marietta?" LuAnn asked.

"I've always wanted to visit this place. My grandparents' grandparents—or something like that—lived here. I want to visit their graves. I think they're in a place called the Mounds?"

"The Mound Cemetery?" LuAnn asked. "It's not far from here."

"Cool. I'd love to find out more about their lives during the Civil War. My grandmother told me they were involved somehow—but you never know if she's telling the truth."

"Does she get a little confused at times?"

"Nah, she just likes to embellish stories, trying to make them more exciting." He chuckled, and LuAnn could tell he enjoyed his grandmother's stories. "It's hard to know what in our family's history is true. I spent my whole life thinking we were Irish. When I finally looked it up, I found out we're Scottish." He shook his head.

LuAnn chuckled.

"Anyway, when the opportunity came for me to head over here for a few days, I took it."

"Opportunity?"

He shifted his weight. "Just an unexpected few days off work."

"That's always fun." LuAnn ran his credit card. "And if you want to learn about your family's history in Marietta, there's an amazing historical society here."

"Thanks. That'll be a big help."

LuAnn handed his credit card back along with his room key and a flyer for the Taste of Marietta. "It's a fun event. You'd be surprised how many great restaurants we have here that offer low-price samples at this event."

"I like food." He chuckled again. "I hope they use biodegradable containers. Outdoor festivals are notorious for the trash they leave. And if it gets into the river, that's just bad for the wildlife down there—bad for all of us, really."

LuAnn agreed. "Marietta's city council is very sensitive to the health of our two rivers. All the restaurants are encouraged to avoid plastic and Styrofoam. And there's a pretty extensive volunteer crew that will help clean up the event grounds during and after."

Seth smiled. "I like hearing that." He picked up his backpack.

"I'll show you to your room." LuAnn came around the desk and met him at the bottom of the stairs.

After taking Seth to his room, LuAnn checked on Dahlia. She sat on the couch in the ladies' common room with her laptop open. Tom was sprawled against the warmth of her leg. LuAnn wondered how many times Dahlia had to shoo their resident cat off the keyboard before he finally settled down. On the coffee table sat an empty mug and bowl and a plate with crumbs on it—probably from a special lunch made by Winnie.

"Have you been up here all day?" LuAnn asked, hoping her new friend wasn't growing deeply depressed over her missing aunt.

"Oh, hi," Dahlia said, startled, apparently not having noticed LuAnn's entrance. As she set her laptop aside to Tom's protests, she heaved a breath, as if the weight of the day had gotten to her. She glanced at the dishes on the table. "After I went out for a while, I came back and fell asleep. When I woke up, the food was here." She smiled as Tom resituated himself. "So kind."

A warm rush filled LuAnn's chest. "We are blessed to have Winnie—she won't let you go hungry while you're here. I'm sure she's the one who left the mysterious lunch. She's always thinking about how to make our guests feel welcome. Her main love language is food."

Dahlia grinned. "Her peanut soup and homemade rolls sure spoke welcome to me." She pinched her lips and slowly shook her head. "Best ever."

LuAnn nodded. "I thought that's what I smelled when I came in. She's spoiled me for others."

"I can imagine."

"How was your day?" LuAnn sat down next to her on the couch. Are you doing okay?"

Dahlia nodded. "I'm okay, now. Earlier I was getting a little down. That's why I went for a run. My mom used to tell me exercise is the best way to overcome stress."

"Exercise does help. Especially on a day as lovely as this one."

"Yeah, I like being outdoors."

"So, your mom...where is...?"

Dahlia ran her hand along Tom's silky fur. "She passed away not too long ago."

"Oh, no." LuAnn's mother had died early last year. She still missed her. She supposed she always would. "I'm so sorry. Margaret is your great-aunt, correct?"

"Yeah. She basically raised my mom. My mom's mom died when my mom was only a toddler. Her father was there but emotionally absent. After my mom died, I really wanted to find the woman who raised her. I don't have anyone else."

LuAnn tilted her head, wishing she could find a way to comfort Dahlia. "We'll find her. I'm so sorry."

"Thanks." Her tense shoulders didn't seem to relax at LuAnn's words. She sat silently a moment, then broke the silence with a sigh. "I would like to have family. I never knew my dad either. I don't actually want to, to be honest. He's a real jerk, from what my mom told me." A tear escaped her eye, and she quickly brushed it away. "Maybe family isn't in the cards for me."

"I believe in prayer," LuAnn said as gently as she could. "I'll pray that God will bring you the right family, okay?"

Dahlia shrugged, but her eyes looked hopeful. "Okay."

LuAnn's phone pinged. It was a text from Janice. *Getting supper going.* Then another text came through. *And Roy is here. Did you know he was coming?* This was followed by a smile emoji.

LuAnn glanced at Dahlia. "Janice says Roy is here for supper..."

"Oh!" Dahlia stood. "That's my fault. He mentioned how he'd like to get to know you ladies better, and I said something about maybe you all would invite him over for a meal sometime. He seemed so lonely, I just had to say something encouraging to him." She grimaced. "I had no idea he'd interpret that as an invitation for supper tonight. I'm so sorry."

"Don't worry about it. When did you see him?" LuAnn asked.

"When I was on my run, I ended up at the historical society to check on things. Roy was there. He's a nice man." She smiled.

"Yes, he is."

"If it's a problem, he and I can go to a restaurant or something."

LuAnn motioned her to come on. "No worries." She led her toward the stairs. "We always have more than enough."

Dahlia relaxed. "Thank you."

"You're welcome. He could probably use some company."

When they walked down the stairs, they saw Roy sitting at a café table. As he rose to greet them, the bell on the front door jingled. This time it was Officer Randy Lewis. Janice, who stood at the desk, greeted him. LuAnn stepped next to her.

"What brings you here?" Janice asked. "Do you have news about Margaret?"

He shook his head. "I'm sorry, I don't. But I wanted you to know that Margaret isn't the only elderly woman who's gone missing."

Chapter Six

Dahlia gasped from where she'd parked herself beside LuAnn. Roy stepped toward them, anxiety and questions written all over his face.

Tess, who must have heard their voices while working in the office, arrived at the desk. "There's another woman missing?"

Randy nodded. "Yes. A Mrs. Eileen Reynolds. She's been missing for a week now."

"What happened?" Roy asked.

"We know Mrs. Reynolds didn't just wander off. And the family has confirmed that she does not have Alzheimer's as was originally reported." He took out his notebook and pen. "Do you mind if I ask you a few questions about Mrs. Ashworth?" He gazed at Dahlia. "You were the first to realize she wasn't where she should've been, is that right?"

"Yes."

"I'll need her age."

"I think she's seventy-six," Dahlia answered.

Janice shook her head. "Who would kidnap a woman in her seventies?"

"That's what we're trying to find out." Randy gave Janice a reassuring smile. "Can you email me a recent picture of her?"

He handed Dahlia a card and pointed. "To this address. It'll come directly to me."

"Of course." Dahlia reached for her phone. "We took a selfie yesterday."

"We know she spends a lot of her time at the historical society. Does she go anywhere else on a regular basis?"

"She shops at Warrens. Goes every day because she likes fresh produce. On special occasions she goes to Jeremiah's for breakfast."

"Does she take walks or go to movies?" Randy continued. "Any friends she visits?"

Dahlia frowned. "I honestly don't know her that well. We just met, actually. Just a week ago."

He wrote something in his notebook. "I see." Then he gazed at LuAnn and her friends. "Can you tell me anything?"

"That's all I can think of," LuAnn answered. "We already called the station about a book that someone left in my pocket that we think is about Margaret going missing."

"Yes, I was told about that," Randy said wryly. "The feeling at the station is that if that's from the kidnapper, they're going about this the hard way. Police aren't big believers in clever criminals. We find they pretty much take the easiest path to letting us know what they want." He checked his notebook again. "What about church? Did she attend?"

"Yes, she goes to Christ Fellowship with us," LuAnn said.

"Okay, can you give me a list of people from there who she may be visiting or who may know about her whereabouts?" He jotted something down. "Any other friends?"

"She didn't have many friends, I don't think," Janice answered.

"I'm her friend," Roy said. "But I've only been here a few months." He coughed. "I had a hard time breaking through that sharp outer layer at first—oh, who am I kidding? She was downright persnickety. But once I did, I found a charming woman hiding there."

LuAnn glanced at him. "I feel the same way about her."

"Do you know what she was wearing?" Officer Randy continued his line of questioning.

"I didn't see her this morning," Dahlia answered. "So I don't know. But she usually wears some kind of cardigan."

"And her afghan was missing from the historical society," LuAnn added. "She always keeps it there in her office."

"And the last time you saw her?"

"Last night." Dahlia hugged herself. "When I said good night."

"Okay." He paused a moment, then glanced back at Dahlia. "You say you only recently met her?"

Dahlia shifted her stance. "Yes."

"Why is that?"

A shadow came over Dahlia's face. "She and my mom had a falling out when my mom was pregnant with me, from what I understand."

"Could she have gone to see your mother?" he asked.

"She's passed." Dahlia's lip quivered, and LuAnn put her arm around the young woman's shoulder.

"I'm sorry to hear that."

An awkward silence followed, interrupted by Roy coughing again.

"Finally, how's her health? Is she in any danger, or does she have any major health issues?"

"She has a heart condition," Dahlia answered.

Randy made a note, put his pen and pad back into his pocket, then gazed at Dahlia. "We'll do everything we can to find your aunt."

Dahlia's eyes filled with tears. "Thank you."

"He's good at what he does. We go way back." Janice smiled at her.

Randy smiled also. "That we do."

"Randy," LuAnn said, "do you think Margaret's disappearance has anything to do with Mrs. Reynolds' disappearance?"

He nodded. "Yes. That's one reason why I think we need to file this report about Margaret right away. Two kidnappings of older women within a few days of each other—"

"You think they're connected?" LuAnn asked.

"Could be. We need to look into that."

"Who is Eileen Reynolds?" Tess asked.

Randy checked his notebook. "She and her husband have been fixtures in Marietta for fifty years or more, until he passed away a couple of years ago. They used to own half the town, practically. She still pretty much runs her company, despite her kids' clamoring to take over."

"Wow," LuAnn said. "And she's missing?"

"Yeah. Like I said, it's been seven days now. She said she was going for a walk and never came back." Randy's phone buzzed. After glancing at it, he faced the group again. "I have to go. Please feel free to call me if you have any questions or if you remember anything that might help in the investigation."

"We will," LuAnn said.

As the door closed behind him, the whole group let out a relieved sigh.

"Is anyone as hungry as I am?" Janice finally said.

"I sure am," LuAnn said.

"Good. But you know what?" Janice said. "I barely started dinner when Randy came. I say I put away the chopped veggies and order some pizza."

Tess patted Janice's shoulder. "That's the best thing I've heard all day."

"I agree," LuAnn said. "But I'm going to slip into the office and see if I can find the Reynolds' information. I'd love to meet with them tomorrow and see what they know—if anything."

"Good idea," Janice said. "I'll call Over the Moon for the pizza while you do that."

In a few minutes, LuAnn had found the website for the Reynolds' company. Under the Contact Us section, she found a list of email addresses. One was for the vice president of operations, Craig Reynolds.

"Did you find anything?" Tess said, leaning her head through the doorway.

"I think so," LuAnn answered. "I found an address for Craig Reynolds. He's the vice president of operations. I'm sure this address will go directly to his assistant, but it's worth a try."

"It can't hurt to have it waiting in their inbox first thing in the morning," Tess agreed.

The two joined Janice and the others at the long harvest table in the café, and soon the pizza arrived. LuAnn had tuned Winnie's radio to an oldies station and opened the kitchen door so they could hear the music as they ate.

"So," Tess started as she handed out colorful paper plates. "What do you do, Roy?"

"I'm retired now. I used to be a fisherman up in Washington State."

"What a beautiful place," Janice commented. "Did you grow up there?"

"No, I—"

"A fisherman?" Dahlia asked, before Roy could answer. "That's a hard job."

Roy smiled. "Well, it's physically hard." He held up his hands, which were rough and misshapen. "Lots of pulling on ropes will do that to you." He put his hands back in his lap. "But the fresh air, the exercise, the satisfaction of the catch..." He sighed. "Nothing compares."

"You like to study history and read and..." Dahlia smiled. "I wouldn't have thought you were a fisherman."

"I do love book studying," Roy answered. "But you can learn a lot from the sea as well."

"What did the ocean teach you?" LuAnn asked as she served the pizza.

"The sea has a mind of its own, you know. It can be breathtaking, with its vastness and tranquility." He leaned back. "I remember many sunsets, the salmon sky reflecting on the glassy water, and thinking myself to be overly blessed by the Creator—just to be taking in such a sight."

"There's nothing like a glorious sunset," Janice agreed.

"Other times the sea would kick our backsides." He laughed heartily. "Like a toddler in a tantrum, unpredictable, tumultuous." He shook his head. "No way to tame it. When the sea was storming, our only hope was to pray it would let us ride it out."

"Sounds amazing," Dahlia said. "Like every day was an adventure."

Roy picked up his piece of pizza. "Don't let me glamorize it too much. Lots of hard work, lots of smells!" He chuckled.

"Constant fish smell, I bet," LuAnn guessed.

Roy tipped his head. "The men were worse than the fish." He laughed again.

"But you didn't tell us what you learned from it all that you couldn't learn in books." Dahlia leaned forward. "I love books, so I'd like to know what could be better."

Roy's face calmed like the tranquil sea he'd described. "Ah." He paused, as if collecting his thoughts. "I learned many things from those days and nights feeling the pulse of the ocean, but the greatest lesson—which confronted me with the consistency of the tide—was that no matter how many years I rode the great sea's waves, I could never control those currents." He fixed his gaze on Dahlia. "A constant reminder that I don't have control over my life either. I like to think I do, but I don't. Nobody really does. Sure, we can make decisions in the short term, but what does the Bible say? 'God determines our steps.' God's a lot like the sea. Can't control Him either. But He always does what's best for us."

Dahlia sank back into her seat.

"That's a good lesson," Janice said.

"Took me a lot of years to learn to trust Him," Roy said. "Not that I'm so great at it now, but I try, and He forgives me when I fail—that's the amazing part!" He took in a peace-filled but shaky breath.

"Thank you for sharing that with us," LuAnn said.

"The Lord's care for my life may have taken me a long time to figure out, but one thing's not taking me too long." Roy took a bite. "This is good pizza!"

"It sure is," Tess agreed as she loaded another slice onto her plate.

"When did you retire, Roy?" LuAnn asked.

"Oh, a few years back. Fishing was tough on the body, but I did it as long as I could."

"I'd love to hear more of your stories," Dahlia said, emerging from her musing. "Maybe after I finish my book about Marietta, I could write your story. I bet you have lots of exciting tales to tell."

Roy shook his head, a sullen look clouding his eyes. "I don't know about that."

"Aw, come on," Dahlia persisted. "We could do it together."

"Maybe," he answered. "Maybe."

Dahlia smiled. "Good. Because I think it's a great idea."

As they finished up their dinner, a knock sounded on the back door, and Brad walked in.

"Hey," he said as he entered. "Sorry. I could hear you all having dinner, and I didn't want to make anyone get up. The door was still unlocked."

"No problem, Brad." Janice smiled. "You're always welcome. You don't have to knock. You know that."

Brad's grin seemed half-hearted as he paced to the table.

"Would you like a piece?" LuAnn asked. "We were finishing up, but there's plenty left." She pointed. "There's pepperoni." She grabbed a plate and started to scoop him up a slice, but he shook his head.

"No. No thanks. I already ate." He rubbed the back of his neck. "With my lawyer."

A pit grew in LuAnn's stomach. "Didn't go well?"

Brad sighed but didn't answer.

LuAnn needed to do something to encourage him. "Hey, why don't we all go for a walk? It's nice out. It won't be long till the weather will turn, and walks will be less appealing. What do you think?"

Brad's eyes softened. "I actually love that idea. Fresh air. Good friends." His gaze landed on LuAnn. "It'll do me good."

LuAnn glanced at the others. None of their faces said yes.

Roy wiped his mouth and laid his napkin on his plate. "I'd better be getting on home."

"I'm pooped," Dahlia said. "And I also want to get back upstairs. I've put several notices on different social media sites. I should check and see if anyone has seen Aunt Maggie. When I mentioned that she didn't have her pills, people were up in arms."

"Ladies?" Brad threw Tess and Janice a smile.

They glanced at each other.

Tess went first. "I have to finish working on the books. I've got a couple of invoices that need to be paid before they're overdue, plus, I should reconcile the receipts."

LuAnn peered at Janice. "How about you, Janice? I'll help clean this up, and we can go?"

Janice smiled apologetically. "I would love that, but Stacey's going to call." She glanced at the microwave for the time. "Oh my! She's calling in ten minutes. I'm sorry."

"That's okay." LuAnn smiled.

"You two should go anyway," Janice said.

"Yeah," Tess agreed. "Don't worry about us."

LuAnn frowned. "Now I'm feeling bad for leaving you two to do all the work again."

Janice, who had been gathering the paper plates, threw them in the trash, then approached LuAnn. "You should go. You both could use the fresh air." The look in her eyes told LuAnn that she spied the stress in Brad's demeanor as well.

LuAnn shifted her gaze to Brad. "What do you think?"

"I'd love to go for a walk with you."

Five minutes later, LuAnn, cozy in her light sweater, meandered next to Brad. She found it hard to believe that she hadn't trusted him when they had first met, had doubted his integrity even. She laughed inwardly at how wrong she'd been. He was the most trustworthy, kind, honorable man she had ever known.

"Do you want to talk about the lawyer meeting?" she asked as they walked. She could see him clench his jaw. "I understand if you don't want to."

"It's okay. It's better to talk about things, especially when it's with someone who's a good listener." He glanced at her as they walked. "Like you."

"I agree." LuAnn smiled.

"Have I told you what the lawsuit is about?"

A breeze swept up from the river. "Not yet. Is it serious?"

"A client is saying I didn't disclose that there was mold in a house I sold a couple of years ago."

"And they're just now noticing?"

Brad's hair, usually perfectly in place, tousled in a breeze from the river. It matched his mood, LuAnn thought.

"I sold it to a young woman," he said. "She recently got married, and her husband has been sick ever since he moved into the house. They're saying it's because of the mold."

"Oh no. I'm sorry he's sick. Is it bad?"

"I think so. He loses strength in his muscles at times. Other times he's fine, but then he'll black out. He hasn't been able to work..."

"Oh, Brad, are they sure it's because of the mold?"

"They seem to be sure, but I don't know." He paused and leaned on the railing overlooking the river.

LuAnn joined him and watched a couple of evening kayakers glide under the bridge, mesmerized for a moment by the oars' rhythm in the lapping water. "Does your lawyer have any suggestions?" she finally said.

"They have to prove that I knew there was mold or that I failed to check."

"You didn't know about the mold though." LuAnn faced him.

"It has to do with the inspector. Our regular guy was on vacation, so we used someone different. He was highly recommended, but they're saying he missed it."

"But how is that your fault?"

"It's not, but the law wants to keep real estate agents honest, so some of the liability falls on the agent."

"I see."

"The agent can be liable if he or she didn't vet the inspector properly." He released a breath.

"Did you..."

"I did." His eyes widened. "I absolutely did. I called his references. I checked the Better Business Bureau. Researched his license."

"So how can they sue you?"

"The guy doesn't care that the law's on my side. He seems to want to bring me down. Or the company. It feels really senseless." He blew out a breath. "Plus, the damage to my reputation."

"That's so unfair."

"The laws are written to protect the consumers. I can understand that, but it's tough to be in this position."

LuAnn didn't know what to say. Everything seemed gloomy.

"Nothing like this has ever happened to me before."

"Of course not. You're an honorable man."

"I thought if I did my best to be honest and serve my customers, I'd avoid this kind of thing." He shook his head. "Now I'm wondering if Grant and I are going to have to leave our real estate business behind. Find something else to do." He stared at his feet as they walked.

LuAnn wondered how Brad's brother and business partner was taking the news. He was quite a bit more laid back than Brad, so she imagined that Brad was the one dealing with the issue.

They strode in silence for a few minutes, then came to the park by the river. Kreamy Kreations, one of the town's ice cream shops, was still open, so LuAnn headed that way. "I know it won't solve anything, but would you like some ice cream? I'll treat."

Brad smiled gratefully. "Sounds good. I've been wanting to try their pumpkin spice ice cream."

"It sounds amazing."

After getting their ice cream, LuAnn and Brad settled on a bench near the water.

"My lawyer says the only hope is to discredit the guy, but digging into someone's life seems…underhanded. Especially since he's sick."

"Yeah, I can't imagine you doing something like that just to win, but is there any chance he's lying?" She tightened her sweater as the cool evening air wafted over her. "I'd think it wouldn't be unethical to make sure he's telling the truth."

The outside corners of Brad's eyes lifted. "You're probably right. The lawyer thinks it's worth a try. I just don't want the stress to make him sicker."

"I understand, but he's the one who started the lawsuit." She licked her ice cream. "Have you met him?"

"No. We only communicate through the lawyers, which seems so impersonal. I'd love to sit down and hash it out face-to-face before it goes any further."

"Has he filed?"

"No, actually. So far it's just a threat. My lawyer's trying to work it out to avoid a suit, but it's not going very well."

"I'm sorry," LuAnn said again. "I don't know how to help with all this, but I'm here if you need me." She tilted her head, her silver hair falling just over her shoulder.

"That means so much, Lu."

LuAnn appreciated her friendship with Brad. He'd been there for her and her friends many times since they'd bought the inn—and even that wouldn't have happened without him. "We're all here for you. There's not much we can do, but you're always welcome at our table or to talk."

Brad inched closer as he gazed at her. "Thank you." He reached out to touch her hand, LuAnn thought, but was interrupted by a loud rustling in the bushes. A dark figure moved toward the water and out of sight.

LuAnn and Brad looked at each other. They'd both heard the rustling. Then the man yelled, "Whoa! Whoa!" And they heard a splash.

They raced to the edge of the bank.

"There!" LuAnn pointed to a figure expertly gliding through the water. He was swimming away.

"I see him," Brad said, staring at the man. "What on earth is he doing?"

"I don't know. He's wearing street clothes. It can't be easy to swim." She continued to watch as he swam away. "That was weird," she said. "Was he hiding in the bushes while we were talking?"

"He must have been. I wonder if he lost his balance and fell into the water."

"I almost feel sorry for the guy." LuAnn chuckled.

They stepped toward the bench, but then LuAnn stopped. "Wait," she said, pointing to the shoreline. "Do you see that?"

It was a cell phone.

LuAnn picked up the phone. The screen was black. "I hope it's not out of battery."

"Does it have a passcode?" Brad asked.

LuAnn swiped it, bringing up the lock screen. "It has power, and it is password protected, but…" She showed Brad the screen, continuing to glance at it herself. It read: "If found return to Cole Harrison." And had a phone number.

Brad took in a breath. "That's the guy who's threatening to sue me."

Chapter Seven

LuAnn reviewed the details of what had just happened. "So, he can swim."

Brad nodded, then after a moment, his eyes perked up. "He swam pretty well for a guy who is supposed to be terribly sick."

"Exactly."

They started walking toward the bridge.

"Can I see it again?" Brad asked, and she handed the phone to him. They studied it together. The photo under the lock screen was a picture of a young man and woman in front of a fireplace. "I recognize the brickwork on that fireplace. That's the house I sold her, and that's my client." Behind them on the mantel, obviously meant to be part of the photo, was a framed photograph of a young woman's profile laughing with a toddler. Brad studied her face for a long moment. "The woman in the frame looks familiar." He shook his head. "It's probably nothing."

"Hmm. You should take a picture of this with your camera, in case the memory comes back to you." She examined the picture again.

Brad took out his own phone and snapped a picture, as she suggested. "Well," he said after a moment, "he looks like a nice enough guy."

"He does. You can never tell what's going on behind the front people put on though, especially in pictures."

"True," Brad agreed as they walked.

They wound down the street to the inn and stood at the front door.

"Thanks for the walk." LuAnn gave him a quick hug.

Before Brad could answer, the door opened, and Tess stood gaping at them.

"I'm so sorry." She chuckled nervously. "I didn't realize you two were standing out here."

"Hello, Tess," Brad said. "I was just leaving."

"I'll see you later?" LuAnn asked.

"You bet." His demeanor seemed less heavy than it had when he first arrived. "Thanks for the company. Did me some good, I think."

"You're welcome. I'm glad I could be here to listen."

"Oh, and don't forget. Are we still on for kayaking on Friday?"

"We sure are." LuAnn smiled. "I'm looking forward to it. And so are Tess and Janice."

Brad raised an eyebrow. "Janice? Really?"

"She just doesn't know it yet."

Brad waved and left, and LuAnn joined Tess inside.

"What were you doing?" LuAnn asked.

"I heard noises out there. I was only checking. I should have known you'd be heading back around now." Tess covered her cheeks with her hands. "I'm sorry."

LuAnn waved her off. "No, no. We were saying good night. We had a nice walk and talk. I think he feels better."

"I'm glad he knows he doesn't have to journey through the lawsuit alone," Tess said. "If there is one, I mean. We're here for him."

"Yes, he seems to know that."

"Good. Where did you guys go?"

"Ice cream. Where else?" LuAnn grinned.

"You indulged? I'm shocked."

"I know, but even a healthy eater can splurge once in a while. And it was yummy."

"Well, I'm going to bed." Tess glanced at the clock. "I know it's not even nine, but..."

"I get it." LuAnn yawned. "We have early mornings, and that's the only reason. It's not that we're getting older."

"Definitely not that!"

LuAnn made a pit stop in the office to grab the *McGuffey Reader* before taking the elevator to the fourth floor. She passed Dahlia on the couch in the common room and said good night to her. After getting ready for bed she crawled between the sheets and opened the book to the pages with the alphabets. Nothing other than the marks she'd already seen caught her attention, so she carefully turned the page.

Around the borders of the next page, she found twenty-four faint hash marks. She wrote that number in her notebook. She turned the page and found no marks at all on that one or on the several pages following until she reached page twenty-four.

"Oh," she muttered to herself. "Twenty-four marks. Page twenty-four."

She looked around, excited. She needed to share this with Tess and Janice. She wrote a note in their group text, hoping they'd still be awake. A moment later, her two groggy friends stumbled into her room.

"Were you sleeping?" LuAnn asked.

"Pshaw!" Janice grinned. "It's only nine thirty. Who goes to bed that early?"

"Not you," Tess teased.

"I'm sorry," LuAnn said. "But I had to show you this."

Tess and Janice studied the page she held up to them.

"Did you find something?" Janice asked.

"Yes, and I think it might lead to something more important. That's why I called you in here."

"Of course. We wouldn't want to miss the discovery of a clue!" Tess sat on LuAnn's bed, and Janice plopped on the other side.

LuAnn showed them the twenty-four hash marks and how they seemed to indicate a page number.

"So what's on page twenty-four?" Janice asked.

LuAnn rubbed her hands together expectantly. "I don't know yet." The three examined the page. There was a picture of a wood carving of a cow standing in a creek with children on the creek bank.

"Delightful," Janice said. "To think these books were enjoyed by children in our country for decades."

"So many grew up with them," Tess added. "It was a different time."

"Okay, so this chart includes the letters used," LuAnn observed.

"No letters underlined there," Janice said.

"The underlines seem to start in the little story." Tess read it aloud.

O Kate! the old cow is in the pond: see her drink! Will she not come out to get some grass?

No, John, she likes to be in the pond. See how still she stands!

The dear old cow gives us sweet milk to drink.

"It really is precious, isn't it?" Janice said.

LuAnn eyed it more closely. "And look at that punctuation."

"It's so different than what we're used to." Tess shifted positions on the bed.

LuAnn pointed to the first line. "Even the spelling. Today we would never use the word 'O' like that, but back then it was a form of address."

"Right," Janice said. "Fascinating—especially for an English teacher, I bet." She smiled at LuAnn.

LuAnn chuckled. "Yeah, I could study this book all night, but let's get back to the marks."

"There are underlined letters in the first line, the second line, and then not until line six." Tess pointed to the story.

LuAnn wrote as Janice read, "*O, C, I, N,* and *S.*"

"The next line has a long line under the word *get.* I think it means the whole word, don't you?" Tess asked.

"I agree," LuAnn said.

"The last line has another long line under *old* and then one under *G.*"

LuAnn held out her notebook for them all to see. *O, C, I, N, S GET OLD G*

"Look at the first group. Do the letters make a word?"

"Coins!" Janice blurted.

LuAnn smiled. "I think you're right."

"Coins get old?" Tess worked it out. "Wait. If you move the *G* it says gold!"

"Coins get gold," Janice said. "What does it mean?"

"What if we move *get* to the front?" LuAnn said. "It reads, 'Get gold coins!'" She ran her finger over the lines under the letters. "It's the same dark ink as the other message."

"Free MA," Tess recalled.

"If we want to free Margaret, we need to find the gold coins," LuAnn mused. "Do you think that's what it means?"

Janice nodded. "I do."

"Me too," Tess agreed.

"How are we supposed to find them?" Janice folded her arms and exhaled. "We have no clue where they could be."

September 22, 1863

Prudence was sure Cynthia had never seen such a distrustful look come from her eyes before. But when it had to do with the safety of those she vowed to protect, when it came to keeping their route to freedom secret, erring on the side of caution was called for.

Cynthia glared back at Prudence with almost as much intensity. "You don't know what you're dealing with," she said in a rough voice. "Give me the reading device." She again reached for the cipher, but Prudence again pulled it away.

Prudence pointed to the letters CSA. "I will reveal thy duplicity to all of these soldiers." She waited a heartbeat then opened her mouth to scream, "Spy!" but Cynthia slammed her hand over Prudence's mouth and tugged her to the back of the Millers' cabin.

"Be quiet!" Cynthia said, still covering Prudence's mouth. "I'm not a Confederate spy."

She loosened her grip on Prudence's mouth, and Prudence started to scream again.

Cynthia tightened her grip again. "Stop this!" she rasped. "You're putting the whole camp in danger. I'm not working for the South." Keeping her hand over Prudence's mouth, she pulled back and gazed into her eyes. "I'm working for the North."

Then why did she have a cipher from the South? Prudence wanted to ask.

"We've gotten our hands on some of the enemy's ciphers." Cynthia answered Prudence's unspoken question. "They do us no good, though, unless we have the key word. We think there's going to be a major activity the next few days—today even. I'm trying to figure out the code. That's why I'm here, and to find the spy who is involved."

Prudence wasn't sure if she could trust this woman she barely knew, but her explanation was not completely unreasonable. Cynthia loosened her grip again, and Prudence decided not to scream. Instead, she caught her breath.

"Thee works for President Lincoln?" Prudence spoke as quietly as she could.

"And you are a conductor, aren't you?"

Every muscle in Prudence's body tensed. "What? I care for those poor souls, but why would thee think such a thing?"

"I know for a fact the gentleman who put that note in your hand earlier is a conductor. I believe you are too." Cynthia straightened her simple dress. "I will keep your secret if you keep mine."

What choice did Prudence have? She nodded.

"The coins are somewhere in Marietta, the newspaper clipping said." Tess leaned on her hand. "Not too helpful."

LuAnn glanced back at the page. "Wait, do you see that?" She pointed to a small mark at the bottom right corner of the page.

"It's just a pencil smudge," Janice said.

Looking closer, LuAnn noticed something different about it. She reached into her bedside table drawer and retrieved a magnifying glass. She trained it over the smudge and then showed her friends.

"They're letters," Janice said. "Tiny letters. I can barely tell which ones they are."

"*X, L, V, I,I,I.*" LuAnn wrote them in her notebook.

"That sure doesn't spell anything. Do you think they're Roman numerals?" Tess asked.

"I think they could be." LuAnn tapped her fingers on the table. "Forty-eight. That's what it is." LuAnn started flipping pages. As she scanned the pages, she noticed something. The lessons were numbered using Roman numerals. "It's the lesson number." Racing ahead, she found Lesson XLVIII.

"I don't see anything," Janice said. "Do you think if we find more marks, it will spell out where the gold coins are?"

LuAnn shook her head. "I don't know."

Tess's brow wrinkled. "But why would the kidnapper go to all the trouble to get this to us when he could just solve it himself?"

"Maybe he couldn't for some reason," LuAnn guessed.

"We need to keep studying this, but"—Janice eyed the clock—"I'm sorry, ladies. I've got to get to bed."

Tess stood. “Me too. And so should you, LuAnn. Get a good night’s sleep, and you’ll be better able to figure this out in the morning.”

“I suppose.” LuAnn closed the book.

They left, and LuAnn leaned back against her headboard, thinking they were right, she should get some sleep. But she couldn’t help taking one more look. Opening the book to Lesson XLVIII, she spotted something she hadn’t seen before and released a small gasp, but as she tried to figure it out, her eyes grew heavy and soon she too was asleep.

Chapter Eight

LuAnn's phone woke her the next morning. Before answering it, she glanced at the time. Five fifty-five. Five minutes before her alarm. After staying up late the previous night, she sure could have used those five minutes. The name on the caller ID didn't look familiar, so she didn't answer. Woken up for no reason, she lay back. Maybe a couple of minutes past six wouldn't put her too far behind.

After a moment, her phone buzzed. She grabbed it from her side table. The person who called had left a message. "Hello, this is Craig Reynolds. I understand you want to talk to me about my mother's kidnapping and a possible connection to another kidnapping in the area. I don't know how I can help, but I'm available this morning at eight fifteen. You can meet me at the house." And then he hung up.

LuAnn glanced at the phone. What an odd message. Awake now, she moved to Tess's room next to hers. Janice was already downstairs. She knocked, and Tess popped her bed-head-messy head out. "Again, you wake me?" She smiled.

"I'm sorry to wake you..." LuAnn knew Tess was teasing, but she cringed anyway. "I got this weird voice mail." She played it for Tess.

"That is weird." Tess shifted her stance. "So formal. No emotion in his voice about his missing mother..."

"Or Margaret for that matter," LuAnn said. "And eight fifteen? Who has a meeting at that time?"

"Yeah. And he didn't leave an address."

LuAnn chuckled. "Right? 'You can meet me at the house.' Like I'm supposed to know where 'the house' is."

Tess lifted her chin. "Well, I guess we better hurry and get ready if we're going to meet him at his appointed time."

LuAnn smiled. "That's what I was hoping you would say."

Forty-five minutes later, LuAnn and Tess had dressed, found the address, and filled their stomachs with coffee and Winnie's omelets.

"I'll see you later," Janice said as they left the kitchen. "Don't worry about us. We've got it covered."

"Thanks!" LuAnn watched Janice get sidetracked by Seth, who was asking for a coffee refill. He too was an early riser.

As they stepped outside the back door, LuAnn noticed a large bubble-wrapped envelope, like one used to ship a book in, on the welcome mat. Picking it up, she saw that it had no name or address on it.

"What's that?" Tess asked.

LuAnn shrugged, then looked at her phone. "I don't know, but we don't have time to find out."

She slipped it inside the mudroom on a shelf next to the door, and the two got in LuAnn's car and drove away.

As LuAnn and Tess drove through town, the sunlight angled through the leaves beginning their color change. "I love fall," LuAnn commented.

"Me too," Tess answered. "But I like all the seasons. Summer's a ton of fun. Don't you think?"

"I do, but we can have fun in fall too...which reminds me. We're supposed to go kayaking with Brad tomorrow afternoon. Did we agree to that?"

"I think we did." Tess's smile sparkled. "It'll be fun."

"I wonder if Janice will back out. She didn't seem too into it."

Tess chuckled. "Nah, she'll come. She's been much more adventurous since we got the inn."

"That's true. It's been good for her to expand those horizons."

"Definitely." They drove in silence for a moment, and LuAnn's mind trudged through the events of the last couple of days. Her brain felt like a ball of yarn had tangled itself inside. She needed help to untangle it. Tess's face revealed a similar feeling.

"Is Dahlia okay?" Tess finally asked, her thoughts seeming to land there. "How is she spending her time? I'm afraid I haven't had a chance to check in on her very much."

Good. Dahlia's situation was a topic LuAnn had hoped to discuss. "I think she's spending most of her time on the internet. She sends out notices everywhere asking people to help find Margaret. She could be anywhere by now." LuAnn's stomach sank.

"Yeah, it's so scary."

LuAnn turned the fan on. "Yesterday Dahlia spent a good amount of time at the historical society and Margaret's house. She wants to make sure everything is taken care of, including Margaret's parrot. It's neat how connected she feels to her aunt even though they've only known each other for a short time."

"I haven't wanted to say anything, but I was wondering about that." Tess raised her eyebrows. "It's terrible of me to say, but can she really be that close to Margaret? After only just a week?"

"Maybe Dahlia longs for family so much that she overlooks Margaret's persnicketiness." LuAnn grinned.

"That's probably it," Tess agreed. "We all overlook things when it comes to family."

"Yeah. And that's a good thing." LuAnn's GPS told her to turn right on Elm. As she turned down the street, she pondered something that had been gnawing at her ever since the first time she met Dahlia. Something not about Margaret. "She's also been talking a lot about writing."

"That's right. I noticed that at dinner last night."

"She wants me to help her with it." Dread sank into LuAnn's chest—she wasn't sure why. "She's writing a book about Marietta, apparently."

"Oh?"

"A time-travel book where the characters go back and forth from modern day to the Civil War."

"That sounds kind of cool, actually."

"It does..." Emotion thickened in LuAnn's throat.

Tess picked up on it. "What's wrong?"

"I was talking to Roy yesterday about regrets. He says he has lots of regrets, but he's trying to make them right."

Tess frowned. "Sad that he has regrets... I guess we all do, but some, well, some have real heartbreak in their past."

"That's the impression I got from him. He wasn't specific, but he hinted at a life-altering decision he wished he hadn't made." She sighed. "But I was inspired by his determination to try to make things right."

"Yeah?"

LuAnn nodded. "I was thinking about my old files... the ones with the notes about my book."

Tess slapped the dashboard. "Your book? The one you were working on a few months ago about the inn's history?"

LuAnn shook her head. "Not that one. It was an idea for a novel I had a long time ago."

"I think I recall something about it from college days. Is that what you're talking about?"

LuAnn nodded.

"It's coming back to me now. You wanted to be a writer. Oh, LuAnn, you were so passionate about it. You worked hard on that book. What was it called?"

LuAnn shook her head. "Don't ask."

Tess tapped her finger against her lips, thinking. "Something about history. Oh! *A Man and His*... What was it?"

LuAnn wished she wasn't driving, so she could curl into a ball and disappear. "*Heart*," she managed to choke out. "*A Man and His Heart.* It was about a Civil War soldier who lost his leg, and his wife who stuck by him. So embarrassing."

"I don't think so," Tess said. "It's a great idea for a story. I can't wait to read it. You're going to finish it, right?"

LuAnn let out a long sigh. Her stomach lurched at the idea, caused by the fear of failure, she supposed. But at the same time, her heart raced with the excitement of expressing herself and bringing life to the characters who had been buried inside her all these years. "I don't know. Maybe. I don't want to have regrets, but..."

"I hope you do write it. Why not? You're retired from teaching. I know we're busy with the inn, but I think you could find time."

"I wouldn't want it to get in the way of my work at the inn."

Tess peered over her glasses at her. "I have no doubt about your commitment to Wayfarers."

"Thanks." LuAnn released a breath. "I don't know. I'm thinking about it, and praying about it."

"Okay." Tess patted her arm with kind reassurance. "I'll pray too."

They moved into the "rich" part of town—the hills overlooking the old original homesteads, dating back to before the Revolutionary War. Brad had told them that many of the sprawling historic homes in the area had been kept in families for a century or more. LuAnn hadn't heard about the Reynolds family, but if they lived up here, they were certainly rich.

The GPS on her phone told her that her destination was on the left. Since there was only one huge home—not quite a mansion, but close—taking up the left side of the street, she assumed that was it.

"Whoa," Tess said as they approached the driveway. "This is quite a place."

LuAnn wasn't sure if she should park in the driveway or on the street. Both seemed awkward. Fortunately, she didn't have to decide. There was a gate with an intercom. She pulled up next to it and rolled her window down.

"Hello?" she said.

"Yes," a woman's voice answered.

"I'm, uh, here to talk to Craig... uh, Mr. Reynolds."

In answer, the gate buzzed and slowly opened.

LuAnn rolled up the window and glanced at Tess. "I'm suddenly nervous. I feel like a country bumpkin going to visit the rich relatives."

"Me too, but let's get our confidence on. They're no better than us."

"You're right. We're here to ask a couple of questions, not to get anything from them."

"Exactly."

LuAnn pulled her car next to the red Mercedes sitting in the driveway, and she and Tess got out and sauntered to the door.

Before LuAnn knocked, a woman opened the door. "Good morning," she said coolly—or maybe simply professionally.

"Mr. Reynolds is expecting you." She smiled and seemed a bit softer. "He's out back, exercising the dog." She led them inside and through a vast parlor. A portrait hung on the wall of a striking older woman with silver hair and a confident gaze.

"Stunning," LuAnn said. "Is this Mrs. Reynolds?"

"Yes, it is," the woman said. She continued to lead them through the library and dining room to the back door.

They followed her outside to a stone patio edging a yard lined with maple trees. The morning sun highlighted a manicured lawn. Craig, a thirty-something man, was watching his black labrador retrieve a stick.

"Hello," he said without looking. The dog ran back, delivering the stick, and Craig threw it again.

"Mr. Reynolds," LuAnn began. "I'm LuAnn Sherrill, and this is my business partner, Tess Wallace. We—"

"Nice to meet you." He glanced at them, then returned his attention to the dog, who was having trouble finding the stick. "There, Spirit." The dog ran in circles before finally finding it and scampering back. "Good boy," Craig said. "I think that's enough."

LuAnn relaxed. She didn't know how she was going to talk to him with his full attention on the dog.

The blond woman who had answered the door appeared and called Spirit away. Craig walked to an outside sink and washed his hands, then finally focused on the women.

"Forgive me. If Spirit doesn't get his morning exercise, he's a terror. Do you have dogs?"

The thought of scruffy little Huck compared to sleek, athletic Spirit nearly brought a giggle, but LuAnn held it back. "We have a dog and a cat," she said.

"Good friends, aren't they?" He moved toward a table with four cushioned chairs and sat in one, so LuAnn and Tess joined him.

"They truly are," Tess answered.

"Mr. Reynolds—"

"Call me Craig."

LuAnn wondered if she would ever get a sentence out without being interrupted. "Thank you. Craig—"

"So you're here about the kidnapping," he stated, the lines in his forehead tightening. "My mother." He let out an aggravated sigh. "She's not easy to handle, shall we say."

"I'm sorry to hear that," LuAnn said.

His gaze veered over the tree line of the yard and up at the sky. "I do love her though. One always loves one's mother. I'm terribly worried."

"I'm so sorry." LuAnn leaned forward. "I can't imagine. Officer Lewis said that she was taken several days ago. When did you notice she was gone?"

"She went out for an errand, but she never came back." He shook his head. "She liked to have her sparkling cranberry juice with her morning biscuit and sausage, and we were out of it." He sniffed. "Lila, our housekeeper, was on an errand elsewhere. Mother couldn't wait for her to come back. I was busy taking care of the business. We got in an argument—over cranberry juice. So ridiculous." He waved a hand as if brushing his mother's feelings away like a fly. "And she went to get the juice herself."

"And the business?" Tess asked. "May I ask what type of business it is?"

"Our family has lived in Marietta for centuries." He looked at them directly. "My great-great-great-great-grandfather served in the Union army out of Camp Putnam."

"Interesting."

"So our business was manufacturing back in those days. Reynolds Iron Works. We made parts for trains. We forged weapons for the soldiers. Pots, pans, everything you can think of."

"What an honorable business," LuAnn said.

"Yes, well, now it's an outdated business. We barely make ends meet from it, despite Mother's rich friends."

LuAnn glanced around. It hardly seemed like they were struggling financially.

"Do you still have a manufacturing plant?" Tess asked.

"Yes. Very high quality. High standards." He rolled his eyes. "High costs. Now that I'm CEO, I'm going to make some changes. There's no need for the sky-high standards my mother insisted on."

LuAnn tilted her head. "You're CEO?"

"Well, not officially, but with Mother gone, who else is able to run it?"

LuAnn's face must have shown what she was thinking.

"If you're wondering—no I did not kidnap my mother in order to get the position."

He certainly had a motive. LuAnn chose to drop that line of questioning. "Has your mother disappeared before?"

"No. She normally wouldn't leave this place. Tied to it like a moth to a flame."

"Did your father live here too at some point?" Tess asked.

"My father died when I was in college. It was devastating." He seemed genuinely sad.

"I'm sorry," Tess continued. "I don't know her, of course, but I wonder if your mother cherished her home because of the memories with your father."

LuAnn gazed at Tess. She knew Tess understood that struggle.

"Perhaps." He folded his hands. "Probably."

LuAnn was surprised by his sudden softening. Perhaps the mention of his father triggered something. "I think we've taken enough of your time." She stood. "I greatly appreciate your willingness to meet with us."

"My pleasure." As he walked them to the front door, he seemed sobered by their conversation. Not as cocky as when they first arrived.

"Thank you again," LuAnn said as she and Tess turned to go.

"Do you think you'll find your missing friend?" he asked.

"We're doing everything we can."

"Have you found any links between her disappearance and my mother's?"

LuAnn glanced at Tess. "I'm not sure yet."

"You'll let me know if you do?"

"Of course," LuAnn said.

They walked back through the house and to the driveway. As they approached the car, LuAnn glanced at Tess. "Do you mind driving?"

"No, why?"

LuAnn tossed her the keys. "Last night I was studying the *McGuffey Reader* again."

"You mean after Janice and I left?" She feigned a glare. "Didn't we tell you to go to sleep, young lady?"

LuAnn smiled sheepishly and stifled a yawn. "I needed to see one more thing."

As Tess unlocked the car, LuAnn slid into the passenger seat, took the carefully wrapped book out of her bag, and laid it on her lap. "Anyway, I studied lesson forty-eight a bit more, and I found more underlined words."

"You did? Did you figure out the message?"

"This time the marks were different. Barely visible. Until I used my magnifying glass, I didn't even notice them."

"So they weren't put there by the same person who marked the other ones. Is that what you think?"

"Yep." She opened the reader to lesson forty-eight and pointed to the page. "These marks are almost like water stains, they're so faded. I would guess really old."

Tess squinted at the letters. "I can barely see what you're talking about. Very faded and different than the ones we discovered earlier. Did you find a pattern or a word?"

LuAnn shook her head. "Not this time. Just a bunch of jumbled letters."

"Sounds like we need to take a closer look," Tess said as she started the car.

By the time LuAnn and Tess got to the inn, the early-morning rush had slowed. They walked into the kitchen where Janice had just entered from the café.

"It's that short break after the early birds finish breakfast." LuAnn rolled up her sleeves to help with the dishes.

"Yep." Tess grabbed the broom. "Just enough time for us to clean up before the late sleepers roll in."

Janice plopped into a chair. "It was a busy morning," she said. "I hope you don't mind if I sit for a minute before helping. Taylor's classes were canceled this morning, so he's helping Robin."

"Of course not," LuAnn said. "You've been working all morning without us. Where's Winnie, by the way?"

Janice took a sip from the mug of coffee sitting in front of her. "She slipped into the office for a minute to check on the order for the Taste of Marietta. She's getting pretty excited about it. It should be fun."

"Right. That's coming up in a couple of days." LuAnn set a pan on the stack of dishes to dry. "If the weather holds, it'll be a great event."

"So how was your meeting?" Janice rubbed her forehead. "What was the guy's name?"

"Craig Reynolds," Tess answered as she swept a pile of dirt into the dustpan. "Quite an interesting fellow."

LuAnn chuckled. "And quite a place he lives in. It's an old Revolutionary War house. It looks like it's been expanded and remodeled."

"Probably by Mrs. Reynolds," Tess put in.

"Yeah, well she did an amazing job. It was beautiful." LuAnn put the last pan on the stack and grabbed a clean towel to dry. "I would love to meet her someday. She's had an interesting life—not easy."

"What do you mean?" Janice asked.

"They are the family that owns that big Iron Works building in the old downtown. It's been here since before the Civil War."

"Wow."

"Yeah. And her husband died several years back. It sounds like the son is a bit difficult to deal with." Tess poured herself and LuAnn a cup of coffee and sat across from Janice.

"I feel sorry for her." Janice's face shone with compassion. "And now to be kidnapped. Who would do that?"

LuAnn finished drying and settled next to Tess, cupping the mug in her hands and inhaling the comforting aroma. "I don't know, but the son said something about them needing money."

"I caught that too," Tess said. "Do you think he kidnapped his own mother to get money?"

"He did mention that she has rich friends," LuAnn said. "If he was desperate... maybe he would in order to get them to pay."

"He sure seemed self-absorbed," Tess pondered. "Especially at first."

The midmorning sunlight shone through the windows, and Janice got up to adjust the blinds. "Do you think there's a connection with Margaret's kidnapping?"

"I wonder if he ever checks out that Marietta history page," Tess said.

LuAnn nodded. "I was thinking the same thing. If he saw the post I put up about the gold coins, he may have gone to the historical society to research them, found Margaret, and kidnapped her."

"In hopes of getting information about the coins from her?" Janice asked.

Tess shifted in her chair. "We're missing something."

A wave of frustration hit LuAnn. "It's the motive. He may want the gold coins to help with their money troubles, but I can't imagine Margaret not simply telling him any information he wanted."

Tess and Janice both sighed.

"Yeah," Tess said. "Kidnapping Margaret doesn't seem to fit."

"Not really, unless, like I said, we're missing something." LuAnn took another sip of coffee, hoping for clarity.

"Do you think he'd kidnap both of them?" Janice asked after a moment.

"Honestly?" LuAnn set her mug down. "He didn't seem like a ruthless human being, but he did seem like the kind of guy who gets what he wants. If something got in his way, I could see him justifying his actions for his own purposes."

Tess shrugged. "At the end of our conversation he did seem sincerely worried about his mom. Although I guess it could have been an act. It's hard to tell."

"I agree," LuAnn said.

Janice sighed. “Poor Margaret has spent two nights away from home. If this is the guy who took her, we need to know ASAP.”

“Absolutely,” LuAnn agreed. “Or at least rule him out.”

As she sat pondering what to think about Craig Reynolds, something orange sitting on the shelf in the mudroom caught her eye. “Oh!”

Her friends must have been deep in thought as well because this startled them.

“What is it?” Janice asked.

LuAnn raced to the mudroom and retrieved the package she had found on the back porch before she and Tess left earlier that morning.

“I forgot about that,” Tess said as LuAnn sat back down.

“A package?” Janice asked. “Who is it for?”

LuAnn turned it over so Janice could see that it had no name on it. “Let’s open it and find out.” She carefully peeled back the flap and peeked inside, then gasped. “I know what this is!”

Chapter Nine

September 22, 1863

Without finishing their deliveries, Prudence and Cynthia returned to the schoolroom to discuss the situation.

"Thee knows about the spy here then?" Prudence asked after laying Moses down on a bench for a nap.

"I do." She sat next to Prudence. "What do you know?"

Prudence eyed her. "What does *thee* know?"

"It's good to be cautious, but if we both have the same goal, it would be best to work together." She spoke with skilled quietness. Someone walking by would never hear her words. "I'll start. I know there are rumors of a Confederate spy here in the camp. The spy is supposed to meet someone soon and exchange information and..."

"And?"

"We've heard rumors that a Confederate sympathizer in the North is sending a parcel of gold coins—a wealth of gold coins—to help support the South. Since they were so decisively defeated at Gettysburg, they're losing confidence that they will win. They're getting desperate."

This was worse than Prudence had imagined. The side with the most financial strength would have great advantage over the other. "Does thee know anything about the spy?"

Cynthia nodded. "We know his family has a connection to a business in this town. We're not sure if he himself is from Marietta or has relatives here."

"That should narrow it down though." Finally, something encouraging.

"Yes. I've been looking into the backgrounds of the soldiers, as well as asking questions in casual conversation. I can't go directly to the commanding officers, because we don't know whom we can trust."

"Does thee have any leads?"

"Only one." A cloud came over Cynthia's face. "Austin, the man who was talking to Moses this morning. His family owns the mercantile. Of course, that doesn't make him guilty, but there are few soldiers left in town who have a connection with a local business."

An ache formed in Prudence's chest. "He seems like such a nice man. I hate to think he would do something so treacherous."

"I've grown fond of him as well—before I realized he may be the spy, of course." Cynthia placed a hand on her chest, then refocused her attention. "And now will you share what you know?"

"Not much more than that. I just received a message that a spy is near. I've heard nothing about the gold coins."

"Is that all?"

The last part was the worst, and Prudence hesitated to even speak the words. "The message I received is that this will happen tonight."

Cynthia's eyes widened. "Tonight? Are you sure?"

Prudence nodded.

"How are we supposed to find…" She seemed to rein in her emotions. "Well, it's only just past noon. We have this afternoon to find the spy." She peered at Prudence. "Will you help?"

As she spoke, two soldiers' voices sounded from outside. The door opened, and a redheaded young soldier entered, followed by Austin.

"I'm sorry, ma'am," the redheaded soldier said, not caring which ma'am he was addressing. "We have to confiscate your firewood."

"Come on, Reynolds." Austin stood between him and the woodpile next to the iron woodstove. "You're stealing firewood from the schoolchildren?"

"We are the ones who will be fighting in a few weeks." Reynolds reached around Austin. "We deserve it more than they do."

Austin shook his head. "They're children."

"It's really all right." Cynthia tried to break in. "We can find wood somewhere or—"

"See? They'll survive a little cold." Reynolds moved past Austin and picked up the box of firewood.

Carrying the firewood, Reynolds strode out. Austin removed his hat as he approached Cynthia. "I'm sorry, Miss Knight. I'll find you some more firewood. That fellow is out of line. Too used to his rich family taking whatever they want."

Cynthia chuckled. "Don't worry about that," she said, seeming to choose her words.

"So, I guess I'll be..." He glanced at Prudence. "I'll be going." He tilted his head as his gaze returned to Cynthia. "It was nice seeing you." He reached forward and shook her hand with an awkward grin.

Cynthia's eyes softened. She seemed to be inspecting his face, searching to see if he was sincere or a lying spy. The look passed, and her countenance returned to normal. "I thank you for your efforts on behalf of our firewood."

"You're welcome," he said as he backed out. "I will bring you some more as soon as I can."

"It really isn't a problem," Cynthia said. "It's chilly only in the mornings. By noon we are warm enough."

"Still. I'll bring you some." He smiled, and Cynthia's face remained serious, but Prudence spotted a hint of blush again.

After he left, Cynthia looked at Prudence and exhaled. Prudence's heart went out to her. She knew the pressures of keeping one's actions and thoughts hidden. She prayed the war would be over soon, so she and Cynthia and all others in this country could go back to living simple lives filled with justice and mercy and walking humbly with their God. "Does thee think he is the spy?" she finally asked. Prudence did not want to think so. He seemed honorable and kind, but she knew spies were experts in deceit.

"We need to find out as quickly as possible."

"How?"

"I will follow him. Search his things. See if I can find anything."

Cynthia spoke of invading someone's privacy so easily. Prudence clasped her hands together. "How will thee do that?"

Cynthia eyed Prudence. "I will sneak into his tent, somehow." Her eyes hinted urgency. "Today. This afternoon. As for following him, we could follow him as we finish our deliveries, but I fear we don't have time for me to search his things and also do that. Could you possibly . . . ?"

"Follow him while I make my rounds checking on people and gathering supplies? Is that what thee suggests?"

"Yes, keep an eye on him. See where he goes. Who he talks to. And report back to me. You would not have to confront him."

"Just watch him as I do my rounds?" She paused to pray. *Father, would Thee have me do this?* The image of little Charles and Sarah waiting in the secret room for someone to rescue them infiltrated her mind's eye. The war was to save souls like theirs, so future generations would not have to flee bondage in the cold, dangerous night. She thought of the damage a wealth of gold in the enemy's hands could render. She placed a hand on her chest. "Yes. I will do this thing."

LuAnn pulled the object from the envelope.

"Oh, wow," Janice said. "What is that?"

Inside the orange envelope was a thin, round piece of wood, old wood. LuAnn took a moment to study the device. It was about four inches in diameter and had an outer wheel that freely spun when she moved it and an inner wheel that was stationary. Both had letters etched along their perimeters. LuAnn's heart raced as she showed it to the others.

"It looks like a child's toy," Janice observed.

"What are these letters in the middle?" Tess asked. "CSA."

LuAnn's excitement grew. "It's Confederate..."

"... States of America!" Janice finished.

"Yep," LuAnn said.

"So, what do you think it is?" Tess asked.

LuAnn grinned. "I used to teach about these in my history classes. It's a cipher from the Civil War."

"Whoa." Tess's eyes widened. "Do you think it will make sense of the jumbled letters you found in the *McGuffey Reader*?"

Janice furrowed her brow. "What?"

"I found more underlined letters—but the marks were really faint, like they were older ones," LuAnn answered. She received the cipher back from Janice. "I can't wait to try this out." As she reached in her purse for the *McGuffey Reader*, Robin poked her head into the kitchen.

"Are any of you ladies free to wait on tables?"

LuAnn glanced at the clock. It was only nine forty-five. "Yes, of course we are."

The three popped to their feet, and LuAnn hurried to put the cipher and the book in the safe. "Until we return," she whispered as she shut the safe door.

After the morning rush, there were rooms to clean. LuAnn, and she assumed the others, ached to figure out whether the cipher worked with the letters she had found in the reader. But the rooms wouldn't clean themselves. As LuAnn approached the stairs to go to her apartment and change into her work clothes, Seth came barreling down, almost knocking her over.

"Oh, I'm so sorry!" he said, turning to her. "My mind was on other things. I should have been paying more attention. You okay?"

LuAnn smiled. "Really, I'm fine. I thought I saw you in the café earlier." He and LuAnn stepped toward the desk. "Did you already go out?"

"Yeah, I did. I was doing some research on my family, and then I, uh, forgot something, so I came back." He started to leave.

"Have a good day," she said. "And if you don't mind, I'd love to hear what you've been learning about your ancestors from the Civil War. I'm a big history buff."

Seth's eyes lit up. "Yeah, I've found some interesting stuff. I'll tell you about it—maybe later?"

"Of course."

And he left.

As the door closed behind him, Tess and Janice meandered to the desk.

"I'm sorry," Janice said. "I was supposed to be manning the desk. I didn't think anyone was around."

"It's okay," LuAnn answered. "I just happened to bump into Seth as he was leaving. Sort of strange..."

"Seth?" Janice asked.

"No." LuAnn chuckled. "I don't mean him, just the conversation." She shook the feeling away. "He was in a hurry. That's probably all it was." She glanced at the others. "I should get working on the rooms."

Tess nodded. "Me too. There are three needing cleaning, and guests coming this afternoon to fill them back up."

Janice glanced around the parlor. "Why don't I help with the rooms, since we're running a bit behind today? We'll hear the door jingle if anyone comes, and Robin will be done in the kitchen very soon."

LuAnn relaxed. "That would be awesome."

As they climbed the stairs, LuAnn's phone dinged. It was a sales call, but she noticed a previous text from Brad.

"Hey," she said to her friends, "I never told you about my time with Brad last night."

Janice paused walking and looked at her. "Something happen?"

LuAnn tugged her to keep walking. "It did. Something very odd." They reached the first landing, and Tess grabbed three cleaning supply buckets from the storage closet—one for each of them.

"We walked to Kreamy Kreations—"

"Yum," Janice inserted. "Did you try their pumpkin spice? I've been wanting to try it."

"I don't know why people like that flavor." Tess wrinkled her nose. "It's bitter..."

"Anyway." LuAnn attempted to refocus the conversation. "We did try the pumpkin spice." She slipped a quick smile to Janice. "It was great."

Janice grinned.

"We were sitting on a bench next to the river, and we heard a splash."

"What was it?" Tess's eyes widened.

"It was a man. He started swimming away from us until we couldn't see him anymore."

"With his clothes on? That is odd," Janice said.

"I know," LuAnn answered. "He must have been hiding in the bushes, listening to our conversation."

"Why would he want to do that?" Tess asked.

LuAnn reached into her pocket. "We found this on the bank."

"Is that his phone?" Janice asked.

"We think so," LuAnn said.

Tess reached for the phone. "Did you figure out whose it is?"

LuAnn handed it to her. "See that picture on the front?"

Janice leaned next to Tess to see. "Yes."

"The man in the picture is the one who's threatening to sue Brad. He's saying the house Brad sold his wife—the house in the picture—has mold in it, and it's making him sick."

"Wow," Janice said. "The phone belongs to the husband?"

LuAnn nodded. "He's the one who's behind the lawsuit," she repeated.

"You're saying the guy thinking of suing Brad was hiding in the bushes listening to you, and then he jumped in the river and swam away?" Tess asked.

LuAnn shrugged. "I think he must have fallen, because we heard him yell out before we saw him in the water."

"What are you going to do with the phone?" Tess picked her bucket up.

"I don't know yet." LuAnn picked up hers. "I was thinking of giving it to the police, but I'm not sure. I mean, do the police want a lost phone?" She leaned on the broom Tess handed her. "And he didn't do anything illegal."

"Stalking!" Janice blurted.

"We can't prove that," LuAnn said.

"I don't think one incident of hanging out in the bushes constitutes stalking," Tess added.

"Have you looked this guy up? Found out anything about him?" Janice was not letting this go.

"I haven't had a chance." LuAnn glanced at the bucket. "It's been a busy morning."

"I see there's a number to call in case it's found." Janice's forehead gathered in worry. "I don't think you should call, though. He could be dangerous. He's making up all this trash about Brad."

LuAnn appreciated her friend's concern. "It won't hurt to call him. Maybe I can talk to him. Ask him why he's doing this to Brad."

Janice's face still reflected worry. "I don't know..."

"It'll be okay," Tess assured her. "But...maybe it would be good to call from some other phone, so he doesn't get your cell phone number."

Janice nodded. "That's a good idea, but don't use the inn phone either. We don't want him coming here if he gets upset." She tapped her fingers on her broom. "Use a pay phone."

They all chuckled. "Do they even have those anymore?" Tess asked.

"Actually," LuAnn said, "I think there's a for-real pay phone at the gas station on Fifth Street. I'll call from there."

"One of us will come with you," Janice stated as though it was not optional.

"Okay," LuAnn agreed. "Now back to work."

They turned to continue up the stairs, but then LuAnn paused again. "Oh, and one more thing. Brad thought he recognized the woman in the framed photograph in the picture on that guy's phone. Isn't that weird?"

"Who does he think it is?" Tess asked.

"He wasn't sure. It's not a very clear picture. Could be nothing."

"How's he doing, by the way?" Janice asked.

"He's understandably upset—actually, he was more down than I've seen him. But you know Brad, by the end of the evening he was his positive self again."

"He's a good guy," Tess said.

"We should make him some cookies." Janice smiled.

"I think that's a great idea." LuAnn started up the stairs. "I'm afraid I've made us even more behind schedule."

Tess followed her. "We'll get it done. Don't worry."

It was only eleven thirty, but as she trudged up the stairs to the fourth floor, LuAnn felt like she'd already worked a whole day. Entering the living room, she was surprised to see Dahlia there, still in her pajamas, engrossed in her laptop.

"Hi there," LuAnn said as she approached the couch.

"Oh, hey." Dahlia typed something on the computer then closed it. "How are you doing?" She rubbed her eyes and leaned back.

"I'm fine. Are you okay?"

Dahlia glanced at the antique clock on the mantel. "Oh, wow. It's late. I had no idea." She glanced at her pajamas and blushed. "I don't usually do this. I've just been engrossed in stories about kidnappings. I think if I read about every one that's ever been solved, I'll find some kind of hint about where my aunt is."

"That's understandable," LuAnn said. "You're worried about her. I am too."

"Have you found anything leading to her? I mean, you guys have been working on it, right?"

"Yes, we have, but..." LuAnn's stomach lurched. "I'm afraid we're not much closer to finding her. I'm so sorry."

Dahlia's lower lip trembled. "It's okay. Not your fault."

LuAnn patted Dahlia's shoulder, desperately wishing she had the words to take away her pain. She sent up a prayer. "God is with you," was all she managed to say.

At that moment, Janice came in. As soon as she stepped into the room, she gave LuAnn a questioning look. LuAnn nodded, and Janice padded across the room and settled in the big chair.

Dahlia dabbed her eyes and took in a breath.

"I was thinking," Janice said. "The clue in the *McGuffey Reader*..."

"What about the *McGuffey Reader*?" Tess asked as she entered.

"We found that it said 'gold coins,' right?" Janice continued.

"Yeah," LuAnn agreed.

"I think we need to research that more. I know that bin of clippings and files was stolen from the historical society when Margaret was kidnapped, but there might be other information there."

"That's smart thinking," Tess said, laying her head back on the sofa cushion and closing her eyes. "We should find out everything we can about those coins."

"I agree." LuAnn sat forward. "Should I go?"

"How about I go with you?" Janice said. "And we can go to the pay phone afterward and call the guy about his cell phone."

"Okay," LuAnn agreed. "That sounds like a plan."

Tess perked up. "You two go. I'll man the inn."

"Can I tag along?" Dahlia asked. "I'd like to check up on the historical society, as well as Margaret's house." She glanced at LuAnn. "I can walk there from the historical society."

"Sure," LuAnn answered. "And we can drive you if you like. How long till you're ready to go?"

"Give me thirty minutes?" She blushed again. "I'm sorry. I can't believe I lounged in my pajamas so long."

"No worries."

Half an hour later Dahlia emerged from the bathroom, showered and ready to go. After waving goodbye to Tess, the three drove to the historical society.

When they got to the door Dahlia reached into her pocket and produced a key. "My aunt keeps a spare key in her desk at home. I feel kind of weird carrying it, but I figured someone needed to be able to get in."

"Of course," Janice said.

They stepped inside, and LuAnn gazed around the dark-wood interior, so, so rich with remembrances of those who had stepped there before. The meeting room, which had teemed with history-loving souls just a few nights before when LuAnn had given her lecture, now sat in cold silence. LuAnn relished this place for its treasure trove of historical relics. And she'd grown to care about Margaret, realizing her persnicketiness was really only a crusty exterior hiding a kind, generous heart—most of the time. Still, she'd never realized until now that the heart of this place wasn't the historical nuggets, but Margaret herself.

She glanced at the others, who seemed to be pondering their own reactions to this realm that was missing its queen, and moved toward the staircase.

The stairs squeaked as they stepped deeper into the darkness, and LuAnn got a chill. Dahlia entered the basement first and stepped out of the way as she flipped on the light switch.

When the lights came on, what they saw made them stop dead in their tracks.

Chapter Ten

How did that get there?" LuAnn rushed to the table where the exact bin that had been sitting on that very table the night Margaret was kidnapped—and which had been gone the morning Margaret went missing—sat before them.

"I have no idea," Dahlia answered. "I haven't seen it since that night."

"The cover is missing," said LuAnn.

Janice stepped to the table. "You mean this is the bin that disappeared?" She peered inside. "Are you sure? And there was a cover on it before?"

"There was." LuAnn looked inside the box. A newspaper clipping about the missing gold coins sat on top. It was a different article than the one Margaret had shown them. "The label on the side of the box was the same, so yes, this is the same bin."

"Is there any way it was misplaced that night?" Janice asked. "Could someone have set it back in its normal spot? Maybe Margaret put it away that morning, before..."

LuAnn shook her head. "I looked everywhere for it. It wasn't here."

"I can vouch for her," Dahlia said. "I couldn't find it either."

"Plus, we know it wasn't on the table." LuAnn eyed the bin's exterior. "Even if it was misplaced, how did it get back on the table?"

"That's a good point," Janice conceded. "If you're sure it's the same bin, then how strange that it came back."

"It sure is," LuAnn agreed. "Do you see this?" She pointed to a small film of white powder on the bottom of the plastic bin. "Do you remember it being there before?" She turned to Dahlia, who was looking in the box.

After examining what LuAnn had pointed out, Dahlia shook her head. "No. I don't remember any white powder. What do you think it is?"

"I don't know." LuAnn slowly peered around the room. "But I don't see any in this room."

"It must be from wherever the bin was taken to," Janice said.

Dahlia's eyes widened. "And maybe where my aunt is?"

"Maybe." LuAnn stepped back. "We should call Randy. He can check for fingerprints and maybe even get the powder analyzed, unless he can figure out what it is."

"Good idea," Janice agreed. "I'll call."

"I'm going to go check on Margaret's house." Dahlia cinched her bag over her shoulder. "You don't need me here, do you?"

"Go ahead," LuAnn said. "Do you want a ride?"

"No thanks. I'll walk." She stepped toward the stairs. "And if Roy shows up—it's weird that he's not here yet—tell him to text me, okay? I'm sure he's fine, but..."

"We will." LuAnn liked the idea of the two of them taking care of each other. "You all are getting along really well, aren't you?"

"Yeah. He's a sweet man. Acts like he's really interested in me as a person, you know? I like that."

"I'm happy to hear it."

Dahlia left as Janice finished her conversation with Randy. "He'll be here in about ten or fifteen minutes."

"Perfect," LuAnn said. "That will give us time to research the coins." She gazed longingly at the bin with all the pertinent information. "We can't touch this stuff though. Not until Randy gives us the okay."

Janice let out a breath. "So where should we start, O history professor?"

"Well, we should start with this article." LuAnn looked into the bin and read the headline out loud. "'Few Answers Found in Gold Coin Heist.'" She scanned the print underneath the headline.

"What did they find out?" Janice asked. "Did they catch whoever took the coins?"

"I don't think they caught them, but it says here a Confederate spy was supposed to hand them over to another spy who was embedded in the Union Army at Camp Putnam. The coins were sent by someone in the North who sympathized with the South."

"Camp Putnam?" Janice repeated. "Is that around here? I don't remember seeing it. There's Fort Harmar from the Revolutionary War. I've heard of that."

"I think Camp Putnam was only around for a little while, during the Civil War. I'd love to talk to an expert on it."

"Margaret would know everything about it." Janice sighed.

"She would, but..." LuAnn moved to Margaret's desk. "I bet she also knew the best expert in town." She flipped through Margaret's vintage Rolodex. "Camp Putnam expert!" she exclaimed. "I found it."

"Of course Margaret would have it, and only she would file it that way. What's the name?"

"Thaddeus Culverson," LuAnn answered. "That name sounds familiar." She pondered a moment. "I think he's the guy who runs the steamboat tour. He talked to Ashley and me when we were having lunch yesterday."

"That's perfect. You already have a connection with him."

"Not much of one, but at least I know who he is."

"Where does he live?" Janice asked.

LuAnn skimmed the card. "It doesn't have an address, but she has a note saying to find him around the steamboats down by the river. Listen to this. 'Take one of his tours, and he will tell you more than you ever wanted to know about Marietta, and especially Camp Putnam.'"

"Perfect." Janice smiled.

"Let's go there after this," LuAnn suggested.

Janice's eyebrows rose. "You mean after we call our friend Cole Harrison?"

"Oh, right, we need to get that cell phone back to the twilight swimmer." She let out a mirthless chuckle. "After that, then?"

"I'm up for it. Maybe after lunch, though. We forgot to eat before we left. I'm getting hungry."

"Me too," LuAnn said. "Now, back to this article." LuAnn gazed at the clipping. There was a picture of gold coins, apparently as an example. She took out her phone and snapped several pictures of the article. "Common coins from the time, I assume, since they couldn't be the ones that were never delivered or found."

"Right."

"I wonder how much these would be worth today." LuAnn zoomed her camera lens and took another picture.

"How many was the spy trying to deliver?" Janice asked. "Does it say?"

LuAnn kept reading the text. "It's hard to read this old print."

Janice used the flashlight on her phone to illuminate the page for LuAnn.

"That helps." She read down the page then looked at Janice.

"What does it say?"

"It says they estimate there were ten thousand dollars in coins."

Janice blinked. "That seems like a lot. How many coins would that be?"

LuAnn looked around the room. "I bet Margaret has a book on Civil War coins." She walked to the tall bookshelf that rested on the wall next to the desk and scanned the titles. "Here it is." She pulled out *The Official Blackbook Price to United States Coins.*

"Thank goodness for Margaret's thoroughness," Janice said.

LuAnn sat down at the table, opened the book, and found that each gold coin was worth ten dollars during the 1860s.

"So that would mean there were..." Janice glanced at the ceiling a minute. "A thousand coins! That's more than I expected. How much would they be worth today?"

LuAnn scanned the page. "It looks like they sell for about one hundred dollars apiece now." She sat back in her chair.

Janice gazed over her glasses. "So that means these coins are worth one hundred thousand dollars."

"If they're actually these kinds of coins. There were different ones, some were only worth five dollars each, some two fifty. And they weren't sure of the amount, but..."

"But no matter what, it's a lot of money." Janice's shoulders drooped. "This seems more serious, suddenly."

LuAnn's heart ached even more for Margaret—and Mrs. Reynolds too, if she was kidnapped over the coins. "For this amount of money, someone could possibly be willing to..." She didn't want to finish the sentence.

Janice folded her hands. "Is there anything else important in the article?"

LuAnn pushed to her feet, stood over the bin, and finished reading. "Not really, just reactions of the townspeople. Nobody had any clue what happened to the coins, according to this."

"Hmm."

"But wait, the photo is kind of interesting." She studied the grainy picture of some townspeople standing around an old schoolhouse. "Look at this."

"So interesting to see how they lived back then," Janice said.

"Yeah, and I think the schoolhouse was near Camp Putnam."

Janice eyed it silently for a moment. "Look at that woman." She pointed to a young woman standing in front of the schoolhouse.

"I was looking at her too. She looks frazzled. Her hair."

"I wonder if she was the teacher."

LuAnn got her phone out and took another picture, focusing especially on the woman. After she took it, she pressed two fingers on the screen to zoom in on it. "Hey," she said, "there's someone else in this picture. Look at the woman holding the basket." She held the zoom on her screen and showed Janice, who raised her hand to her chest.

"It's..."

"I think so."

"It's Prudence."

Before they could discuss it further, Randy came down the stairs.

"Hello, Janice." He gave her a familiar smile. "LuAnn."

"Hi, Randy." Janice took his hand. "Thank you for coming. Before you get started, tell me how that little one is doing."

Randy smiled and pulled out his phone. "This is my little girl." His face beamed with pride and a hint of weariness—from lack of sleep, LuAnn guessed.

LuAnn and Janice gushed over the pictures as he scrolled through them. "What a sweet baby," LuAnn said. "Those kissable cheeks."

"She's definitely getting a lot of kisses." He put his phone away and donned his officer face. He looked at Janice. "You said a bin was missing and has returned?"

LuAnn pointed to the bin on the table. "Yes. The other morning when we found that Margaret was missing, this was also gone. It had been here the night before, so we thought the kidnapper must have taken it."

"Okay." He wrote a note in his notepad. "Who has access to this building?"

"Margaret has a key. I believe Roy does. Now Dahlia has the spare one. I don't know who else. Someone on the board maybe? I expect Margaret let the cleaning crew and grounds people in..."

"So we need to rule Dahlia and this Roy person out then." He seemed to be writing a to-do list.

"Dahlia?" Janice said, sounding surprised. "I don't think she would kidnap her aunt. She seems really concerned about her."

Randy nodded. "I understand. We're not accusing her of anything, we just need to rule her out."

"I see," Janice said.

"Are she and Margaret close?" Randy asked.

LuAnn didn't like this line of questioning. She wanted to trust Dahlia, but maybe her fondness for the young woman had diminished her objectivity. "They haven't known each other very long, but I agree with Janice. Dahlia seems very concerned."

"So, they were at odds before, right? Didn't she say something about her mother and Mrs. Ashworth having a falling-out over something?"

"That's what she said," LuAnn answered. "They argued about something before Dahlia was even born."

"Do you know what Dahlia's mother's name was?"

"No, but I think she's only recently deceased, which is why Dahlia started searching for Margaret."

Randy didn't say anything else about it, but LuAnn wondered if his thoughts were winding the same direction as hers. She also questioned why she hadn't realized that Dahlia's less than ideal past with Margaret could hide a motive. Her thoughts were interrupted by Randy asking another question.

"And this Roy..."

LuAnn looked at him blankly. It suddenly occurred to her that she didn't have the slightest idea what Roy's last name was. "I—I don't know much about him. I just know he was helping Margaret organize things down here. I met him yesterday morning for the first time."

Janice came to her rescue. "I think the best person to ask about him is Dahlia."

Randy took a deep breath. "Okay, so this bin..." He put on his gloves and examined it. "The white powder on the bottom. Was that there when you saw it the other night?"

"No," LuAnn said. "I'm sure it wasn't there."

"We checked around and didn't find anything like it here," Janice added.

He pulled an evidence bag from his satchel and scraped some of the powder into it. "I'll get it checked out."

"Thanks," LuAnn said.

"Have you two touched the bin?"

"We tried not to." Janice leaned against the table. "I don't think we did."

He smiled. "Good. You innkeepers are actually getting good at investigating."

LuAnn chuckled. "We've had a few opportunities."

Randy took out his fingerprinting kit and dusted the bin and its contents very thoroughly. He seemed to be finding some.

"Okay," he said once he finished his work, "I've found several prints. Some partial ones and some seeming to be pretty fresh. Most are probably Margaret's. We'll run them through the system."

"That's great," Janice said. "If there are any that aren't Margaret's, we'll be able to know who took it."

"Not necessarily." Randy shook his head. "The other prints could be there for legitimate reasons. If this Roy was helping Margaret, he might have handled this particular bin. Also, prints won't show up in our database unless the person has a criminal record, so if they've never committed a crime, it won't help."

"Right," Janice said. "But it could possibly point us in the right direction."

"It could."

He packed up his evidence bags and hefted the bin. "I'm sorry we haven't found Margaret yet. I know you're worried."

"We are," LuAnn said. "It's hard to imagine her being tied up somewhere or locked in a room..."

Janice shuddered. "We've been praying for her."

"Me too," Randy said. "I'll bring the bin back when we're done with it." He waved goodbye and left.

"Well, I think we've done all we can do here," LuAnn said, picking up her purse.

Janice tightened her sweater around herself. "Should we be off to the magical pay phone?"

"Yes," LuAnn said. "It'll be good to get that over with."

"What about Dahlia?"

"I'll text her that we're leaving. She can always walk back to the inn if she needs to. It's not that far. I'll let her know we can pick her up on our way back if she wants."

"Sounds good." Janice headed toward the stairs.

LuAnn paused and said a silent prayer that they'd be able to find their friend. Knowing the great worth of the coins made their quest to find her even more urgent.

They reached the gas station with the pay phone. LuAnn parked, and they strode to the relic. LuAnn got Cole Harrison's number from his phone and dialed.

"Hello?" The person answered on the first ring, and LuAnn's pulse sped up.

"Is this Cole Harrison?"

"Yes." His voice sounded annoyed, harsh. "I don't know how you got this number, but I'm on all the no-call lists. You shouldn't be calling me. I don't want what you're selling."

"I'm not calling to sell you something. I have your phone." LuAnn glanced at Janice for support. "I found it at the river last night after you, uh, swam away—"

"You have it?" His voice changed from annoyed to... LuAnn wasn't sure, but possibly nervous. "I need my phone back."

"Of course. Where can I meet you?"

"The library."

"Oh." His abrupt answer unsettled her. "Marietta Library? When? We, I mean, my friend and I—"

"Brad Grimes?" Now his voice reflected anger. That was easy for LuAnn to read.

"No, no. Another friend." She didn't want to give him Janice's name. "Not Brad."

"Okay then. I'm at the library now."

"Can we meet him now?" LuAnn whispered to Janice, who nodded. "Sure," she said into the phone.

"Meet me in front of the main entrance."

"We'll be there in..." She glanced at the time. "About ten minutes, maybe fifteen, depending on traffic."

"Fine." He hung up.

LuAnn glanced at the phone, then to Janice. "We're supposed to meet him at the library in ten minutes." She replaced the receiver, and they walked back to her car.

"Do you know what you're going to say?" Janice asked as they slid into the car.

"I'm going to ask him why he's doing this to Brad. I think the direct approach is best. From what I could tell, he's not the type for small talk."

"Good plan," Janice said.

They reached the large red-brick library, parked, and headed along the path bordered by pristine lawns and up the steps toward the front entrance. Several people were coming and going between the colonial-looking white pillars of the entryway, but no one who had the build of the guy LuAnn had seen swimming last night.

"Hmm," she said as she scanned the area. "I don't see him." Glancing toward the other side of the building, she saw a tall maple. Leaning against it was a young man in a gray T-shirt. LuAnn recognized him from the picture on the phone. It was Cole Harrison. He glanced up at the women then indicated that they should come over.

LuAnn glanced around. The tree itself was pretty isolated, but the sidewalks around the yard were fairly busy. With Janice beside her, she felt safe talking to him. She and Janice trudged through the damp grass to the tree.

"You have my phone?" he said once they'd reached him.

"I do." LuAnn left it in her pocket for the moment. "I was wondering..."

"I just want my phone."

She took it out. "I... Could you tell me why you're doing this to Brad?" She handed him the phone, and he snatched it from her hand. "He's a good man."

Cole let out a snort. "Well, you don't know him then."

LuAnn straightened. "I think I do."

"You his girlfriend?" He looked at her closer. "Hey, I know who you are. I've seen your picture in the brochures around town for that, what's it called... Wayfarers something or other."

The directness of the question unsettled her. She had wanted to be the one asking the questions. She glanced at Janice. "I... no. I'm not his girlfriend. Just a friend. But I do care about him, and I know him well enough to know he's a good man. His reputation..."

"His reputation?" Cole's chest rose and fell. "He puts himself out there like he's Mr. Perfect." He rolled his eyes.

Janice cautiously stepped forward. "Could you tell us what you have against him?"

His eyes seemed blank for a moment, as if Janice's question had sent him somewhere. His face became increasingly stern—eyebrows drawing together, jaw clenching, lips pinching. LuAnn thought he might explode.

"Oh, I don't have anything against him," he finally said, obviously sarcastic. "Maybe you should ask my *mom* what she has against him." He turned to go.

"What?" LuAnn asked. "What do you mean?"

He hesitated. "Thirty years ago. Did you know him then?" He went on without waiting for an answer. "He wasn't the super-perfect, entrepreneur/philanthropist he makes himself out to be now."

"I don't understand." LuAnn's heart pounded like a locomotive in her chest. "Please, what do you mean?"

"Brad Grimes killed my mother. That's what I mean."

Chapter Eleven

LuAnn was too stunned to try to get Cole to explain more and simply watched him rush over the yard to the sidewalk and disappear behind the trees outside the parking lot.

Janice placed a hand on her back, releasing her from her trance.

"Well." LuAnn tried to smile. "That was unexpected."

"I'll say," Janice said. "Of course he's lying. He must be."

LuAnn leaned against the tree, collecting her scattered thoughts. "He had so much emotion. He seemed so hurt. You know? The kind of hurt that makes you angry."

Janice nodded. "He definitely seemed that."

"So I don't think he was just lying. He believed what he was saying. Besides, what would be the purpose of lying about something like that?"

"Right. It's hard to imagine what he would have to gain by accusing Brad of killing his mother."

Memories of her time spent with Brad breezed through LuAnn's mind. She couldn't think of any instance that would give her a clue to him having a past like this young man described. No red flags came to mind. No light bulb saying,

Now that makes sense. "We've known Brad over a year now," she finally said. "Can you think of anything about him that would make something like this in his past make sense?"

Janice shook her head, and LuAnn's stomach remembered that they needed to get on with their day. "Let's get some lunch." She started walking, and Janice came along.

LuAnn kicked a pine cone as she walked. "I don't want to blindly think Brad is perfect—I don't. But from what I know of him, I think Cole is mistaken... or misinformed."

They reached the car, and LuAnn pressed the unlock button on the fob. "I'll be glad when I can talk to him about this." Despite her reasoned response, a nagging ache nipped at her. Talking with Brad would be the only thing to drive it away.

Janice got in the car. "Until then, keep reminding yourself what a good man he is, okay?"

"You're right." LuAnn drove out of the parking lot. "And at least we can be pretty sure this guy has an ulterior motive to his lawsuit."

"That's right." Janice's voice perked up. "So, we're on our way to find the expert guy now, right?"

"Yep," LuAnn answered. "But I'm actually starving. Where should we eat?"

"How about Rev's by the River?" Janice smiled.

"Chili dogs sound perfect. And it's near where we're supposed to find Thaddeus."

A few minutes later they were standing outside of Rev's, lunches in hand.

As they silently filled their hungry stomachs at a picnic table, LuAnn perused the beach. Even though it was September, and the summer tourist season had died down, it still vibrated with life. All ages gravitated to this park. It had everything—history, water sports, hiking, biking, food. LuAnn felt grateful to live so close. Her gaze moved to the river where a couple of kayakers skimmed across the water.

"Kayaks." Janice must have had the same thought.

LuAnn eyed her friend. "Yes, that's going to be us tomorrow afternoon. Isn't that exciting?" She grinned, hoping Janice would pick up on her enthusiasm.

Janice reflected the smile, but LuAnn knew it wasn't heartfelt. "I'm, uh, looking forward to it." Then she gave up the charade and shook her head. "I'm really not."

LuAnn wiped her mouth with her napkin. "You've done some awesome things since we opened the inn. Remember how scared you were of ice skating?"

"That was different."

"You ended up being the best of all of us. And, more importantly, you had fun. Right?"

Janice nodded reluctantly. "I guess you're right about that."

"Will you at least try kayaking then?"

Janice glanced at the water. "It does look like fun. I just imagine myself turning upside down and not being able to get out of that hole you sit in. And then I'm trapped, and then I drown."

"I've seen lots of kayakers on this river. Never have I seen one turn upside down and the person in it not be able to get out. And the kayaks we'll be using have really big holes you sit in. You can't get stuck. Besides, it's not like we'll be braving the rapids. Just a peaceful, calm, sunset cruise. You'll love it."

"That does sound nice."

"So you'll try it?"

Janice nodded a little less reluctantly. "I'll try."

"That's awesome. It will be a nice break from all the stress we've been under." LuAnn moved to pick up their trash. "We need to find our expert. Thaddeus Culverson."

"Hey," Janice said as she stood to help. "Isn't that your friend Ashley?"

"Where?"

"Over by the dock."

LuAnn looked and, sure enough, Ashley was standing next to the long wooden dock talking to someone. "I wonder what she's doing at the park."

"Isn't she in town to research the Castle?"

"Maybe she came here for lunch, like us. She mentioned that she likes to get outside."

"That could be," Janice said. "Who is that she's talking to? It looks like..."

"It looks like Seth, doesn't it? Yeah, it is him. I didn't know they knew each other."

"Maybe they just bumped into each other here." Janice stepped toward the trash can. "Do you want to go say hi?"

LuAnn nodded. "I do. Maybe I'll try to plan another lunch date."

They headed toward the dock where she stood, but as they walked, a tall, scruffily-dressed older man was walking directly toward them. LuAnn recognized him from when she and Ashley had bumped into him. "That's our expert," she whispered to Janice.

LuAnn eyed her friend over by the dock but figured she might not have an opportunity to talk to this man again. She would call Ashley later. The man had nearly reached them, so she stepped toward him.

"Mr. Culverson?"

He did a double take, then eyed LuAnn suspiciously. "You talking to me?"

LuAnn smiled as graciously as she could. "Yes, I was wondering if I could talk to you for a minute."

"What about?" His gruff voice fit his sudden standoffish demeanor.

"I just want to ask you a question about the history of Marietta. I understand you're the expert in town."

A hint of a grin spread over his face. "I have a bit of knowledge about the place. It's true."

"I don't mean to interrupt. You seemed to be headed somewhere."

He smoothed his gray beard. "I was on my way to visit a sick friend, actually."

"We wouldn't want to keep you from that," Janice said.

His short-lived annoyance passed, and he smiled. "Well, how about this? Why don't you ladies walk with me? It's just up the street a bit and around the corner." He pointed up Second Street and then curved his hand to the left.

LuAnn glanced at Janice, who nodded. "Sure," she said. "Thank you."

"What do you want to know?" he asked as they began their trek.

"We were wondering about Camp Putnam," LuAnn said. "Can you tell us about that place?"

"Oh, sure," he said. "I've been hearing about Camp Putnam my whole life. My grandfather's grandfather served there."

"Your family's been here for a long time," Janice said.

"Yup, before that even. We Culversons were some of the first to homestead."

"What a great legacy," LuAnn said.

"So when the South seceded, good President Lincoln, he called for standing armies to be formed in all the states. They didn't have bases around like they do now. So, the governor called for Camp Putnam to be formed."

"Interesting." LuAnn shifted her gaze to the two rivers converging—the Ohio and the Muskingum. "I suppose this was a pretty important location, with the two rivers right here."

Thaddeus threw her an approving wink. "That's right. My ancestor and his troop were charged with guarding the river against any Southern river attack."

"That makes sense," LuAnn said. "Were the men trained on the river or mostly as foot soldiers?"

"Most were trained as foot soldiers. Only for a short time before they were sent to fight."

"That's too bad," Janice said.

"Yes, many young men lost their lives." He leaned his head back, letting a breeze ride through his gray hair. "Some were sailors though. Some of the locals who grew up on the river with the steamboats and canoes knew the river so well, they stayed to take care of the Union Navy ships that were here, as well as to keep watch in case of an attack."

"Is the camp still here?" LuAnn asked. "Was it preserved for history?"

"I wish." He shook his head. "They tore it down in the late 1800s. It was over there where the fairgrounds are now." He pointed as if LuAnn would know exactly which direction the fairgrounds were.

"So has it been excavated over the years?" LuAnn asked.

"Oh, yeah."

"There are no buildings left?"

"Unfortunately, no."

LuAnn was thinking about the gold coins. They must not have been buried at Camp Putnam, or they would have been found by now. She decided to ask him the question she really wanted answered. "You don't know anything about a load of gold coins that was lost there, do you?"

"Ah!" The man slapped his forehead. "Don't tell me you're treasure seekers too."

"No, sir," Janice said. "Don't worry."

He glanced at them suspiciously. "Sure, you're not. That's what they all say."

"Really," LuAnn assured him. "Our friend—you know her—Margaret Ashworth. She's been kidnapped, and the gold coins seem to have some connection."

His face drooped. "Margaret..." He sighed. "My friend, Margaret. Yes, I've heard about her disappearance. I'm worried sick."

"We are too," Janice said.

LuAnn nodded. "That's why we're trying to help find her."

"You ladies are?"

LuAnn leveled her shoulders. "Yes. And it's really important we find out about the gold coins. We have reason to believe the kidnapper may be after them."

He shook his head. "People have been looking for those coins for more than a hundred and fifty years. What makes you think you can find them?"

"Even if we don't find them, the more we learn about them the better," LuAnn said. "Maybe it will lead us in the right direction at least."

"Makes sense, I suppose," Thaddeus said. "I'll tell you one thing." He leaned into them as if he was going to share a secret. "I do know who found out about the Confederate spy. Not many people know it was a schoolteacher."

LuAnn exchanged a glance with Janice. "What?"

"She taught in the school, but she was actually working for the North, and she's the one who found the spy."

"How do you know this?"

His brow furrowed. "You doubt me?"

"Of course not," LuAnn said. "But we saw a picture of a schoolteacher in a newspaper clipping from that time, and I'm wondering if it's the same one."

"I know about the schoolteacher from my grandmother, and she heard about it from her grandmother." His steps slowed as they approached a small house. "This is where I have to say goodbye. I hope I was of some assistance to you."

"You were," LuAnn said with a smile. "Thank you."

He ascended the three steps, knocked, and without waiting, opened the door. "Roy?" LuAnn heard him say as he leaned in. "There you are. How are you doing today, my friend?"

Chapter Twelve

Did he say Roy?" LuAnn asked Janice as they climbed the stairs behind Thaddeus.

The door was still open, but Thaddeus had closed the screen. LuAnn peeked in. Thaddeus must have sensed the movement, because he turned toward the door.

"I'm so sorry," LuAnn said. "Did you say Roy?"

Before he answered, she spotted Roy lying on a sofa facing a TV. A few pillows were tucked behind his head. He lay on a sheet and was covered by a blanket. He was tilting his head, trying to catch sight of who was talking, LuAnn suspected.

"Who's there?" Roy asked.

"Roy?" LuAnn called. "It's LuAnn and Janice from Wayfarers Inn."

"Oh!" He pushed himself up on the couch. "It's good to see you ladies. How'd you find me?" He glanced at Thaddeus.

"I didn't know you knew them," he said.

"Don't just stand there." Roy beckoned to them. "Come on in."

LuAnn and Janice paced inside, pausing at the spot where Thaddeus stood.

"Well, come on," Roy continued. "Pull up a seat. You know each other?" he asked as LuAnn, Janice, and Thaddeus settled into chairs in the small living room.

"We just met," LuAnn said. "You know each other?"

Roy smiled. "We haven't known each other long either."

"Not until I found you passed out at the diner." Thaddeus frowned.

"And you so kindly took care of me."

"Despite your protestations." Thaddeus crossed his arms. "We all need help sometimes. Only fools don't know when to accept help."

Roy bowed his head. "True, true."

Unspoken questions swirled around the room. LuAnn didn't know where to start, so she paused, taking in the scene. Next to the couch on the side table sat an array of medicines, and an IV stand stood next to it as well. It didn't seem to be hooked up at the moment.

Roy must have seen her gaze, because he smiled softly. "I'm sick."

A wave of sadness flowed over LuAnn. "Not just low blood sugar?"

"I'm sorry." The corners of his eyes sagged. "I didn't want to worry you." He coughed. "I didn't want to worry anyone."

"We understand," Janice said. "I'm so sorry you're sick."

"It's cancer—colon."

"Can we help you?" LuAnn didn't know what to say. "Should you be at a hospital?"

"Yes," Thaddeus answered.

"I have my reasons for not." His voice rasped, heavy with emotion.

LuAnn sat quietly, remembering how much she appreciated times when her friends supported her just by being there, even when no words of wisdom would help. She hoped their company would comfort him.

"Dahlia..." he said.

Thaddeus glanced at him. "You sure you want them to know?"

"If I don't have a chance to tell her," he said, "I wonder if they would." He turned to LuAnn and Janice. "The doctors say I don't have much time left—months, weeks, maybe. I had hoped to spend more time with Margaret and Dahlia, to tell them, to..." His chest rose and fell. "I wanted to reconcile or at least apologize."

Still LuAnn didn't say anything, just waited.

"I'm Dahlia's father."

LuAnn took in a breath. "She said her father left when..."

"That's right. I've done wrong. That's why I want to make it right before I..." He shook his head. "I wish I had something to leave her, to help her," he continued. "She's on her own. Well, she has Margaret, if she's found."

"She'll be found," LuAnn said.

"I hope so."

Even more questions knocked at the door of LuAnn's mind, but she hesitated, respecting his privacy as well as his health. She didn't want to overwhelm him.

"I'm hoping to get back on my feet, at least for a little while." He sighed. "I'm hoping to tell her then."

"Do you want us to tell her you're sick? She's been wondering where you are," Janice said.

Roy shook his head. "I can't bear the thought of burdening her."

LuAnn barely knew this man who was asking her to keep his secrets. Aside from the fact that she had been growing fond of Dahlia over the last couple of days, she also cared about Dahlia because Margaret was a friend. She was not comfortable keeping a secret from the young woman. She liked Roy, but he was asking a bit much. "She was worried when you weren't at the historical society. She's grown fond of you. We could bring her to visit you."

A warm smile swept over Roy's face. "Oh, how I hope she's grown to like me." His smile was replaced by a frown. "But I'd really rather she not know. She's already so concerned about Margaret." He sat up a little straighter. "Please tell her that I'm not well, so she knows why I haven't been there, but nothing about the...you know." He sighed. "Talking to you has reminded me how much I want to at least spend a few more moments with my daugh—Dahlia. The doctors' temporary solution—we'll hope it works enough to get me off this couch for a few days. Okay?"

"Okay," LuAnn said reluctantly. She would respect his wishes, but it would be difficult to keep this from Dahlia.

"If it doesn't, then I'll let you bring her here."

"Fair enough." LuAnn stood. "We don't want to wear you out." She moved to his side and touched his shoulder. "We'll be praying for you, Roy. I promise."

"We sure will," Janice agreed. "And we'll bring you soup."

His eyes glowed like they hadn't the whole time they'd been there. "Yes, pray for me. And Dahlia. And Margaret."

LuAnn moved toward the door. "We will."

The sun had sunk low in the sky when LuAnn and Janice stepped down the few concrete stairs in front of Roy's rental. A breeze swept up from the river and blew a strand of hair into LuAnn's face, and she brushed it aside as she took in what had just happened.

"Poor man," Janice said.

LuAnn's heart ached for him. "A life filled with regrets is a sad thing. Now I know what he meant when he said he was trying to make things right."

"I'm so glad he's trying."

"I hope he has time," LuAnn said. "He didn't look well at all."

"No, he didn't."

A leaf lingered on the breeze and fell to the ground in front of LuAnn's feet. "I guess that's why we should remember to do our best to live each day to the fullest."

"We've learned that, haven't we, Lu?"

"We have. Which makes me think how much I wish he would tell Dahlia. I understand why he wants to wait, but I think it would be better if she knew and could spend as much time with him as possible." She thought about when her mother died. How hard that was.

"Yeah. Moments are precious at times like these."

"On the other hand, we don't know how Dahlia will respond. She seems to really want family relationships, but being abandoned by a father is not an easy thing to forgive. I felt that growing up...and saw it as a teacher."

Janice's eyes showed compassion. "I saw it too," she said. "He may be worried about that, and having the time together without her knowing is better than no time at all—if she were to reject him."

LuAnn pondered the heartbreak. "I'm glad it's never too late to try and make things right."

"Me too."

"It'll be good to get back to the inn," LuAnn said as they approached the car. "We have a lot to tell Tess."

"Yeah, and I'm looking forward to dinner." Janice smiled.

As they entered the car, LuAnn's phone buzzed. It was a text from Brad.

Want to stop by my office for some coffee? It's been a long day. I could use some company.

A knot formed in LuAnn's stomach remembering what Cole Harrison had accused Brad of—killing his mother. It just wasn't possible. She showed the text to Janice. "What do you think? Should we stop by?"

Janice's shoulders slumped. "I think we should. He needs to know about that guy's accusations."

"I think so too. Tess will have to wait a bit longer for the scoop on our day. Will you text her and tell her we're running late?"

"Sure."

Ten minutes later LuAnn and Janice pulled into the parking lot of Brad's office.

As they entered the reception area, Saffron Navratilova, Brad's niece who worked there part-time, greeted them with a smile. "Oh, hi, LuAnn. Hey, Janice."

"Nice to see you, Saffron," LuAnn answered. "How are you doing?"

Her slender form leaned against the desk. "I'm good. Working a lot, but good. Are you here to see Uncle Brad?"

LuAnn smiled. "We are. Is he available?"

"Yep. Go on in."

LuAnn and Janice guided themselves to Brad's office.

"Knock, knock," LuAnn said as she poked her head in. "Is this a good time?"

Brad glanced up from his computer. His face, tight and creased a moment before, relaxed. "Of course. This is the perfect time. Come in." He pressed a button on the intercom to buzz Saffron.

"Yes?"

"Will you bring us some coffee, please?"

"Sure," she answered.

LuAnn and Janice found their seats as Brad pulled his chair around to the front of the desk so he could sit near them.

"I've had a stressful few days," he started. "As you know." He glanced at Janice. "LuAnn filled you in?"

"She did," Janice answered.

"And this morning was the worst. Lost two buyers and one seller." He took in a breath. "Cole Harrison put negative reviews on all the sites."

"I'm so sorry," LuAnn said.

Brad smiled. "Don't be. It'll all be okay. I know it will, but I thought, I don't have to go through this rough day all by myself. I have friends who care about me." He eyed Janice and LuAnn, lingering just a breath longer on LuAnn. "And I knew seeing you would lift my spirits."

LuAnn's cheeks warmed a bit. "I'm glad we can be here for you. That's what friends are for."

Brad nodded slowly. "That's right."

Saffron delivered the coffee in smooth brown mugs, and LuAnn cupped hers in her hands. Brad's relief at seeing them was making her doubt her determination to tell him about the Cole incident.

"So," Brad said, "I've told you about my day, as depressing as it has been. How was yours?" His eyes grew serious. "Any news of Margaret?"

LuAnn's mind weaved through the events of the day. Where to start? "Actually, we did get some important information about the gold coins, and Camp Putnam, and—"

"Camp Putnam? I know about that place. Remember, I used to be a tour guide on the trolley tours. I know Marietta pretty well."

"That's right," Janice said.

LuAnn leaned forward. "Do you know anything about Camp Putnam?"

"I know it was by the fairgrounds. There was a school next to it. There was a scandal at the school. Apparently one of the teachers married a spy." He grinned. "Tourists love those kinds of stories."

"Is it true?" LuAnn asked.

"As far as I know. It's hard to tell, being the history is from so long ago, but the tour group got their information from Margaret, so it must have been vetted."

Janice looked as confused as LuAnn felt. "That's different from what we heard from Thaddeus. He said the teacher was a spy for the North."

"Thaddeus?" Brad asked. "You mean the guy who gives tours on the river?"

"Yes," LuAnn answered. "We talked to him today."

Brad leaned back in his chair. "That guy's notorious for making up stories for his tours. I would take what he says with a grain of salt."

"I guess we'll have to research," LuAnn said.

"You'll hate that," Brad teased.

LuAnn chuckled.

"What else did you do today? Oh, I almost forgot to ask you. That phone we found last night and our impromptu swimmer—did you hear anything from him?"

LuAnn sucked in a breath. She couldn't avoid the subject anymore. "Actually, yes, we did hear from him."

Janice nodded. "He's quite a fellow, this Cole Harrison."

"So, what happened?"

LuAnn took a sip of her coffee. "I called him at that number on the lock screen," she began. "And we set up to meet at the library."

"The library?" Brad tilted his head. "Is he a book guy?"

"My guess is he was using the computer," Janice put in.

"Right," LuAnn said.

"So you met at the library?"

"Yeah, outside on the lawn. And he was pretty angry."

Brad nodded. "He's got a grudge about something. I don't know what."

"Well, that's where the crazy part comes in. He says you..." LuAnn paused, thinking how best to say it. "Knew his mother."

Brad frowned and tilted his head, asking for more.

"He said you killed her," she finally managed to get out.

Brad blinked as he shook his head. "*I* killed his mother?"

"That's what he said," Janice said softly.

"Why would he—" Brad stopped midsentence as he seemed to scan his memory. Then a sick expression came over his face.

Before Brad could say any more, LuAnn's phone rang. Glancing at the screen, she saw that it was a call from Dahlia.

"I'm sorry," she said to Brad and Janice. "It's Dahlia. I should probably take this." She tapped the ANSWER button. "Dahlia? Are you okay?"

"LuAnn?" Dahlia said. "You need to come to my aunt's house right away. Aunt Maggie is in serious danger."

"We'll be right there," LuAnn said.

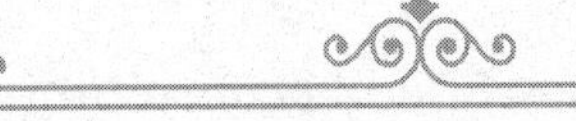

Chapter Thirteen

September 22, 1863

The sun hung high in the sky as Prudence finished her rounds. She'd ended up at the mess hall, which was really a long tent with tables inside. She'd given the leftover food to the cook. Outside the opening was a firepit where a man with a handlebar mustache sat quietly smoking a pipe.

Austin had been called to his regiment to practice maneuvers. Since they did this on the large parade grounds in the middle of camp, Prudence was able to watch him as she entered and exited the tents and cabins along the perimeter. So far the young soldier had done nothing suspicious. He performed his training duties with vigor. He was respectful to his superior officers. She even heard him encourage some of the new recruits.

She sighed as she stopped inside the entrance to the mess hall. She was no closer to discovering if he was the spy than before, and time was running out. A lump formed in her throat. She'd hoped to either rule him out as a spy or uncover proof that it was him. She'd done neither.

As she stood there, Moses playing beneath a nearby tree hitting leaves with a stick, Austin's regiment was released for the midday meal. Suddenly her lonely post surged with hungry soldiers. She eyed Austin as he tramped toward the mess hall with the others. He neared her position, and she planned to greet him, but before he reached her, he detoured to the man with the pipe. From where she stood, Prudence could not make out their hushed words.

Needing an excuse to move closer, she walked to the tree where Moses played, just behind Austin and the other man sitting by the fire.

"That's right, Corporal," the older man said. "They'll be repairing the stone wall tonight, understand?"

Austin nodded. "Yes, sir." he said, and got up and joined the others for lunch.

As quickly as she could, Prudence grabbed Moses's hand and rushed to the school. Entering, she gave Moses a slate to draw on in the back of the room and joined Cynthia at her desk.

"Prudence," Cynthia said. "Tell me you learned something."

Prudence attempted to catch her breath as she sat in a chair next to the desk. "I overheard him and another man."

"What other man?"

"An older man, probably an officer, with a handlebar mustache and a pipe."

Cynthia's face registered recognition. "Oh?"

"Does thee know him?"

"I may have seen him. What did they say?"

"It may be nothing, but I think they spoke in code. The older man said the stone wall was being repaired tonight." Relieved to have delivered the information, she glanced at Cynthia. "I do not think there is a stone wall around here, definitely nowhere near this camp, nor on the river. Not that I know of."

Cynthia's eyes brightened. "You did it, Prudence! You are brilliant!"

"What does thee mean?"

"'Stone wall,' Prudence." Cynthia pulled the cipher from its place behind the blackboard. "Stonewall Jackson. Their hero, who is more revered in his death than he was in life. Stonewall is the key word, I'm sure of it."

She removed a scrap of newspaper clipping from her boot and laid it on the table. Prudence could see that she was going back and forth from the clipping to the wheel and writing down a series of letters. When she finished, she showed them to Prudence. "This is where they will drop off the coins."

As the words left Cynthia's lips, the door opened, and Austin walked in.

Although he startled her, Prudence kept herself calm, as did Cynthia, who painted a warm smile on her face.

"Hello there, Austin." She pushed the cipher and papers into the top drawer of the desk.

Austin's eyes narrowed, and he didn't return her smile. Instead, he stepped to the desk, opened the drawer, and pointed. "You are a spy, Miss Knight, are you not?"

"I am not," Cynthia said. Then with a quick movement, she pulled a gun from her dress pocket and aimed it at him. "But you are."

LuAnn pulled into Margaret's driveway and noticed a FOR SALE sign in the neighbor's yard. It had Brad's and Grant's smiling faces on it and said, "Grimes Realty."

"That's nice to see." Janice gazed the same direction.

"It really is." LuAnn put the car in Park. "They're great real estate agents. I need to remember that losing three clients isn't the end of the world. They have a stellar reputation in this town."

"They really do," Janice agreed. "It's hard to see them treated so unfairly."

"It is." LuAnn ached for Brad.

The sound of the car doors closing must have alerted Dahlia to their arrival, because she opened the front door. "I'm sorry," she said as she let them in the house. "I'm probably being paranoid, but I was cleaning the house, and I found these." She pointed to a cupboard in the kitchen that was left open. A row of medicine bottles lined the shelf in a perfect row.

"Her meds?" LuAnn asked.

"And look at this." On the door to the cupboard was a schedule of when Margaret was supposed to take each one.

Two were for every day. On the side of the paper in all caps was a handwritten note.

DON'T FORGET CARVEDILOL AND LISINOPRIL

"See?" Dahlia pointed. "Those are the ones she takes every day, and I looked them up. They're for her heart. It's not good for her to be without them. She could have a heart attack."

LuAnn wanted to comfort Dahlia, to tell her not to worry, but she was worried too. She'd heard that it could be dangerous for heart patients to miss their meds, but she didn't know for sure.

"Before we panic," she said, "why don't we stop by the pharmacy on the way home and see what the real situation is. It's only been at the most between thirty-six and forty-eight hours. Missing them may be a problem, but it may not." She gazed at Dahlia. "Okay?"

Dahlia's muscles seemed as tight as ever, but she agreed.

LuAnn took a picture of the bottles with her phone so she could show them to the pharmacist.

"I can understand why you're worried," Janice said. "It's hard to imagine where she could be, what she's doing, and now without her medications, but LuAnn's right. Let's go to the pharmacy. And then back to the inn. We'll get some dinner. Are you hungry?" She glanced at her phone. "Tess texted me earlier that she's making chicken divan. It's a delicious dish with chicken and broccoli and cheese. It's one of my favorites."

"That sounds amazing." Dahlia's frown loosened into a slight smile. "Thank you so much."

Dahlia locked up the house, and as the three strolled to the car, LuAnn noticed a man standing in the yard next to Brad's sign.

"Hello," LuAnn greeted him. "How are you tonight?"

The man smiled. "Good. And you?"

"I'm fine. I see Brad Grimes is your real estate agent—"

"Wish I never met the man," he blurted before she could finish.

LuAnn felt like she had been punched in the gut. "May I ask why?"

"Did you hear what he did to that poor couple? Sold them a house overtaken by mold. Now the man is sick. They say he may never fully recover. I hope they sue and get everything he has." He yanked on the sign.

"You can't believe everything you read on the internet," LuAnn said, her voice sharper than she intended. "Anyone can accuse anyone of anything." Her heart raced. How could someone be so quick to judge?

"What? You know the guy?" he asked. "Don't let his charm fool you like it did me. I should've known someone that polite couldn't be for real. I believe the sick guy." He finally managed to pull Brad's sign out, letting it fall on the ground "Why don't you take this. Save me a trip to the dump." He kicked the sign in LuAnn's direction, then strode toward his house.

LuAnn stood in shock for a moment before she looked at Janice and Dahlia. "Can you believe that?" she finally said.

"That was insane." Dahlia helped Janice get the sign to the car as LuAnn rushed ahead to unlock it and open the trunk.

A few minutes later they were settled into their seats and headed to LuAnn's pharmacy.

Fortunately, the pharmacy was nearly empty, probably a lull before the after-work rush.

LuAnn led the others toward the back past the candy, makeup, toys, and natural remedies to the pharmacy counter. Her normal pharmacist wasn't there. Instead a young man who looked fresh out of college was working at a computer terminal. He looked deep in thought.

She approached the counter. "Hi." She leaned her head toward where he stood. "Excuse me?"

He jolted to attention, looked at her, and smiled. "I'm sorry. I didn't see you." He walked to the counter. "How can I help you?"

LuAnn took her phone out of her pocket, found the picture of the two pill bottles, and showed them to him. "Are you familiar with these medications?"

He glanced at the photo. "Sure," he said. "One is a beta blocker. The other one helps manage blood pressure. Is this you?" He pointed to the name on the prescription. "It can be confusing to start a new medication. Are you having side effects?"

LuAnn shook her head. "No, no. Thankfully, these aren't mine. They belong to our friend."

"I see. Well, they are good medications for heart issues. Often prescribed. They can cause drowsiness at times, but other than that, there aren't many side effects." He handed the phone back to her. "They should be taken with food."

LuAnn put her phone back in her pocket. "Uh, thank you. We were actually wondering what would happen if she suddenly stopped taking them."

"Why is your friend not taking them?" He frowned. "I would do everything you can to get her to follow her doctor's instructions. She could experience serious heart problems such as severe chest pain, an irregular heartbeat, or even a heart attack."

Dahlia sucked in a breath.

"If she doesn't want to take them anymore," he continued, "have her talk to her doctor. He can wean her off of them over a few weeks. Perhaps give her a different prescription."

LuAnn's gut clenched. "Thank you." She took a step back. "How long does it take for the negative effects to happen?"

"It's hard to say, but abruptly stopping something your body is used to can be dangerous. Do you think you can convince your friend to keep taking them?" he asked.

"I'll try," LuAnn answered. "Thank you."

"Thank you," Janice repeated as the three of them walked away in silence through the store and to the car.

Back at the inn, LuAnn and the others trudged into the kitchen where Tess was making dinner and listening to forties tunes on her phone. The lyrics "accentuate the positive" rang out, but LuAnn sure didn't see any positive to accentuate, except maybe the divine smell coming from the oven where Tess's chicken divan was surely just about ready.

"Could we listen to something else?" she said as she plopped into her chair at the table. "I'm so tired."

Tess's smile morphed into worry. "Of course." She turned off the tunes, then returned to the three of them sitting at the table. "Rough day? You got back late. It's past seven."

LuAnn was too exhausted to go into everything that had happened, so she just nodded. "And we're hungry." She felt like a child coming home from a rough day at school.

"Well, I've got a comforting meal waiting for you." Tess grabbed an oven mitt out of the drawer and opened the oven, letting the smell and heat drift to the waiting recipients.

"Thank you, Tess," Janice said, closing her eyes as she seemed to soak in the delicious aroma.

Dahlia sat quietly, her hands folded on her lap. LuAnn couldn't tell what she was thinking—her mind seemed miles away.

Tess's hot dish delivered the comfort she had promised, and soon LuAnn's wilted body and soul perked back to life. "So," she said as she finished her meal and laid her napkin across her plate, "we have a lot to tell you."

"I can see by the looks on your faces that you do, but guess what?" Tess said with a hint of a grin.

"What?" Janice asked.

"I also made dessert." Tess took a flowered tea towel off a plate sitting on the counter. A rich chocolate scent wafted through the room.

"Brownies?" Dahlia asked.

"You are a rock star," LuAnn said as Tess placed a plate with a brownie in front of her.

"Thanks!" Tess offered cups of milk to go with the brownies. "Now, tell me about your day."

Janice sighed. "I don't know about you, LuAnn, but I feel like we uncovered more questions than answers."

LuAnn nodded. "Me too."

"We still don't know where Aunt Maggie is." Dahlia took a bite of her brownie, then a sip of her milk. "I don't think we're any closer to finding her."

"It does seem that way," Janice said. "But sometimes all the little things fit together to guide us to the solution."

As Dahlia swallowed the last bite of her brownie, her eyelids drooped. "I'm going to get on my computer before I get too tired," she said. "I want to check the chat boards and see if anyone has posted about Aunt Maggie. I'm wiped out." Her chin quavered. "I can't think anymore."

"You've had a hard day," LuAnn said. "Why don't you use my sitting room so you can have some peace and quiet? Let us know if you need anything."

"Poor thing," Janice said as Dahlia left the kitchen. "She's been through a lot."

LuAnn stood, went to her bag, and retrieved her notebook. She turned to a fresh page and wrote, *Suspects.*

"What are you doing?" Janice asked.

"Everything seems a little garbled in my mind," LuAnn answered. "I think it will be helpful to lay it all out."

Janice leaned on the table. "Good thinking."

"Who are our suspects?" LuAnn asked.

The others looked at her blankly.

LuAnn wrote *Dahlia* on the paper, then cringed. "I'm sorry. Dahlia seems really convincing, but there are too many questions about why she and Margaret haven't met before now. What happened between Margaret and Dahlia's mom?"

"Okay," Tess said. "I can see that."

"So, does that mean Roy could be a suspect?" Janice gave Tess a sidelong glance. "We have a lot to tell you about him."

"Really?" Tess asked. "What?"

LuAnn glanced toward the kitchen door, making sure Dahlia hadn't come back into the common area. "He's Dahlia's father."

Tess almost choked on her brownie. "What?"

LuAnn nodded. "I know. It's crazy, but we saw him today at his house."

"His house? How?"

"It's a long story," Janice said. "He's terminally ill with colon cancer. He says he wants to reconcile with her before he dies."

"Wow." Tess rested her cheek on her hand. "But why does that make him a suspect?"

"If we think the kidnapper is really after the gold coins, then maybe he wants the coins to give to Dahlia," Janice offered. "He mentioned something about having nothing to leave her. If he could give her those, she'd be set for a long time. Maybe his guilt over being an absentee father is greater than his guilt over kidnapping an old woman."

"That's an interesting hypothesis. Is it enough of a motive to make him kidnap Margaret?" LuAnn gripped her pen in her hand.

"Imminent death makes people do all kinds of strange things," Janice said. "And he could have another reason for wanting the coins."

"Yeah," Tess agreed. "Any others?"

LuAnn wrote as she said, "Craig Reynolds."

"The guy whose mother was also kidnapped?" Janice asked. "I was thinking of him too."

"So we have three suspects." LuAnn twisted the pen in her fingers. "Any others?"

They stared at each other for a moment.

"I can't think of anyone else," Janice said.

"Me neither." Tess stood and gathered their brownie plates.

"Well," LuAnn said. "It's a start. We'll need to talk to these three about where they were when Margaret was taken, assuming she was taken yesterday morning after she got to the museum. In Dahlia's case, we know she says she was home, but maybe we can find someone who saw her."

"That's a good idea," Tess said.

"Mostly, I still feel like the answer to all this lies with the gold coins." LuAnn put the cap on her pen and closed her notebook.

"Right. Did you find out anything else about those?" Tess settled back into her spot at the table.

"More questions," Janice commented. "One person told us that the schoolteacher was a Union spy. Another person told us she married a Confederate spy."

"That is confusing," Tess agreed. "What schoolteacher?"

LuAnn smiled at Tess. "When we got to the museum, the bin that was missing was back on the table. Inside was another newspaper article from 1863 about the gold coins. It had a picture of a schoolhouse with the article, and we saw someone we thought could be a schoolteacher standing next to Prudence."

Tess's mouth fell open, and it took her a moment to find her voice. "You found a picture of Prudence?"

LuAnn retrieved her phone and opened the gallery to the series of pictures she'd taken of the article. She handed the phone to Tess. "See what you think, but Janice and I definitely think that's Prudence—the one holding a basket."

Tess studied the picture, and LuAnn could see that she enlarged a couple of the photos as she scrolled through them. Finally she handed the phone back to LuAnn. "I agree with you. That's Prudence."

"We need to look in Prudence's journal," LuAnn said. "It might shed some light on all of this."

"Once again, we're turning to Prudence for help," Janice said. "Just think, a small part of her legacy continues to help us."

As LuAnn pushed to her feet, her phone rang. "It's Brad." Tess and Janice nodded.

"How about we get up early to look at Prudence's journal? Six? My room?" Janice whispered as she and Tess exited the kitchen.

Nodding to her friends and giving Janice a thumbs-up, LuAnn sat back down. "Hey there," she said. "How are you doing?"

There was a pause, and then Brad spoke, his voice heavier than LuAnn had ever heard it before.

"Cole Harrison was right," he said. "I killed his mother."

Chapter Fourteen

LuAnn moved the phone from her ear and double-checked the name. Was this really Brad telling her he had killed someone? It didn't seem possible.

"Brad? What do you mean?" She leaned forward, her elbows on the table.

"I'm a few minutes away. Do you mind if I come over?"

"Of course not. Come on by." LuAnn moved to the stove and turned on the kettle. This called for tea. Tess and Janice had gone to their rooms, and Dahlia was still in her sitting room, so she and Brad would have the common room to themselves.

A few minutes later Brad arrived. She heard heavy footfalls on the stairs instead of his usual bouncy steps. Yet his ever-present smile surfaced when he spotted the teapot, cups, and cream and sugar set up on the coffee table, along with the plate of brownies.

LuAnn poured him some Earl Grey, just the way he liked it, with cream and sugar and a splash of vanilla.

"Perfect," he said as he took a sip. "London Fog. My favorite."

"So." LuAnn poured herself a cup then sank into the couch, leaning her head against the cushion. "What is this about you killing someone? That's absurd!"

Brad let out a slow breath. "It was a long time ago. I was starting out in real estate. In fact, I was showing my first listing."

"That long ago?"

"Yeah. It was an old house—probably from around the 1920s or so. It needed many repairs. Nice layout though. The inspector told me not to take anyone upstairs until we had it stabilized." He took in a breath. "I was so young."

"So you took someone up there?"

"I had a married couple for a client. When I was at the car getting some paperwork, the wife went against my warnings and climbed the stairs. The floor gave out, and she fell..."

"I'm so sorry, Brad." LuAnn patted his hand. "This was Cole's mother?"

"Yes. And he was there when it happened. He was about two years old."

LuAnn exhaled. "Oh, how awful. And now he seems to be holding a grudge against you." She eyed him. "But, Brad, it's not your fault. You warned her, right?"

A shadow passed over Brad's already discouraged face. "I warned her that the second floor wasn't stable, but I didn't warn her about the stairs. She thought she could go up the stairs and just peek at the second floor."

"Did you know the stairs were unstable?"

"The inspector didn't specifically say the stairs were dangerous, just the second floor. But if I'd looked closer, I would have known. If I hadn't gone out to my car, I could have kept her from going up the stairs at all. How many times I've wished I hadn't left her alone in the house..."

"Brad—"

"LuAnn, I know it wasn't all my fault. She chose to go up the stairs, but I do believe it was partly my fault."

"Did…" The question stuck in her throat. "Did the family sue you or anything?"

He nodded. "They did. The court found me not guilty of any negligence or incompetence. Said I couldn't have known the stairs were a deadly risk. There's not even a mark on my record."

"That's good." LuAnn released the breath she'd been holding.

"It was a huge relief, but the fact is, no matter what the court said, I am partly to blame."

LuAnn sat in silence for a moment. "I understand how you could still carry some guilt about this, Brad, but you have to forgive yourself. You weren't directly responsible."

"I know that in my head, and in many ways, I've learned to live with what happened. The months of depression and self-doubt I went through afterward helped me be a better agent. But that sounds trite, I suppose."

"I don't think so. When people make a huge purchase like buying a house—or an inn—" She smiled. "They need someone who cares about them and not just the deal. Someone who is careful, kind, compassionate." She caught his gaze. "You are all those things."

Brad's eyes moistened. "I've gotten past a lot of the struggle, but hearing that Cole Harrison blames me for his mother's death brought that whole time in my life to the surface. I don't blame him for lashing out at me. I wish I could help him somehow."

"Maybe you can." An idea floated to LuAnn's mind. "One of the things that's hard for those who have lost loved ones is the longing for details about them. Since he was so young when his mother died, I wonder if it would help him if you got together and shared with him the details of that day."

"That's a thought. It might comfort him, at least a little, to know exactly what happened that day." Brad smiled. "That's a lovely idea, Lu. Do you still have the phone number from his lost cell phone?"

"I do." LuAnn took out her phone. "I snapped a picture of it. I'll send it to you."

"Thanks."

"I hope this will help him." LuAnn swallowed the last bit of her tea.

"Me too. In a way it's a relief to connect with him and understand where his anger is coming from. I had no idea why he was out to get me."

"Yeah. You're still the best real estate agent in town." LuAnn threw him a glowing smile, knowing he would brush aside the compliment.

"I don't know about that, but by God's grace, I do my best."

LuAnn put her cup on the coffee table. A lawsuit. Two missing women. A desperate father. Stolen coins, Confederate spies, secret code. Were these things all tied together? How?

The next morning, LuAnn's alarm woke her at five thirty. After a quick shower and getting dressed, she grabbed the

McGuffey Reader, the cipher, her copy of Prudence's journal, and her laptop and met her two friends already gathered in Janice's sitting room.

"Good morning, sunshine," Tess said with a smile, handing her a cup of coffee. "How'd you sleep?"

LuAnn sank into a cozy armchair next to the couch. "I slept well, actually." She glanced at the items she held in her lap. "What should we go over first, the *McGuffey Reader* or Prudence's journal? We don't have much time before we have to get ready for breakfast."

"Actually, I texted Winnie last night." Tess placed her cup on the coffee table. "She said she and Robin and Taylor can cover the guest breakfast this morning. They'll need help with the café though."

"That was smart thinking," Janice said. "Gives us at least an extra thirty minutes or so."

"Anyway." Tess held up her copy of Prudence's journal. "I think we should look in this first. I think I remember something about a teacher."

"Me too." Janice nodded.

They opened their copies of Prudence's journal to the date that had been on the newspaper clipping.

"There it is," LuAnn said after a moment. "She was friends with the schoolteacher. It says they delivered care packages to the families at the camp. Some of them had lost their fathers to the war, others were deployed, some just didn't have much to live on. It's just like our Prudence to take part in this."

LuAnn read on. "And she seems to have formed a friendship with the teacher, speaks highly of her."

"I wonder if this is the woman who married a Confederate spy," Tess said.

"We don't know if that's true or not," LuAnn responded. "Remember, it was Thaddeus who told us, and Brad said he's not always spot-on with his historical facts."

"Oh, right," Tess admitted. "But it could be true, couldn't it? We know there was a spy at Camp Putnam—the one who was supposed to meet the guy delivering the coins."

LuAnn's mind flooded with the possibilities. "Maybe she didn't know he was a spy when she fell in love."

Janice's eyes twinkled. "Or maybe she did, but she loved him so much she didn't care."

"Or maybe she was a spy too." Tess joined in.

"Anyway," LuAnn said, "I wonder whether she knew about the coins. If she had a connection with the spy—which we don't know for sure she did—then it's possible she did know."

"And if she knew…" Tess continued the line of reasoning. "Then it's possible that Prudence did too." She glanced back at the journal in front of her.

Skimming the handwritten lines, LuAnn saw the word *McGuffey*.

As she did, Janice gasped.

"Did you see what I just saw?" LuAnn glanced at Janice.

"I don't know," Janice responded. "She mentions a *McGuffey Reader*."

"That's what I saw."

"You did?" Tess said. "Where?"

LuAnn pointed it out to her then read: "'My teacher friend uses the *McGuffey Reader* for her students. It's a grammar book written by a man from Ohio.'"

"That's really cool," Tess said.

"And look." LuAnn kept reading the journal. "'I am reminded today of the futility of earthly wealth. "Your gold and silver is cankered; and the rust of them shall be a witness against you, and shall eat your flesh as it were fire. Ye have heaped treasure together for the last days." James 5:3. I pray for the souls of those who use the gift of gold to perpetuate slavery.'"

"Sounds like she's talking about those gold coins," Janice said.

"It sure does," Tess agreed.

"We seem to be on the right path." LuAnn's gaze stayed fixed on the journal. "Do you see anything else about the coins or more about the teacher? I have a hunch the teacher has something to do with all this—wait." Having read a few pages both before and after the date of the newspaper clipping, she scanned the margins. At the bottom of the second page after that date, she found something written in tiny print. If she hadn't been looking, she wouldn't have noticed. "What's that?" She pointed it out to her friends.

"I can't read it," Tess said. "It's too small."

LuAnn went to her room and returned with her magnifying glass. The glass revealed three words.

KEY MOSES WILLARD

"Key. Moses Willard," Janice spoke the words out loud. "What does it mean?"

"I would guess that 'key' would be a key to understanding something, don't you think?" LuAnn asked.

"That's what the context seems to point to," Tess agreed.

"So." LuAnn's heart pounded. "That's it." She gazed at her friends then back to the journal. "Moses Willard is the key!" She grabbed the *McGuffey Reader* and opened it to where she had placed a bookmark at Lesson XLVIII. The page where she'd found the older, faded underlines. She set the opened book on the table.

Tess picked it up and showed it to Janice, who hadn't been there when LuAnn had shown her the underlines. "Do you see those marks? That's where LuAnn thinks the next clue is."

"I can barely see any marks." Donning her reading glasses, Janice took the book from Tess and looked closer. "They must be really old to be that faint."

LuAnn opened her notebook to where she had written down the marked letters.

YIT BMQ

Then she picked up the wooden cipher.

"What are you thinking, Lu?" Tess asked. "Your mind seems to be in full figuring-out mode."

LuAnn pushed a strand of hair behind her ear. "I remember from the history classes I taught that many times a cipher will have a key word that's needed to use it. I think 'Moses Willard' is the key to the cipher." She glanced up at her friends.

"But how does this cipher work with the key?" Janice asked.

"I'm not sure," LuAnn said. "Maybe we can find something on the internet about how the ciphers worked." LuAnn opened her laptop and powered it up. She opened a browser window and typed "how to use a cipher disk" in the search engine. "There." She clicked on a video and the trio watched a demonstration of deciphering a secret message using a cipher wheel.

"Wow," Tess said. "That's so cool."

LuAnn wrote in her notebook.

MOS ESW ILL ARD

YIT BMQ

"The guy said they separated the words into groups of three or four letters," LuAnn said. She picked up the cipher, examining the inner and outer ring marked with the alphabet and the CSA in the middle. "Now, let's see."

"The outer ring is the coded text, right?" Janice asked.

"Right. They used the *A* of the inner wheel as a pointer. So..." She moved the inner *A* to point to the first letter in the key word, *M*, on the outer ring. "Now I find the first letter in the secret message, which is *Y*." She pointed to the *Y* on the outer ring. "The letter on the inner ring below the *Y* should be the first letter in the message."

"It's *S*," Janice said. "This really is cool. And so clever."

"I know." LuAnn allowed herself a second to revel in the awesome history moment, then she refocused.

"Now you'll point the *A* to the second letter in Moses, right?" Tess asked. "The *O*?"

"Yep." LuAnn turned the ring so the *A* in the inner ring pointed to the *O* in the outer ring.

"And find the second letter in the message on the outer ring, which is *I*."

LuAnn traced around the cipher to the *I*.

"The letter below the *I* is the next in the message, right? It's *U*."

"You got it." LuAnn smiled at Tess.

"It's pretty simple, actually," Janice said.

"As long as you have the key. Without 'Moses Willard,' you couldn't decode this. That's what made these decoders so useful."

"I see what you mean." Janice nodded.

LuAnn continued, with Tess and Janice checking her work, until they finished.

The words that came up were *SUB MUS*.

"What is that supposed to mean?" Janice asked.

Tess shook her head. "Not what I was expecting."

LuAnn sat back in her chair. "Me neither."

Chapter Fifteen

The three women stared at the words until the sound of footsteps and a door opening and closing jolted them from their trance.

"That's Dahlia getting up," Tess said.

"Yeah," LuAnn agreed. "I'll go check just in case she needs anything."

"We'll go downstairs. It's time to help with breakfast anyway." Janice glanced at the word again.

LuAnn gathered the items from the table. "Let's simmer on the words for a while. Maybe our minds will come up with something if we give it a few hours."

"Sounds good, since it means nothing to me at the moment." Tess stood and straightened her slacks.

"Me neither." Janice smoothed the afghan over the back of her sofa.

"We'll figure it out," LuAnn said. She tucked the items in her room before knocking on her bathroom door to check on Dahlia.

After Dahlia assured her she didn't need anything, LuAnn went downstairs. Reaching the last flight, she saw Seth near the desk. He seemed to be aimed toward the café, but he lingered.

"Hello, Seth," LuAnn said as she reached him.

"Hi. I was wondering if the café's open yet."

LuAnn check the grandfather clock in the parlor. It was 6:59. "The guests' complimentary breakfast is just starting," she said with a smile. "The café for paying customers doesn't open until eight."

"Sounds good," he said. "I'm glad I got up in time."

"Let's see what's on Winnie's menu for you today." She led him into the dining room to a table near the window with a view of the river. Sunlight angled through the clouds, reflecting on the water. LuAnn never got tired of the view.

"This is a beautiful place," Seth said. "I can see why my ancestors found their home here."

"Oh, have you learned more about them?"

Seth nodded. "They served here during the Civil War—my great-great—you know, *great*—grandmother helped with the Underground Railroad, and my grandfather was a soldier at Camp Putnam."

"Hmm." LuAnn had been hearing about that place a lot lately. "We've been learning about Camp Putnam."

"It's too bad they tore it down. I guess the people back then didn't realize we'd want to learn its history a hundred and fifty years later."

LuAnn smiled. "That's right." She pointed to the buffet table. "Feel free to load up your plate." As she moved away, she remembered something. "Oh, hey," she said as she returned to his table. "We saw you yesterday at the river."

"You did?" He smiled. "I, uh, like to walk around by the banks. It's peaceful."

"It really is," LuAnn said. "You were talking to my friend Ashley."

Seth looked up as if trying to remember, then he slowly nodded. "A brown-haired woman who works at one of the historical sites?"

"That's right. Do you know her?"

"No. I just bumped into her, and we started talking about history, genealogy, that kind of thing."

"That makes sense. She would be a big help in your research. She's a smart lady. One of my former students."

"You were a teacher?"

"I was. For many years I taught English and history to high school students."

"That's so cool. I loved my history teacher. I think it would be a fun job."

"Definitely fun," LuAnn said. "I miss it sometimes, but I don't miss grading all those papers." She smiled.

"Well, my great-great-great-grandmother—the one we've been talking about—she was a teacher too, so maybe it's in my blood, even though I've never done it." He chuckled.

"She was a teacher?" LuAnn jumped on his statement. "Where?"

"Here in Marietta. At the schoolhouse near Camp Putnam. It's how she and her husband met."

LuAnn's mind began to spin. "That's so interesting."

He must have noticed a perplexed look on her face. "Interesting? How?"

"It's kind of neat that love sprang up during such a dark time." That was definitely true.

"Yeah. They seem like pretty amazing people, from what I've been able to learn. I'm glad they found happiness."

"Yes, that is truly wonderful." She glanced at the buffet table. "Well, I should let you eat. You don't want to miss Winnie's blueberry pancakes."

"No," Seth said. "I sure don't."

A few hours later, LuAnn and the others finished up their morning chores and congregated in the kitchen.

"Well," Winnie said as she removed her apron. "Another busy morning. Lots of customers."

"Yeah. It seems like we've been having a pretty steady flow lately," LuAnn agreed. "It's nice."

"People are used to us now. They must like our service." Janice glanced at Winnie. "And our food."

Winnie smiled, accepting the compliment.

"The more consistent flow of money into the inn's account is nice too." Tess picked up a dish towel and wiped the island. "Speaking of which, I should work on the books today. I have a few invoices to pay." She turned to Winnie. "Do you have everything you need for the Taste of Marietta tomorrow?"

"I believe I do. I'll spend some time this afternoon preparing, and we'll be good to go." She grabbed her jacket from the hook. "I'll see you all," she said as she left.

LuAnn looked at the clock from her spot at the table. "It's just about time for my writing session with Dahlia. I half expected she would cancel after everything that's been going on."

Janice tilted her head. "I think spending time with you doing what she's passionate about will be comforting to her."

LuAnn wanted to help Dahlia, so why was she dreading this meeting?

"What's wrong?" Janice asked.

"I don't know…"

"Is it the writing thing?" Tess paused her mission to do the books and sat down next to LuAnn. "What we talked about on the way to the Reynolds'?"

LuAnn tensed. "Maybe. But it also feels a little like I'm going backward, kind of. She wants me to teach her to write. I loved teaching, but it's not me anymore. Ugh. I should be happier to help her. And I am. I really am. It's just stirring up feelings about other stuff."

"Dreams and regrets and hopes?" Tess smiled.

"Yeah. All of that."

"Are you thinking about taking up writing again?" Janice asked.

LuAnn paused before answering. Ever since Dahlia mentioned that she wanted to write a story about Marietta, ideas for her own story kept niggling at the edges of her mind.

Characters, places, plot ideas, even whole scenes. Thinking about these imaginary people and places brought joy to her heart. She was falling in love with the idea. She looked at her friends and nodded. "I really am." She laughed as relief came over her.

Her friends' encouraging smiles boosted LuAnn's spirits.

"We're behind you, 100 percent." Janice patted her back.

"Definitely," Tess agreed. "I can't wait to read it."

LuAnn took in a breath. "Honestly, I can't wait to write. Thanks, friends. What would I do without you?"

"Probably be cold and lonely on the street," Tess teased.

"Friendless," Janice joined in.

LuAnn rolled her eyes. "All right, let's not get too crazy." She pushed to her feet. "Dahlia and I will work at a table in the café. That way I'll be able to catch anyone coming in the front door, and you two can be free to get other things done."

The other two stood up, each preparing to tend to her business, when Dahlia came into the kitchen. Her hair was pulled back in pigtails, and she was carrying a backpack.

"Hey." She greeted them brightly, but LuAnn noticed a heaviness in her eyes.

Tess and Janice greeted her before exiting the kitchen.

"Hi there." LuAnn approached her. "How are you doing today?"

Dahlia smiled weakly. "I'm good. I mean, I'm still worried about my aunt." She sighed.

"Are you ready to talk about writing?" LuAnn thought changing the subject might help.

"I am," Dahlia said.

"Let's go to the café and work," said LuAnn. She followed Dahlia out of the kitchen, and they settled at a table on the outside edge of the café, near the front desk.

Just as they were getting started, LuAnn heard the front door open. A young man walked in with dark curly hair. He held a notebook. She heard Dahlia say under her breath, "What's he doing here?" but before she could ask her what she meant, another man came in right behind the first one.

The pair had stopped in the middle of the lobby when the door opened again and three middle-aged women shuffled in, followed by a teenage girl dressed in maroon and black.

LuAnn rose to her feet and walked toward them. "Welcome to Wayfarers Inn. May I help you?"

One of the women spoke up. "We're here for the writing class," she said.

LuAnn froze. Writing class? She stared, dumbfounded, at Dahlia.

Dahlia, her face a deep red, stood and walked to the group. She addressed the young man. "Brayden, what are you doing here?"

Brayden looked confused. "You said there was a woman at Wayfarers Inn who could help with writing novels. You said she was an English teacher and knew a lot about writing, and she was going to help at ten fifteen Friday morning."

Dahlia glared at him. "I said she was going to help *me.* I didn't say she was going to help just anybody." Her face flushed again, and she looked around the group, shaking her head. "I didn't mean that the way it sounded. But, really—"

LuAnn heard the door open again but barely glanced up, she was so discombobulated. Then she mentally shook herself, gathered her wits, and decided to rescue her young friend. "It's all right, Dahlia. I might as well see what I can do, since you all are here already." She pointed to the café and the table with Dahlia's backpack and notebook. "Why don't you all sit down? We'll learn each other's names, and just talk about writing."

When they were all seated she moved to the front of the group, situated at four of the small tables. "Okay, let's introduce ourselves. Tell me what you want to write."

"I want to write about the man who killed my mother." LuAnn startled. She had heard that voice before.

LuAnn's stomach sank. "Cole? What are you doing here?"

The man who accused Brad of killing his mother glared at her from the far table. "I'm here to continue our discussion from yesterday."

LuAnn wasn't going to let him ruin this time for the other students—even though she hadn't expected them. "Then you're not here for the class?"

He snorted. "Hardly."

LuAnn didn't want to make a scene, so she forced herself to smile. "As you can see, I'm busy right now. You're welcome to stay and listen, if you'd like, and if you can do so without causing a disturbance."

Some of the students glanced at each other. LuAnn could tell they were uncomfortable, but she also knew from experience that, when dealing with a potentially rowdy student, it was just best to nip bad attitudes in the bud. She must still have the touch, because even though Cole folded his arms across his chest, leaned back in his chair, and glared at her, he kept silent.

After the students had shared their story ideas—everything from a historical romance to a modern-day suspense story to a retelling of a grandparent's life—LuAnn decided to take questions to get a feel for what they were looking for.

"I'm curious about your writing experience," one of the women asked.

LuAnn should have realized they'd want to know their teacher's background. "Well, I was an English teacher for many years."

"That's why I asked her to help me," Dahlia put in.

"Have you been published?" Brayden asked.

The question sent LuAnn's mind to a time in her twenties when she submitted several articles to magazines. A few did find their way to print. She smiled, remembering the feeling of an acceptance shining through the darkness of many more rejection letters. "Yes. A few articles and short stories."

"Have you written a book?" the teenage girl asked.

"I have." LuAnn nodded. "Well, it's not quite finished."

"Do you think you'll finish it?" the girl continued.

"I'm not sure." She thought about her love story from the Civil War. The character who lost his leg. The passion with which her female protagonist fought for him. The joy and heartache of their relationship. She was even tempted to betray her own beliefs to get him to safety…a flaw LuAnn had to reckon with. Remembering that story sparked thoughts about the teacher and the soldier that might have been at Camp Putnam. What if the soldier was the spy, and the teacher, Prudence's friend, defected to the other side for him? She itched to tell her friends her thoughts, research her suspicions, and figure it out together. But eight eager writers and one angry son sat in front of her, so she returned her focus to them.

"Okay," she said. "Let's talk about characters."

Thirty minutes later, LuAnn thanked those gathered for coming.

"Can we do this again?" Dahlia asked. "It was great."

"It really was," one of the women added. "I could meet every week if we did it in the evenings."

"I could too." The teenager in maroon and black closed her notebook.

LuAnn leaned against the table. "I'll have to let you know. I wasn't expecting more than one"—she glanced at Dahlia—"session."

"Why don't we write our names and emails down, and if you decide to continue, you can email us?" another woman suggested.

LuAnn smiled and nodded. "Of course. That's a great idea."

The others packed up their things and plodded to the sign-up sheet that the woman quickly drew up, thanking LuAnn as they left.

Cole hung at his table, head down, until everyone but Dahlia had left.

"Who is that guy?" Dahlia whispered.

LuAnn shot a glance at her young friend. Cole's presence set her on edge, and she didn't want to talk about him. "I'll tell you later."

"He's just sitting there." Dahlia didn't take the hint. "Do you want to add your email address to the list?" she asked him.

He finally glanced up. Redness edged his eyes, and he looked pale.

Dahlia chuckled. "Did you fall asleep?"

He eyed LuAnn. "I'm not well," he said. He stood up but had to sit down again.

"I'm sorry—" Dahlia muttered. "I didn't mean to be rude. I didn't realize you were sick."

LuAnn stepped next to his table. "I didn't either. I thought you were just waiting—I am sorry. Dahlia, why don't you get him some ice water?"

LuAnn sat down at the table with him.

"You probably thought I was faking being sick, didn't you?" he said weakly.

To be honest, she had thought that very thing. Looking at his frail state, she now doubted her doubts. Maybe he really was ill, but that didn't mean it was Brad's fault. "I'm sorry," she said. "I admit, I thought you might be faking as a way to get back at Brad for—"

"Killing my mother?"

At that moment Dahlia returned with the water. "Wait." She set it down. "Who killed your mother?"

He rolled his eyes, apparently not wanting to bother with an explanation.

"No one did," LuAnn answered. "Brad told me about it. It was an accident."

There was an awkward pause, and apparently, Dahlia took the hint. She gathered her notebook, pens, and backpack. "Okay, uh, thanks for the class, LuAnn." She looked at Cole. "And I hope you feel better." She turned and hurried up the stairs.

He took a drink of water. "If it wasn't for Brad Grimes, my mom would still be here." His voice rose as he spoke, and his energy seemed to be coming back, maybe from angry adrenaline. "I remember her—even though I was only two—I remember seeing her lying on the floor." He took in a shaky breath.

"I'm so sorry," LuAnn said. "I know Brad would like to get together with you and talk about all this—if it would be a help."

"He called me already." He coughed, and LuAnn wasn't sure if it was legitimate or out of sarcasm. "Says he wants to help me find closure. Like I'll ever have that. Is that even possible?"

LuAnn shot up a prayer for the right words to come. "I don't know. I think you'll always miss your mom—and the void you have of growing up without her—but maybe hearing Brad's account of what happened would help take away a portion of the hurt. Even a little bit of relief would be something, wouldn't it?"

His features softened but then hardened again. “He only wants to convince me to drop the case.”

“I can promise you.” LuAnn shook her head and looked him in the eye. “That is not his reason. Brad feels horrible about your mom’s death, and he would like to do anything he can to help you.”

At that moment, Brad came in from the kitchen. “Did I hear my name?” he said. “Who can I help? I’d be happy to—” Then his smile faded into concern.

At the sight of Brad, Cole rose to his feet, scowled at him, and rushed out the front door.

Chapter Sixteen

Brad stood dumbfounded, staring after the man who was threatening to sue him.

"Brad..." LuAnn began. She stepped closer. "Are you okay?"

Brad blinked back to the present. "Yeah. That just took me off guard. What was Cole doing here?"

"He said he wanted to continue our discussion from yesterday." She grimaced. "He didn't know he'd be interrupting my writing class."

"Writing class?" He tilted his head, confused. "You didn't tell me about that."

The strange happenings of the last hour almost made LuAnn laugh out loud. "I didn't know about it myself. I told Dahlia I'd give her some writing advice."

"That makes sense," Brad said. "The former English teacher."

"Right, but when the time came, about eight people showed up, expecting me to teach them how to write a novel."

Brad raised his eyebrows. "Did you have material prepared?"

"No." She exhaled. "But I think it went okay. Anyway, it was all a misunderstanding, and Cole showed up at the same time.

He looked sick, and I think maybe he wanted to convince me it was for real."

"What did you think?"

"I don't know." LuAnn glanced toward the kitchen. "Can I get you some coffee? Let's go in the kitchen and talk." As she finished speaking she received a text message.

"Actually, I only stopped by for a moment. Thought I'd see how the investigation about Margaret was going. See if there's anything I can do to help."

LuAnn's worry for her friend rose to the surface. "I don't know if we're making any progress toward figuring it out. I just got a text from Randy that the white dust is just standard construction dust that could have come from anywhere. There were no fingerprints other than Margaret's and ours."

"That's too bad." He gave her an encouraging smile. "Don't give up. I know we'll find her."

"I know we will. The sooner the better."

"Absolutely."

As Brad headed toward the door, Tess and Janice entered the lobby. Tess held the *McGuffey Reader*.

"Hey there!" Janice called out. "Are you leaving?"

"Yeah, heading out," Brad said.

"We'll see you later for kayaking." Tess shot a glance toward Janice.

"Yeah." Janice smiled hesitantly. "There's still that."

"You're going to do great." Brad smiled. "Don't worry."

Janice laughed. "I'll take your word for it."

Brad left, and Tess poured herself and Janice some coffee from the coffee bar, then joined the others at a café table. "That phrase you found, O great decoder. We've got to figure out what it means."

LuAnn opened her notebook to the page where she had written her notes.

SUB MUS

"Sub Mus," Janice said. "Could it mean Sub Muskingum?"

LuAnn smoothed a strand of hair behind her ear. "Well, what does sub mean?"

"It can mean beneath, right?" Tess suggested. "Like subterranean. Under terra. Under the earth."

"Right, that's what I was thinking too," LuAnn said. "Beneath Muskingum."

"So like, underneath the muddy river floor?" Janice asked. "No wonder no one has ever found it."

"It could mean beneath like on a map," LuAnn suggested. "South of Muskingum." LuAnn wrote the ideas in her notebook. She sighed. "There's a lot of territory south of the Muskingum. Do we have a map?"

Janice traipsed to the office and retrieved a folded map of Ohio. She brought it to the table and spread it out.

"See." LuAnn pointed and traced the Muskingum's path down to Marietta. "The southernmost point is right where it empties into the Ohio."

Tess leaned over the map. "They'd have to mean that the coins are located in the river then, wouldn't they?" She pointed to where the Muskingum flowed into the Ohio River. "There is no land south of the Muskingum at that point. There's a west bank and an east bank, and the river flows south into the Ohio. Any land south of that would be across the Ohio River and in West Virginia, wouldn't it?"

"It would," Janice said. "But I don't know what else it could mean. There's a lot of land running the length of the river that could be considered 'south' of the Muskingum. There would have to be more clues to pinpoint the exact location."

"We should talk to that riverboat guy again, Thaddeus. Maybe he could tell us about the area south of the Muskingum," LuAnn suggested. "He might even take us on a tour."

"I like that idea." Tess said.

"Plus, I promised Roy we'd bring him some soup," Janice said. "We could stop there on the way."

"Should you and I go, then, Janice, after the lunch service?" LuAnn asked.

"Actually, I'm watching Larry for a few hours this afternoon." She glanced at the clock. "They're bringing him around three."

LuAnn eyed Tess. "Do you want to join me then?"

"Sure," Tess answered. "The sooner we find those gold coins, the sooner we get this solved." She stood and folded the map. "And the sooner we get Margaret back."

September 22, 1863

Prudence's pulse pounded in her temples. A gun. How she hated violence. She loathed seeing someone threaten another's life, even if he was a spy. "Please, stop this," she said, but didn't know how to calm the situation. *Please, Lord.*

"All right, Miss Knight. All right now." Austin raised his hands. "Put that down. Let me explain."

"Explain? We know you're a spy. Prudence saw you talking to a known Confederate sympathizer. Turns out we were right to let him linger here. He pointed us straight to you."

"I know it looks bad." Beads of sweat showed beneath Austin's hairline. "But I promise we're on the same side. Put the gun down, and I'll tell you about it."

"Thee better tell her now," Prudence put in. "I do think she will shoot thee."

"She's right." Cynthia's eyes narrowed.

"I'm a double agent." He whispered the words. "Put it down before you draw attention. Someone could come in and see you."

"How do I know you are not simply working for the enemy?" Cynthia asked.

"That's easy." Austin inched forward. "Because I'm here to tell you the location of the drop-off tonight and ask you for help stopping it."

"What?" Cynthia asked. "Why would you do that? What makes you think I can help you?"

He moved closer and spoke softly. "I've known you are a spy for the North ever since I've been here. I was told we had someone in the school."

"Then why wasn't I told?"

"Being a double agent, I couldn't risk it. I was told to only involve you once I knew when the drop-off would be and where. Well, now I know."

"As do I."

"What? How?"

"I overheard thee," Prudence said.

"You did?" He looked at her, then his eyes rounded in recognition. "I saw you there with your son. I should have been more careful."

Prudence nodded.

"The problem is, we don't have a lot of time. The shipment is coming tonight, and I have to get a message to the Union Navy waiting upriver so they can come after we intercept the delivery."

"What do you mean?" Cynthia asked.

"After we get the coins and spies, the Union Navy will sink the Rebel conveyance."

Cynthia shook her head. "You're saying the South is sending the coins by ship? Aren't they worried they will be spotted by watchmen far before they reach this area?"

Austin shifted his gaze. "You don't know?"

"Know what?"

"The coins and information are not coming by ship," he said. "They're coming by submarine."

When LuAnn returned to the kitchen, the rich aroma of bean soup, which Janice was reheating, filled the room as she packed a basket of goodies for Roy. Dahlia and Tess sat at the table.

"Dahlia?" LuAnn peered at the young woman. "What have you been up to? You disappeared after the workshop ended a little while ago."

"Going over and over the message boards about Margaret's kidnapping," Dahlia said. "Lots of weirdos have ridiculous theories, and there's nothing else to go on."

"That's too bad." Janice placed the packed basket on the island.

"One guy seems to be lurking in the background. Someone called CR. He has a drawing of a crown for his avatar. He never creates a new post, but he comments on all the posts. It's kind of weird."

"CR with a crown, huh?" Tess asked. "Thinks highly of himself."

"CR," LuAnn said. "Craig Reynolds?"

Janice gasped.

"Oh!" Tess said. "From the attitude he had, the heir to the throne, practically, I could see him using a crown for his image."

LuAnn nodded. "Me too."

Dahlia's eyes rounded like a confused puppy. "What are you talking about?"

LuAnn turned to her. "Craig Reynolds is the son of the other woman who was kidnapped. They're part of a wealthy family who has lived in Marietta forever."

"And you think he may have something to do with Margaret being kidnapped?" Dahlia asked.

"We're not sure," LuAnn answered. "But he could be. We don't even know if CR Crown is him. CR could stand for plenty of names. But it's something to keep an eye on."

"I definitely will, now that I know." Dahlia's eyes brightened a touch. She seemed to need things to keep her busy trying to find out who kidnapped her aunt.

LuAnn moved to the island to inspect the gorgeous basket Janice had made for them to take to Roy. "Beautiful job, Janice."

A smile spread over Janice's face as she added the jar of soup. "Tell him I hope he's feeling better."

"We will." LuAnn lifted the basket, then glanced at Tess. "Are you ready?"

Tess stood. "I am."

"Are you going to see Roy?" Dahlia asked. "Could I come too? I've been meaning to visit him."

LuAnn's stomach clenched. Dahlia still didn't know that Roy was her father or that he was terminally ill. She glanced at her two friends, who appeared to have the same stomach-clenching sensation. LuAnn longed to tell the young woman. She deserved to know, but it wasn't their place. They had to at least give Roy the opportunity to tell her himself. Well, maybe this would be the opportunity.

"Of course," LuAnn said. "We'd love to have you, and he'll be glad to see you."

In a few minutes the three of them were driving to town to deliver the basket to Roy.

After parking on the street, LuAnn stepped out of the car, and she, Tess, and Dahlia headed to Roy's small house. She climbed the steps and knocked. Like last time, the front door was open, but the screen door remained shut.

"Coming!" Roy's voice called above the sounds of Beatles' music.

In a moment, the man himself appeared, wearing an apron.

"Roy?" LuAnn asked.

"Hello there, ladies." He approached the door with a steady step. "I wasn't expecting you."

"We promised to bring soup," LuAnn answered.

He opened the door, and they stepped inside.

"Well, how about that? I'd forgotten. I'm feeling so much better—" His words halted when his gaze fell on Dahlia following Tess inside.

"I'm so glad to see you," Dahlia said. "When you weren't at the historical society, I was worried about you."

A wistful look came over Roy's face. "That's so kind, but as you can see, I'm fine." He closed the door behind the women, then rushed ahead to clear space on the kitchen counter for Tess to set the basket. "Oh my, what a feast!" he said as he went through it. "How can I thank you?"

"It was Janice who put it together. She gets most of the credit." LuAnn took the jar of soup out. "Should I heat this up? Are you hungry?"

Roy pointed to his apron. "I was just going to make myself grilled cheese and canned tomato soup, but I'd much prefer your feast."

"Perfect." Roy pointed to a cupboard, and LuAnn opened it to find a pan, then poured the soup in and started heating it. "It's great to see you doing so well."

Tess and Dahlia sat on stools next to the kitchen counter.

Roy joined them. "It feels good to feel better. Not that I'm 100 percent, mind you."

Dahlia moved a history magazine that sat on the counter to the side. "LuAnn told me you were sick, but she didn't mention what was wrong. What was it, Roy?"

LuAnn pivoted from the stove where she was stirring the soup. Roy's lips tightened as he paused. She tried to send him a subliminal message. *Tell her. Please, tell her!*

A hint of fear flickered through his eyes. Finally, he smiled and shifted his stool to face her. "It's serious, I'm afraid. Cancer. I'm dying, they say."

"What?" Dahlia's eyes widened. "What do you mean?"

"It's true." His eyes held compassion for her, not sorrow for himself. "And there's something else."

LuAnn froze as she sent up prayers. Would he tell her now?

"I haven't always been who I wanted to be. I've done some bad things, but I need to use the time I have left to make them right. So..." He sighed shakily. "I also need to tell you that, uh, well, I'm the one who was married to your beautiful mother. I'm your father, Dahlia. I'm sorry."

Dahlia's eyes narrowed, and she shook her head. "You're my what?"

"I'm your father." He leaned closer. "I'm sorry for...so many things."

Tears flooded Dahlia's eyes, and LuAnn could tell they were angry tears, not relieved ones or happy ones. "You're my father?" She shook her head again. "No. You're lying."

"I'm the one who married your mother. I'm the fool who left when you were just a child. I'm the one who knows I can never make up for what I did, but I'm also the one who couldn't be sorrier. I don't ask you to forgive me. I don't ask anything from you. I just thought you had the right to know."

Dahlia pushed up from the stool she was sitting on, and it screeched across the floor. She stood and glared at him but didn't say a word, then turned to LuAnn and Janice. "I'm going to Aunt Maggie's." She stormed toward the door.

"Dahlia!" LuAnn called to her, thinking how alone Dahlia was in the world and knowing Margaret would be grateful that LuAnn had been there for her niece. LuAnn hoped someone would be there for her loved ones if she could not. But Dahlia slammed the door behind her and left. LuAnn stood to go after her but stopped herself.

"You should give her some time," Roy said. "Some space to take it in."

LuAnn sighed. "Yes."

"We'll check on her later," Tess said.

After a moment, LuAnn looked at the soup bubbling on the stove. "I think you should eat. You need nourishment."

"I'd be grateful," he said. His cheery demeanor took on a heaviness, and LuAnn prayed, then prayed some more.

Thirty minutes later they pulled out from Roy's street and headed toward Margaret's house. As they passed the general store on Fourth Street, LuAnn thought she saw someone she recognized.

"Wait," she said. "Is that Ashley coming out of the store there?"

"It looks like her," Tess confirmed.

The woman turned as she walked, and LuAnn was sure it was her friend. "This is great. I still haven't talked to her. Do you mind if we stop and say hi?"

"Of course not." Tess answered.

As they got closer, LuAnn noticed that Ashley was crying. She held a bag of groceries in her arms and a cell phone in her hand. As she walked, she wasn't looking where she was going, and she stumbled, spilling the groceries all over the parking lot.

LuAnn, stopped at a red light, called out the window. "Ashley!"

Ashley turned and saw her, then fumbled to get her things and stand back up.

The light seemed to last forever, and by the time they reached the market, Ashley was gone.

Chapter Seventeen

LuAnn parked the car near where Ashley had been. An apple and a box of pre-made scones still lay on the ground, remnants of what her friend had spilled.

"What was that about?" Tess asked as she helped clean up the mess.

"I don't know," LuAnn answered.

"She seemed really upset," Tess said.

LuAnn took out her phone and called Ashley's number. "No answer."

"Did she tell you about anything wrong when you had lunch with her the other day?"

"Not at all. She hinted that things were not going great, but I didn't think it was anything major. She implied the troubles were just the normal stresses of life." LuAnn and Tess walked to a trash can to throw away the apple. "I think I'll go by the Castle after we talk to Thaddeus."

"Are you sure you don't want to go there first?" Tess asked.

"I don't think so. She didn't answer her phone. She probably needs some time alone."

LuAnn and Tess returned to the car and drove to the park. They made their way through the sand to the steamboat where

Thaddeus gave tours, and sure enough, he stood by the gangplank, soliciting passersby to take the tour.

"Hey there!" he said as LuAnn and Tess approached. "Good to see you, Miss LuAnn. Who is this you have with you this time?"

"Thaddeus, this is my other business partner, Tess."

He shook Tess's hand. "Ah, now I've met all three owners of the old inn. Glad to see it back in business after all these years."

Tess smiled. "We're happy to be the ones taking care of her."

"You ladies here for a tour?" He patted the railing on the gangplank. "You'll learn a lot about this old town."

LuAnn recalled Brad's warning about Thaddeus's tall tales. "Sounds like fun, but we actually just have a few questions we were hoping you could help us with."

"If you have time," Tess added.

His beard swayed as he shook his head. "I'm sorry. We're about to push off. If you want to talk to me, gotta take the tour." He eyed them.

LuAnn gave him a teacher look, but then pulled the money out of her purse and paid.

He chuckled. "It's worth it. You'll see."

"We're sure it is," LuAnn said as he led them onto the steamboat.

LuAnn took in the musty scent of the old steamer, and as they paced along the outer balcony on the lower deck, her imagination swirled with images of those who had ridden it in years gone by.

Thaddeus marched to the front of the boat, looked up at the man on the bridge above, and gave a thumbs-up. The motors whirred, and the boat trembled. For a moment LuAnn wasn't sure the old thing was seaworthy, but then it gained momentum, and they moved forward, leaving white ripples through the water.

Thaddeus then walked back to his spot at a podium that had a microphone. "Here." He pointed to a few seats next to him. "This is the prime spot to see everything."

LuAnn and Tess sat down as Riverfront Park disappeared behind them.

Thaddeus welcomed the tourists, told a story about Riverfront Park, and turned back to LuAnn and Tess. "So, what was it you wanted to ask me? Not about the coins, I hope. I've heard enough about them to last a lifetime."

LuAnn eyed Tess. "Actually..."

He rolled his eyes. "Fine then, what do you want to know?"

"We have reason to believe the coins are south of the Muskingum," LuAnn said. "Does that make any sense to you?"

He let out a loud belly laugh. "That's one I haven't heard. South of the Muskingum. How? That's where we are on the Ohio. The only thing directly south of the Muskingum is the Ohio River. It's where it lets out. You think whoever hid the coins dropped them in the muck and mud at the bottom?" He laughed again, even more loudly. "Not too smart those spies, were they?"

LuAnn didn't see what was so hilarious. "Actually, we did happen to look at a map, and we know the Muskingum lets out into the Ohio. We were thinking they meant across the Ohio from where the Muskingum lets out. In West Virginia." She looked at him.

Thaddeus frowned. They had turned, so now they were parallel to the shore. He gazed at the south shoreline. "You think it's over there somewhere?" He pointed. "No one I've known about has searched there before. Why do you think that?"

LuAnn hesitated to tell him about the *McGuffey Reader* and the cipher, but then, maybe he could help.

"We found a clue in Prudence Willard's journal—you know about her, right?"

He nodded. "Indeed. Quite proud to have such a good woman in Marietta's history."

"We decoded it, and we think it means the coins are south of the Muskingum," Tess said.

"Hmm. So you're saying the Confederates brought the coins—by canoe maybe? Or some other form of transportation. Most likely not by land. To the *south* side of the Ohio instead of the north side. We all thought it would be the north side, since that's the side Camp Putnam's on. The spy from the camp would've had to cross the Ohio—by your plan—get the coins, and return to the camp. Sounds like a weak plan, but not impossible."

LuAnn's mind spun. It did seem a bit unlikely that the spies would plan to meet over there. "Or maybe the coins got hidden there for some reason."

"Yeah. But why? Either the spy who brought the coins or the one who was supposed to receive them would've had to cross the river, twice, most likely in a canoe, in order to do that. They would risk being seen. Why wouldn't the spy just take them to a fort on his side of the river?"

"Maybe he thought it was a good enough hiding place that it was worth it," Tess commented.

He grinned. "So, say your guy did hide it on the southern bank. Where? It'd have to be far enough away from the sand that it wouldn't just wash away with the tides. Most of the land over there has been developed. I would think it would've been found by now, or it's completely buried under buildings and roads."

This lead wasn't panning out as LuAnn hoped. She glanced at Tess. "I'm starting to think we may not have interpreted the clue correctly."

"But what else could it mean?" Tess asked.

"I just don't know." She gazed over at the south shore. "There does seem to be a lot of development over there. Where would we even begin looking?"

"Sorry, ladies." Thaddeus looked sincerely apologetic. "I know you think the coins will help locate Margaret." He shook his head sadly. "Any luck with that?"

LuAnn felt the weight of his question. "No, not yet."

"That's too bad." As he moved back to the microphone, LuAnn looked at Tess.

"Maybe there are more clues in the *McGuffey Reader*." She sighed. "I thought I looked through the whole thing, but I could have missed something."

"Let's find some time to go over it again tonight," Tess suggested.

"I like that plan."

By the time the park came into view again, LuAnn and Tess had a new plan.

"We're so grateful for your help," LuAnn said to Thaddeus. "And your wonderful tour."

"I'm glad I could help," Thaddeus said, not seeming to care how he helped, just glad he did.

LuAnn glanced at Tess. "Should we go to the upper deck? I'd love to explore it."

They climbed the stairs, and as they hit the upper deck, the breeze was even stronger, whipping LuAnn's hair in her face. The boat was making a wide turn to head back to the dock, and at the moment they were closer to the south shore than they had been.

LuAnn glanced one more time at that shore, wondering if the coins could possibly be buried there after all, yet she doubted it. Besides the businesses, a few small houses looking as if they were from the World War II era—small, maybe mail-order homes—lined the way. As she stared, someone came into her view. A woman, walking along the shore, her hair blowing in the breeze and a contented smile on her face. She looked familiar.

"Do you see that woman?" LuAnn asked Tess.

"I do," Tess answered. "She seems happy."

"Yeah. Does she look familiar to you?"

Tess squinted in the woman's direction. "Maybe. I'm not sure."

"It's probably nothing."

Before she could puzzle it out, the boat had continued its turn, and they were approaching the dock.

A few minutes later LuAnn and Tess were walking along the beach back to their car.

"I'm off to visit Ashley," LuAnn said as she and Tess reached her car. "I'm worried about her. I can't imagine what had her so upset."

"I hope she'll share what's going on. Struggling alone only leads to more heartache."

"By the way she avoided us, something seems to be really wrong." LuAnn's heart ached for her friend. "I hope it's not her husband or her son."

Tess frowned. "You better go see if you can help." She pointed toward the inn. "I can walk home from here. No need for you to drive me all the way."

LuAnn glanced down the street. "All the way home," she said with a hint of sarcasm. "It's a two-minute walk."

Tess chuckled. "I think I can make it."

Tess was about to leave when LuAnn's phone buzzed. A text appeared from Dahlia.

Margaret's pill bottles are gone.

Chapter Eighteen

LuAnn called a very panicked Dahlia. "I'm going to put you on SPEAKER, okay?" she asked.

"Okay. So, I got here and started cleaning. I know it's already clean, but I just wanted to wipe everything down, to keep dust from building up. I want it nice for her. Then I took care of Lafayette, you know, her parrot? Anyway, when I went to the kitchen, I noticed the cupboard where the pills are kept was a little open. I thought it was strange, so I opened it the rest of the way, and that's when I found the pill bottles missing. I looked everywhere, thinking maybe I moved them when we were talking about them before, but they simply aren't here. Where could they be? Why would someone do this? A drug addict or something?"

LuAnn remained quiet, taking in all Dahlia said. Finally she asked, "Nothing else has been touched or taken?"

"No."

"Go to the door. Does it look marked up, like someone broke the lock? Check the back door, and all the windows too."

A few minutes passed as Dahlia checked. "Everything looks secure," she said when she finished.

"No break-in. Only one thing missing," Tess commented.

LuAnn nodded, knowing what Tess was thinking. "Whoever took the pills must have had a key and been after the pills and nothing else."

"What do you think it means that the pills were taken?" Dahlia asked. "It's so cruel, like someone is trying to scare me."

LuAnn saw it differently. "We know the person who took the pills had a way in. That person must have a key."

"Oh yeah," Dahlia said. "How would they get a key?"

"The person also knew where to find the pills," Tess added. "They didn't mess the place up looking for them."

"How would they know?" Dahlia paused. "Unless... Oh! Do you think it was the kidnapper?"

LuAnn couldn't think of any other conclusion. "I think so."

"But this is even weirder." The tension in Dahlia's voice grew. "Why would they get her pills?"

"I don't know," LuAnn answered. "It could be that the person isn't interested in hurting her, doesn't want an injury on his or her conscience."

"Or on his or her record," Tess put in.

"Or?" Dahlia asked but didn't wait for an answer. "Or they want to give her an overdose of her own medication to harm her."

LuAnn had thought that too, but she didn't want to say so. "Let's think positively. Okay, Dahlia?"

Dahlia sighed, obviously skeptical. "I'll try. I think I'll head back to the historical society. Get out of the house for a bit."

"Okay," LuAnn said. "Do you want a ride there?"

"It's okay. It's just down the street. I'll see you later, okay?"

"Okay." LuAnn was glad Dahlia was going to the historical society. Keeping busy was better than wallowing at home. "We'll see you."

After hanging up, LuAnn glanced at Tess. "I feel for her."

"I do too," Tess said.

A thought wound its way through LuAnn's mind. "She's got a lot on her mind. Having just found her aunt, who is then kidnapped, then she learns this man she recently met is her father. She must be overwhelmed."

"Yeah, she seemed pretty angry," Tess commented. "Something like this could send her down a dark path."

"It would help if we could find Margaret." LuAnn opened the car door.

"It really would," Tess said. "I'll be praying for your time with Ashley."

"Thanks. I think I'll stop by Jeremiah's on the way."

"Good idea. Coffee helps any situation," Tess said, then traipsed down the street toward the inn.

As LuAnn drove toward the Castle, she pondered the look she'd seen on Ashley's face and said a prayer both for Ashley, and that she'd find words to comfort her friend.

"Ashley?" LuAnn knocked on the door to the Castle. The outside still had scaffolding around it and tarps covering the walls, but she could tell they'd been working on the upper levels. The eves had been repaired and painted. Some of the siding looked new. She imagined the folks who ran it were pleased with the progress.

She knocked again, then rang the doorbell and waited. When no one came, she rang it again. If Ashley wasn't there, LuAnn didn't know where to find her. As LuAnn was about to give up, she heard footsteps inside.

"Ashley?" she called. "Is that you? It's LuAnn. Are you okay?"

A moment later the door opened. It was Ashley. Her eyes were red, but she smiled.

"Oh, Ashley," LuAnn said. "I was worried...I brought coffee." She held the two mochas she'd picked up from Jeremiah's.

Ashley's hair fluttered in the breeze that swept in from the opened door. "Come in."

LuAnn handed her one of the coffees and slipped inside the elaborately ornate entryway. "This place is so awesome. I can't believe I've never taken the tour."

Ashley smiled weakly. "It is. Working here has given me a great appreciation for the place." She stepped through the dining room toward the kitchen. "Let's sit in the kitchen. It's actually in working order. The employees use it to make themselves coffee and tea and eat their lunches. It's closed to visitors, so they don't keep it quite as pristine as the rest."

LuAnn followed her. "You mean we can relax a little?"

"Exactly."

They entered the old-fashioned kitchen, right out of the 1920s, it seemed to LuAnn, except for the microwave and modern fridge. And the card table with folding chairs. Modest light shone through the tarp hanging outside the four-paned window.

They sat down, and LuAnn took a sip of coffee, trying to decide where to start. She wasn't sure if Ashley had actually seen her earlier. She thought so, but... "Are you okay, Ashley?"

At the question Ashley's eyes welled with tears, and she dabbed them with a tissue she retrieved from her pocket. "I'm sorry. I'm so sorry. I'm afraid I wasn't honest with you before." Her phone buzzed, and she jumped to answer it, but after checking, she tapped it off and returned it to her pocket.

LuAnn waited, partly unsure what to say, partly giving her friend time to collect her thoughts.

"It's Dustin, Lu," she finally choked out. "He's got cancer."

"I'm so sorry."

"He needs a certain procedure. We've been on the waiting list, but I got a call this afternoon that he's had a setback."

"Oh, no." LuAnn paused. "Isn't he studying in Florida?"

Tears ran down Ashley's cheeks. "We thought he was doing better." Her voice was so thick with emotion, LuAnn could barely understand her. "He desperately wanted to go. How do you say no to your son's dying wish?" She pulled another tissue from her pocket and wiped her cheeks. "That's why I thought it was okay for me to come here, to leave him. But he collapsed on the boat he was working on in Florida. He's home, and I want to go be with him. He told me not to come, but..."

"I can understand why you'd want to be with him." LuAnn patted her friend's shoulder.

"What would you do, LuAnn?"

LuAnn exhaled, not expecting the question. "I don't know. I mean, I don't have kids, but I think I would do whatever I could to help him. Is Paul with him?"

The lines around Ashley's eyes deepened. "Yes, he is." She took a sip of coffee. "Actually, Paul also told me not to come. He said this episode wasn't that bad. That I shouldn't worry. He's probably right. I'm probably freaking out over nothing."

"Oh, friend. Can you tell me what actually happened? Maybe if we talk through it, we can figure out if you should go home or not."

Ashley nodded. "Okay. So he was spending the summer with his friends in Florida. When he collapsed, his friends knew about his cancer and made him go to the doctor. Sure enough, the brain tumor had grown." Her voice trembled as tears lined her cheeks. "I'm sorry. It's so hard to even say those words."

"I can only imagine. Just take your time, okay? I have all day."

Ashley took in a breath. "Okay. Paul went and got him and brought him home right away so he could go to his own doctors."

"So what did the doctor say about the tumor?"

"Paul said they were able to reduce its size quite a bit with medication."

"That's wonderful."

"It is. He wants to go back to Florida with his friends. As long as he takes his medication, he should be good..."

"Really?" LuAnn thought Ashley didn't seem convinced.

"Well, he'll be good for a while. He really needs this other treatment—the one he's on the waiting list for—to find a lasting solution. Otherwise..."

"Did you talk to Dustin?" LuAnn asked. "Does he want you to come home?"

"He said he wouldn't mind. But I think he's just saying that so I don't feel bad." Ashley smiled. "He's so independent. He doesn't like me fussing over him, I know, but he'll let me—more for my peace of mind than his."

LuAnn tilted her head. "He sounds like a great kid. I'd love to meet him sometime."

"I'd love that. He's a math guy, but he tolerates us English and history majors."

LuAnn chuckled. "Do you have your answer?"

Ashley smiled. "I do. I'm not going to leave. I'll stay and finish this job. I'll let him do his thing while he can."

"I think that's a good decision," LuAnn said. "It can't be easy. I'll be praying for you."

Ashley's eyebrows rose, and she glanced toward the window. "Prayer. I haven't done that in a long time."

"Maybe you should start," LuAnn said, as gently as she could. "It helps. Gives me peace, and God does answer prayers."

"I don't think prayer is for me." Ashley sipped her coffee again then cupped her hands around the cup.

"That's okay. I'll be praying for you, anyway, if you don't mind."

"I don't mind."

"It must be difficult to concentrate on your work with that other stuff going on," LuAnn commented.

"It is, but in some ways working helps keep me from ruminating on it too much."

"I can imagine. How's the work coming?"

"Good. I'm learning so much about this place. It almost feels like home."

"I bet." LuAnn finished her coffee, then stood to throw the cup away in a trash can next to the counter. She noticed two other Jeremiah's coffee cups in the trash. "Oh, I see you've already discovered Jeremiah's coffee."

"Oh!" Ashley stood. "Yes. I got our lunches there the other day, remember? I've been going back for snacks and coffee ever since." She closed the trash can, then something on the floor seemed to catch her attention. It looked like part of a scone. "Oh dear. That's not good. The ants will be after that." She grabbed a broom and swept it up.

"We like Jeremiah's a lot," LuAnn said. "But don't forget about the café at that Wayfarers Inn. It's pretty good too." She grinned.

"So I've heard." Ashley grinned back at her. "I promise to try it."

"And I'd love to see you more often, before you have to go back home."

"Me too." Ashley gave LuAnn a hug. "Thank you so much. You've made me feel a lot better."

"I'm glad." LuAnn glanced at her phone for the time. "Oh! It's just about time to meet my friends for kayaking."

"Kayaking?" Ashley raised her eyebrows.

LuAnn chuckled. "I know. It's a first for me, but Brad loves it. He's taking all three of us. Hey, you should join us. It'll be fun."

Ashley shook her head. "I wish I could. I'm afraid I'm behind on my work as it is. I'll be up late just to get caught up."

"Okay," LuAnn said. "I'm glad you're doing better. Will you call me tomorrow?"

"You bet."

LuAnn rushed to her car. There wasn't much time for her to get home, grab a bite, change, and for all of them to meet Brad. In a hurry, she bypassed the main street, hoping to avoid traffic. As she drove along an unfamiliar street, she noticed the impound lot surrounded by a chain-link fence and barbed wire.

"Wait a minute," she muttered to herself. "Isn't that Ashley's car?"

CHAPTER NINETEEN

LuAnn, Tess, Janice, and Brad stood on the dock of the Riverfront Park staring at kayaks as the sun was beginning to set in the fall sky.

"These are two-person kayaks." Brad pointed to one orange and one yellow kayak.

LuAnn thought they looked like canoes except for the pointed bow. "We're not going to be all sealed in like I've seen?"

"You're thinking of one-person kayaks, the ones where you're sort of part of the boat."

"Yeah," Janice piped in. "The ones where if it tips over, you die." She wasn't laughing.

Brad laughed. "Nope. You simply sit in these, like a little boat. And you row and watch the sunset and have a great time."

Janice managed a smile. "I guess it doesn't seem quite as deadly when you put it that way."

"Would you like me to ride with you?" Brad asked. "I've ridden this river my whole life."

Janice grimaced and glanced at Tess. LuAnn knew her scheming friends were thinking that she and Brad should be together. "Oh no," Janice said. "I'm okay with Tess."

"And I've done this a few times too," Tess said. "It's not like we're going to be braving the rapids. Come on, Janice." Tess grabbed her by the elbow. "Should we take the yellow one?" She started to step into the kayak, but Brad stopped her.

"Hold on a second." He walked to a cart with life jackets hanging on it and tossed one to Tess. "Don't forget this."

"I'll take one of those." Janice waved her hands. "Me! Me!"

Brad handed her and LuAnn each one, then put his own on. "Everyone all set?"

"I am!" LuAnn smiled, grateful for a chance to have a little fun.

"Tess, Janice," Brad continued, "I'll hold your kayak while you step in."

Tess grabbed LuAnn's hand and stepped in and sat in the spot toward the back. "You ready, Janice?"'

Janice's lips pinched together, and her eyes narrowed, but she clutched LuAnn's hand and stepped in. She hesitated instead of using the momentum to get in and sit down, and her weight made the boat rock. She stumbled and had to grab Tess's hand too. Finally, gravity pulled her onto her seat.

"You did it!" LuAnn cheered.

Janice chuckled mirthlessly. "That's me, the graceful one of the group." Then she chuckled sincerely. "This might not be so bad, actually."

Brad turned to LuAnn. "You ready?" He reached out his hand for her to hold. "Steady yourself with my hand, and I'll hold the boat still with my other hand."

"Okay."

He bent forward and held the kayak as she used his hand to climb into her spot in the front.

"Now, the way you maneuver in one of these is to row one side at a time." He showed them the proper paddling method. "If you want to turn, you paddle on the opposite side you want to go. Make sense?"

"Got it!" Tess yelled.

"Let's go!" Brad began paddling, and within a few minutes the orange and yellow kayaks had glided through the murky Ohio River to the midsection, yet still close enough to the shore to leave room for bigger vessels.

As they paddled, LuAnn peeked back and saw Tess and Janice floundering, along with lots of giggles. But as she watched, they figured out how to work together to make the kayak do what they wanted.

"This is so fun!" Tess yelled.

"I like it too!" LuAnn shouted back. "What about you, Janice? You liking it?"

Janice kept her eyes on the kayak, concentrating on rowing, but she smiled. "It's fun. I think I'm getting the—whoa!" Wake from a motorboat caused rolling waves to rock the kayak, taking Janice by surprise. She laid the paddle on her lap and gripped the sides of the boat until the waves passed. "Doing fine," she finally said as she started rowing again.

They paddled across the river toward the inn. LuAnn rowed in sync with Brad. "Thank you for taking us. It's nice out here."

He looked back and smiled. "I'm glad you like it." He switched his gaze to the sky that was turning peach-colored. "It's my favorite time to get out here."

"I can understand why." Her gaze followed the shoreline. "And there's our inn. It was nice of Winnie to stay late to keep an eye on things so we could come with you."

"It was. You're lucky to have her."

"We are." LuAnn breathed in the fresh air and settled into the moment—being on the river, her inn in view, Brad seated at the helm. What more could she ask for?

Brad stopped paddling, and LuAnn turned to face him. "I adore all of you. You know that." His blue eyes sent a shiver down LuAnn's spine. "But to be honest, you're the one I wanted to share this with."

LuAnn's face warmed. She didn't know what to say, and Brad didn't seem to expect a response as he began to paddle again.

They paddled in peaceful silence for a few minutes, then something on the water caught Brad's eye. "Hey. Look." He pointed to a rowboat several feet away but parallel to them, closer to the southern shore. "Isn't that...?"

LuAnn tensed. "It looks a lot like Cole Harrison."

Brad steered a little closer. "It is Cole. What's he doing out here?"

"Going for a boat ride, like us?" LuAnn guessed. "He sure doesn't seem sick, like he did earlier."

"Hey!" Cole's gaze snagged on Brad's. "What're you looking at? You following me?"

Brad paddled to straighten the kayak. "No, Cole. I was just trying to see who was there. We'll leave you alone."

"Yeah, I bet you will. It's what you do. Hurt people, then skip out!"

"Listen," Brad said. "Let's talk about this. I'll take you out for coffee—"

Before he could finish, Cole stood up in his boat. "You killed my mother!" He screamed so loudly his voice cracked. "I grew up alone because of you!"

"I'm sorry, Cole." Brad rowed ahead so he passed Cole. Janice and Tess were close behind, just coming up alongside Cole's boat.

"Sorrys don't mean anything," Cole ranted. "They don't bring her back!"

Brad tried to reason with him, looking back over his shoulder. "I'm truly sorry about your mother. I want to help you. Tell me what I can do."

"I'll tell you!" Cole's face contorted. "You can pay for what you've done!" He swung wildly with his oar. At the same time, the wake from another passing motorboat hit his boat He lost his balance and toppled out of his boat, landing on the ladies' kayak. He scrambled to stay on top of it.

The kayak tipped, sending both the ladies sliding to one side. Tess managed to grab her seat and hang on, but Janice wasn't so fortunate. With a cry, she fell into the river.

"Janice!" Tess yelled as she leaned over the side to reach her friend.

"Oh no!" Cole yelled. "Is she all right?"

LuAnn turned around and couldn't help but glare at Cole before watching Brad take off his shoes and jump into the river. Then once again, like the night she and Brad had first seen him, Cole jumped in. He swam around the kayaks behind

Janice where Brad had allowed her to grab his arm to raise herself. Cole offered her his arm, and together they escorted her through the Ohio back to the kayak. They let her catch her breath before trying to climb back in.

"We should let her put her feet in our hands," Cole said. "Then she can leverage herself up."

"I agree," Brad said.

After Janice had caught her breath, Brad and Cole laced their hands together under the water and allowed her to push herself up and back onto the kayak where Tess waited with a hug.

Then Cole swam back to his boat, and Brad helped him climb in. Finally, Brad climbed into the orange kayak.

"That was fun!" Janice said.

Her words made all but Cole burst out laughing.

"You're okay?" Cole asked Janice after the laughing settled down. "I'm so sorry."

"It's okay." Janice sent him a sincere, if shivering, smile. "I'm f-f-fine."

"You're so cold, Janice," LuAnn said. "Let's get back to the inn and have some hot chocolate. I think we could use it."

"That's the best idea I've heard all day," Tess agreed.

Cole started to paddle away, but Brad called to him. "Why don't you join us? I'm sure the ladies can get you a blanket."

"Definitely." LuAnn nodded. "We might even have some men's clothes in the lost and found."

"Maybe we can make a campfire," Tess added.

"Perfect." Brad leaned toward him. "I'd love to have a chance to talk, clear things up."

Cole stared at his hands for a moment. "You'll tell me what happened that day when she..." He paused and lifted his eyes to Brad with a childlike sadness.

"Of course." Brad eyed Cole's paddles. "Follow us."

"Okay," Cole said. "I will."

An hour and a half later, the five of them stood in the backyard around the barbecue. A simple hot chocolate had turned into a dinner of sliders, french fries, and grilled veggies. After enjoying a relaxing meal together in dusk's last light, they moved to the fire circle where Cole was trying to build a fire.

Brad joined him. "Gotta use the stuff that's easy to burn," he said. He grabbed some newspaper. "Start with this, then the kindling." He pointed to a pile of small wood pieces, and Cole carefully placed them in the fire ring.

"I never learned stuff like this. My dad worked all the time. And when he didn't, he was just sad."

From her spot, LuAnn could see compassion wave over Brad's face. "I'm so sorry," he said.

"Yeah, Dad never got over her death. Now he's gone too." His lip quivered. "I've been holding a lot of anger toward you for a long time." His eyes hardened, and LuAnn thought he still clung to some of that anger.

"That's understandable," Brad said. "Losing a parent so young—there's no way to describe the void it leaves."

They got the fire going, and Brad sat down next to LuAnn. Cole sat across from them.

"I'd like to tell you what happened," Brad started. "If it would help."

Cole nodded.

"Your mom was so excited to purchase a historic home in Marietta. She and your father didn't have a lot of money, but they loved doing renovations. She had seen this house in our newspaper flyer. I hadn't even wanted to advertise it yet, but there was a lot of pressure to make my first sale, so I went ahead and put it in, saying it was a 'fixer-upper.' Your mom saw it and called."

"And you took her to the house?" LuAnn asked.

"Her and her little boy." He glanced at Cole.

Cole took a deep breath. "Right."

"You were in a stroller, just a toddler, about two, I would guess."

"I was two-and-a-half when she died."

"So I showed her the downstairs. It was a neat old house, and she loved it. I thought she'd make an offer right then. I actually had to caution her to slow down a little. It needed a lot of work, and she couldn't see the upstairs, because I'd been warned not to let people up there."

"Did she slow down, as you suggested?" LuAnn asked.

Brad sipped his hot cocoa and closed his eyes, then opened them again. "No, she didn't. She was persistent, telling me to get an offer ready. I've seen clients get like this over the years. They make an emotional connection with a house and are afraid someone else will swoop in and take it. Very common...and understandable. A house is the place you make memories, spend your life, raise your kids." He put his cup down. "I cautioned her not to go to the second floor and went to my car to get my briefcase with the paperwork. They train us to write the offer right in the house if possible. It makes the client feel a sense of ownership."

LuAnn nodded. "That makes sense."

He looked at Cole. "When I stepped back through the door, I noticed that the stroller, with you in it, had been moved to the bottom of the stairway. I looked up the stairs and saw your mom almost to the top step. I reminded her it wasn't safe and asked her to turn around and come down. She said not to worry, she wasn't going to go onto the second floor, she just wanted a peek. I told her I didn't think it was a good idea and she needed to come down immediately."

Brad's hands began to tremble. When he continued, his voice was shaky. "She took that last step up. The floor collapsed beneath her, making her fall sideways. The railing she fell against gave way, and before my eyes she tumbled to the ground."

Cole took in a breath. "Did I see her? I remember seeing her, but sometimes I wonder if it's a made-up memory, if I'm just imagining from what I've been told."

Brad faced him, tears welling in his eyes. "You saw. And when she hit the floor, you screamed. I ran to her, of course. I could see she had injured her head, and she was unconscious. I didn't know what to do. We didn't have cell phones back then. The phone in the house wasn't hooked up, so I grabbed you and ran to the neighbor's and called 911."

His lips tightened with these memories. LuAnn wanted to comfort him, but she thought the best thing to do was listen.

"When I got back, she looked really pale and felt cold. I realized she may have been in shock, so I covered her with my suit coat. When the paramedic got there, she was still breathing, but I doubted she would make it. They took her to the hospital. I took the car seat out of her car, put it in mine, and drove you to the hospital where your father was waiting."

"I remember that," Cole said, simply. "The long hospital hallways. My dad holding me, crying."

"I wanted to stay and find out what happened to her, but I felt I was intruding on the family. So I left." He released a breath. "A few hours later I found out that she had died."

The fire crackled, filling the silence.

"I think I've made up explanations in my mind to fill in the holes of memory and what I'd been told." Cole stared into the fire as he spoke. "I saw you as an angry, greedy man who didn't care who he hurt."

"Did your father portray him that way?" LuAnn asked.

Cole shook his head. "Dad didn't talk about it. Ever. What was the point, he'd say. Talking wouldn't bring her back. I assumed the person who killed my mother was evil. I assumed..."

"You were so small," Brad said. "What else could you do?"

Cole didn't answer but looked up at Brad. "It couldn't have been easy for you, either. I never thought of that before, but having that happen on your first sale... How did you handle it?"

Brad rubbed his neck as the firelight cast shadows on his face. "I struggled for a long time. Fell into depression for about a year. Stopped working, turned to unhealthy coping strategies. But eventually, I surfaced again, thanks to the prayers of my grandparents and parents. Thanks to the Lord."

A light flickered in Cole's eyes. "I'm glad you were able to 'surface,' as you say. Sometimes I feel like I'm still floundering. But if you can find peace, maybe I can too."

"I'm sure of it," Brad said.

"Thank you for sharing this with me. I should have talked to you years ago."

"No problem," Brad said. "It's a journey, right? Takes time."

Cole smiled. "Apparently for me it does."

"Nah," LuAnn put in. "For all of us. We're not young anymore." She glanced at Tess and Janice, who had joined them in the circle. "I mean, we aren't old or anything, but even with all the years behind us, we're still always learning."

Cole squinted. "I'm not sure how encouraging that is." He chuckled. "I guess I have a lifetime to learn."

"That's right."

A few minutes later, Janice went inside and returned with her guitar. "I thought maybe we could have some prayer time for Margaret, Eileen, Roy, and Cole"—she smiled at him—"if he'll let us, that is." Cole nodded shyly, and she held up the guitar. "Then maybe we could end with a couple of praise songs."

She sat back down, and Janice led them in prayer. The others followed, and LuAnn's spirits were encouraged as she remembered that they weren't telling God anything He didn't already know and care about. When the last "amen" was said, she looked up and noticed that her eyes weren't the only ones that were wet with tears.

Janice plucked the strings to tune the guitar.

"I didn't know you played the guitar," Brad said.

"Janice can play any instrument she puts her hands on," LuAnn answered, then glanced at Janice. "But I haven't heard you play guitar in a long time."

"I know. It's been a while, but I think my fingers will remember."

She played a familiar praise song, and Cole listened as LuAnn and the others joined in.

"You have a nice voice," LuAnn said to Brad.

"I was in glee club." He took her hand. "How about you?"

She looked at Tess and Janice. "The three of us sang together in college," she said. "We were called—"

"The In Crowd!" Janice and Tess said together.

LuAnn laughed. "Yep. That was the *I-N* Crowd. Now we're the *I-N-N* Crowd."

As the group was laughing together, LuAnn's gaze caught on a dark figure emerging from the darkness surrounding the fire's glowing border behind Tess. The woman wore a long dark dress and had a pale, elderly face.

LuAnn gasped. The others peered at her, and she pointed at the woman.

"Hello," the woman said with an eerie calm. "I have information about who kidnapped your friend."

Chapter Twenty

As the woman moved into the light, she seemed less eerie—and more familiar. Where had LuAnn seen her before? She scanned through her memories of the last few days. Then it hit her. This was the woman walking on the shore when she and Tess were on the steamboat with Thaddeus. At the time, she'd also looked familiar, but from where? It seemed like she'd previously observed a different version of the woman, not the woman herself. In the span of a few seconds, the memory spun through her mind drawing a clearer portrait, until she realized where she'd seen her.

"Eileen Reynolds!" LuAnn blurted. "It's you!" She stood.

The matriarch of the historic ironworking Reynolds family rubbed her hands together. "Brrr. It's chilly out with that wind stirring up."

"Mrs. Reynolds," LuAnn stated again. "What are you doing here? You are Mrs. Reynolds, aren't you?"

Tess and Janice, who were seated closer to where the woman stood, made a way for her to enter the circle.

The woman smiled and joined their circle, seeming to appreciate the heat from the fire. When she sat, the others also sat. She finally returned LuAnn's gaze. "Yes, I am Eileen Reynolds." She lifted her chin like a queen.

"Craig's mother?" Tess glanced at LuAnn.

"How did you know it was me?" Mrs. Reynolds asked. "Have we met?"

LuAnn shook her head. "No, we haven't, but I saw your portrait in your living room when Tess and I visited your son." She smiled. "It was striking."

"Thank you," Mrs. Reynolds said. "I'm sure Craig was a huge help." She rolled her eyes.

"Can I get you some hot chocolate or anything?" Janice asked.

Mrs. Reynolds laughed. "I haven't had hot chocolate since I was a child. I'd love some."

LuAnn was taken by the contrast between how joyful this woman acted and the feeling LuAnn got from Craig's descriptions of her. But one question sat in the middle of the group like the proverbial elephant.

"Mrs. Reynolds," LuAnn started, "weren't you kidnapped?" LuAnn could tell by the look on their faces that her friends were wondering the same thing.

"Oh, no." She again tilted her head back and laughed. "I wasn't kidnapped. My son was driving me to the end of my tether, you see. He's a spoiled, controlling manipulator—so unlike his kind and generous father." The tiniest frown formed on her lips before she continued. "I said I was going to the market, but instead I went to Waterfront Park and met up with my friend Thaddeus. He gives steamboat rides."

"We know Thaddeus," Tess said.

Janice returned with a mug of hot chocolate and handed it to Mrs. Reynolds.

"Thank you." She took a sip with a childlike smile. "Thaddeus looks like an old coot nowadays," she continued. "But he was quite handsome in our youth." Her eyes drifted toward the sky. "A good friend. Anyway, he allowed me to rent his riverside cottage for a few days." She closed her eyes as if basking in the peace she felt there. "It was wonderful. Wonderful! The first time I was free to just be me in many years. Can I tell you a secret?"

LuAnn and the others, enthralled by the woman, nodded.

"A couple of days ago I wore my pajamas all day!"

LuAnn chuckled. To delight in such a simple pleasure certainly was a great joy to her. She was glad Mrs. Reynolds got to experience it.

"I'm sure your son is worried about you," Janice ventured. "Does he know you're okay?"

"Oh, I heard about the rumors of my kidnapping." Mrs. Reynolds's peaceful demeanor hardened. "Serves him right. He was probably more excited than worried, hoping to get his hands on the business. Modernize it. What a dolt! I'm for modernizing but not the way he wants to." She stopped midrant. "I promised myself I wouldn't think about such things."

"It must be stressful for you," LuAnn said.

"Only when I let it be." She lifted her mug. "Just like anything." She took a sip, then continued. "The reason I'm here—well, there are two reasons. One is I wanted to see what you've done with this old place. I've heard the stories about when it was Riverfront House, and I was so glad to hear that someone was restoring the beautiful old lady to her former glory."

As she spoke, LuAnn's heart raced with the joy of history. "I'd love to hear those stories sometime. But you did say you had another reason for coming as well?"

"Yes. I read in the newspaper that there were two disappearances—mine and your friend's. And that they thought they might be connected. I wasn't sure if maybe you and the police were thinking if you solved mine, you would solve your friend's. So, I thought I should let you know that I wasn't kidnapped—just escaped."

"That was thoughtful of you," LuAnn said. "To be honest, we did wonder if there was a connection, but it didn't send us down too many dead ends."

"We're so glad you're okay," Janice added.

"And it's always helpful to be able to rule out a lead," LuAnn said. "These mysteries often come down to a process of elimination as much as anything else."

"You are all very kind."

"What are you going to do now?" Janice asked. "Will you go back to your home?"

A mischievous grin came over Mrs. Reynolds's wrinkled face. "No, Thaddeus is willing to rent me the cottage, so I'm going to live out my days there. In peace." She sighed. "I might even get a cat."

"Sounds wonderful," Janice said. "But of course you know we need to call the police and let them know you're all right."

"Of course," said Mrs. Reynolds airily, waving her hand. "I would be happy for you to do that. Do you think I could combine that with a tour of your magnificent inn?"

Janice helped to her to her feet, and she and Tess led the elderly woman to the inn.

After Brad doused the fire, LuAnn walked him and Cole to Cole's car.

"It was sure nice to talk to you under less-stressful circumstances," LuAnn said to Cole. "I'm glad you were finally able to learn what actually happened that day."

Cole smiled. "Me too. And I'd love to come back to your writing class if that's okay."

LuAnn rolled her eyes. "Well. I'm not sure if it will continue, but I'll let you know if it does."

"Okay." He turned to Brad. "I'm sorry for all the hatred I've held toward you all these years."

Brad shook his head. "It was understandable. And I'm happy to forgive you. Will you forgive me? I regret everything about that day. I regret not finding you, talking to you, helping in some way."

"Of course."

The two men embraced, and LuAnn's heart melted.

"By the way," Cole said as he got into his car. "I'm dropping the lawsuit."

Brad's eyes widened. "I'm glad. I honestly believe I did everything I could to disclose everything I knew. I did a background check on the inspector, I—"

"Then I'll drop it. Plus, I have a feeling letting go of my long-held bitterness might make me healthier."

"You're feeling better physically?" LuAnn asked.

Cole lowered his head. "I am. I may have exaggerated the symptoms. I'm sorry."

"We're just glad it's all behind us," Brad said.

"I truly was sick, but I used it as an opportunity to get back at you." He gazed at Brad. "How foolish of me."

"It's not easy to admit you're wrong," LuAnn said. "We're grateful."

"Thanks."

Cole drove off, and LuAnn and Brad strolled back to the inn.

"What a relief," LuAnn said. "I'm so glad he's dropping that lawsuit."

"You were worried about it, weren't you?" Brad paused walking.

"I was." She lifted her eyes to meet his. "I care about what happens to you."

Brad returned the look. "I know you do."

He took her hand, and they continued walking.

"Did Mrs. Reynolds leave?" LuAnn asked as she and Brad came into the ladies' common area.

"We called the police, showed her the first floor, and invited her back sometime to see the rooms when we don't have so many guests," Tess said. "Then she called a cab and went home." She shook her head. "I hope the police let her son know right away that she's all right."

"Well, at least we seem to have eliminated one of our suspects," LuAnn said.

"That's right." Tess hung a dish towel on the stove handle. "But I don't feel any closer to finding Margaret."

"Me neither." Janice closed the drawer where she had been putting away silverware.

LuAnn went to her room and got her notebook. She opened it to the suspects page and crossed out Craig Reynolds's name. Tess, Janice, and Brad took her cue and sat at the table.

"I guess we're still looking at Dahlia and Roy," Janice said. "Is that it?"

"It's hard to imagine it could be either of them, but yeah," Tess said.

"I meant to ask," Janice said. "What did you find out from Thaddeus about Sub Muskingum? Did he think it means south of the river?"

Brad looked at LuAnn with furrowed brows.

"It's a clue we found in the *McGuffey Reader*," LuAnn explained.

"It doesn't seem possible that the gold coins could be hidden across the Ohio from where the Muskingum flows into it," Tess said. "It's too broad an area."

"And if they were buried there, they probably would have already been found," LuAnn added. "Or if not, they're buried beneath a building or street or something." She sighed. "It sure seems like the clues should be more specific. If they don't lead to the actual coins, what's the point of having clues at all?"

"Exactly what I was thinking." Janice folded her hands on the table.

"Are we sure there are no more clues in the *McGuffey Reader*?" Tess asked.

"I looked through the whole thing," LuAnn said. "Nothing stuck out. The underlines were so light, though, I could have missed something. I'll be right back."

She left and returned with the reader and the cipher.

"Can I see that?" Brad asked, pointing to the cipher, and LuAnn handed it to him. "So you found underlined letters and used this to figure out the code?"

"That's right," LuAnn said. "And there was a keyword in Prudence's journal. Moses Willard."

"How did you know it was the keyword?" Brad asked.

"It was written in the margin," LuAnn answered. "And it said 'key.' We may not be geniuses"—she grinned—"but we were able to figure that out."

Brad grinned back. "It was in the margin?"

"Oh!" LuAnn said. Brad's question sparked an idea. "I didn't check the margins of the reader."

Brad handed it back to her, and LuAnn laid it in the middle of the table. "Let's go through the pages and see if we find anything in the margins."

"I'll get us some more cocoa," Janice said.

After about thirty minutes of slowly scanning each page for any sign of a mark, they came to the last page.

LuAnn sighed. "Nothing." She started to close the back cover. As she did, she felt a small bulge between the corner of the paper that was glued to the back cover and the cover itself. She grabbed the magnifying glass and examined it more closely.

"What do you see, Lu?" Brad asked.

"I'm not sure." She eyed the corner with the magnifying glass and noticed a faint crease, as if it had been folded. She placed her nail carefully under the pointed corner, and it freely folded over into a small triangle. Beneath it, etched in the solid cover, were four groups of letters and one group with the number sixty and one letter. She shifted it so the others could see.

"It's another message!" LuAnn said. She retrieved the cipher and worked the letters using MOSES WILLARD as the key like she'd done before. After a few minutes she revealed what she'd found.

MAR

60F

INE

TDO

CK

"What on earth can that mean?" Janice asked.

LuAnn sighed, frustrated. "I feel like we're letting Margaret down." She slumped in her chair.

Before she could wallow much longer, the bell on the front door jingled. LuAnn looked at the clock. Nine thirty. "Probably Dahlia coming back." She and the others waited to hear footsteps coming up the stairs. When they heard nothing, LuAnn stood. "I'll go see if they need anything."

She stepped into the front room and saw a young woman with light brown hair standing at the desk. "I need to see my husband," she said before LuAnn even reached the desk.

"Who?"

"Seth Jensen. He won't return my phone calls. I know he's here. What room is he in?"

Chapter Twenty-One

As LuAnn reached the desk, she passed Dahlia heading for the stairs. The young woman had a book in her hand, and LuAnn assumed she'd been in the library looking for some reading material. As she was going up the stairs, the others came down, apparently alerted by the visitor's loud voice.

"He left me alone for days with our children. He said he has a job here." Her chin began to quiver. "Why won't he return my calls?"

"Where are your children now?" LuAnn asked. First things first.

The woman pointed to the door. "In the car, sleeping." She looked out the window at a blue sedan. "See. They're fine. I just want to talk to my husband. Where is he?"

LuAnn picked up the lobby phone and rang Apples and Cinnamon. When there was no answer, she hung up and shook her head. "I'm sorry. I don't know. He said he's been doing research on his family..."

"Is that what he told you?" Her voice rose, but she took a breath and continued. "He told me he was doing a dive job here that would get us a bunch of money. It's always the next thing with him. I wish he would just be content with the job he's got. Isn't being a corporate scuba diver adventurous enough?"

LuAnn waved to the café. "Do you want to get the kids and wait here for him?"

"We have hot cocoa," Janice added.

The woman glanced at Janice and the others.

LuAnn pointed to herself and then her friends as she made the introductions. "I'm LuAnn, and this is Janice and Tess. We're the owners." Then she pointed to Brad. "Brad is our friend."

"Nice to meet you. I'm Melissa." She paused and glanced at the car. "If we bring the kids inside, they'll wake up."

"I know that feeling," Tess said. "Did you have a hard time getting them to sleep?"

"As soon as one falls asleep, the other one wakes up, and then they're both awake. This is the first time they've both been asleep for days. Chance is a year and a half, and April is just three months." Her eyes misted. "I'll sit in the car with them until Seth gets back." She turned toward the door.

"Oh dear," Janice said. "You'll get cold."

"How about we help you bring them in?" Tess said. "We'll be super quiet. If they cry, the four of us can take turns holding them so you can rest, if you're okay with that."

Now the woman's eyes did more than mist. "That's so kind of you…I don't know though."

Before she had time to make a decision, the door opened and Seth walked in, looking bewildered. "Melissa? What are you doing here? Is that our car?"

Melissa stood straighter. "Yes, it is. Why haven't you returned my calls?"

He stepped closer to her. "I've been working all day. You know I can't call you."

"It's almost ten o'clock. You haven't had a moment when you could call?"

Seth shook his head. "I haven't, babe. This thing can't wait. I only have till tomorrow—and then I have to go back to my job."

LuAnn glanced at Tess, Janice, and Brad, who looked as uncomfortable as she felt.

"I'm sorry," Melissa said to them.

Seth seemed to notice them for the first time. "Oh, hey."

LuAnn glanced at a duffel bag he held. "Melissa tells us you're a diver."

"I'm going to go get the kids." Melissa slipped out the door.

"That's right," Seth answered. "I dive for corporations. Do inspections, repair, surveying."

"And you're here for another job?" LuAnn's mind was working something out.

"Something like that."

"And your ancestor was a schoolteacher?"

"That's right." He smiled. "I'm descended from her and a soldier she met at Camp Putnam. I've also been researching them while I've been here."

Melissa returned holding a sleeping toddler with his head on her shoulder and a baby in a car seat that attached to a stroller.

Seth turned to Melissa. "I'm sorry." He rubbed her arm. "I should have found time to call."

"You should have," Melissa said. "And you shouldn't have left us in the first place."

"I can't believe you made the drive all the way here. Let's go upstairs and put the kids to bed. I'll get up with them if they wake up, okay? You can rest."

Melissa released a sigh. "Okay."

They looked at LuAnn.

"Is it okay if they stay in my room?" Seth asked. "I only paid for single occupancy. You can go ahead and charge me whatever the extra is."

"Of course they can stay," LuAnn said.

After the family walked upstairs, the group let out a collective sigh.

"What a day," Janice said. "Sleuthing, singing by the campfire, and before that kayaking." She coughed the word, "Swimming."

The others laughed.

"I think we're all pretty worn out," LuAnn said. "Tomorrow we'll get back to all this."

"Tomorrow is the Taste of Marietta," Janice reminded them.

"I almost forgot," Tess said.

"We better get rested," LuAnn said. "I can guarantee Winnie will have us working hard tomorrow."

LuAnn's exhausted body and mind fell asleep as soon as she crawled into bed. Waking with the sun, she caught her thoughts immediately circling the unanswered questions from the night before. The questions brought up by her encounter with Seth as well as their latest discovery in the *McGuffey Reader.*

She showered and dressed and moved past the common room, where Dahlia was still sleeping. It wasn't long before she needed to help with breakfast and Taste of Marietta preparations, so she padded down the stairs and found a spot on the sofa next to the fireplace. She relished the silence for a few moments before she heard movement in the kitchen. A moment later, Janice arrived holding a tray with a carafe of coffee, cream and sugar, and three mugs.

"I didn't hear you come down." LuAnn gratefully received the coffee from her friend and settled back into the sofa.

"You seemed deep in thought," Janice said, settling onto the couch next to her.

"I was."

"Hey, you two." Tess's voice rang softly through the lobby. "I thought I heard someone down here."

"You're up early," LuAnn commented.

Tess grabbed a mug and filled it first with cream and sugar, then with coffee. "I can't stop thinking about Margaret."

"Me neither," Janice said.

LuAnn sipped her coffee. "There's something about that code. I want to figure it out!" She opened her notebook and glanced at the letters they had found a few days ago and the ones from last night. She'd written them in a column.

SUB

MUS

MAR

60F

INE

TDO

CK

She went to the office, grabbed a pad of sticky notes, then returned and wrote each group of letters on a different sticky note. When she was finished, she had seven sticky notes.

"Good thinking," Janice said.

LuAnn smiled and moved a strand of hair behind her ear. "So we think SUB and MUS go together."

"Right," Tess said. "That's where we got the idea that the coins were south of the Muskingum."

LuAnn moved the notes around. "Look," she said. "If I put these here." She laid out the MUS 60F TDO CK horizontally. "Mus 60 ft dock."

"Oh my," Janice said. "That looks like a location."

"It does," LuAnn agreed. She rearranged the remaining sticky notes, and her heart skipped a beat. Her hands shook as she displayed the remaining notes to her friends.

SUB MAR INE

"Can you believe it?" She stood up, then sat back down.

Tess and Janice only gaped at her, confused.

"Submarine?" Tess asked. "Did they even have submarines back then?"

"They did," LuAnn said. "They even had one in the Revolutionary War."

"Really?" Janice sounded skeptical.

"Yes. It was called the *Turtle*. It didn't work very well, but I'm sure they'd improved the design nearly a hundred years later. I need to go to the historical society." She stood up again, then sat back down.

Tess blinked. "This is really exciting." But she didn't sound excited. "I still don't quite understand what this has to do with finding Margaret."

"I'm not sure," LuAnn said. "But I have an idea. If I'm right, it could lead us to her. I need to go to the historical society." She glanced at the grandfather clock. It was still early. "I'll go and be back as soon as I can."

"Don't forget, Dahlia has the key," Tess said.

"Right." LuAnn rushed up the stairs. To her surprise, Dahlia was awake and dressed.

"Hey," she said when LuAnn walked in. "You seem in a rush. What's up?"

"Good morning," LuAnn answered. "I have to run to the historical society. Can I borrow the key?"

Dahlia glanced at her purse. "Sure, but could I come with you? And could we maybe stop at Roy's on the way back? I'd like to see him and...talk about the whole"—she swallowed—"'father' thing."

LuAnn's heart swelled. Dahlia seemed to be softening to the idea of Roy being her father. What an answer to prayer. "Of course. I'd be happy to take you."

September 22, 1863

"By submarine?" Cynthia asked.

"That's right. The South has one, and they thought it would be the safest way to receive the coins."

Cynthia lowered the gun. "I have no choice but to believe you," she said. "If you're lying, you will be sorry."

Austin's entire body relaxed, and he gazed into Cynthia eyes. "I swear to you. I am for the North. Like you." He glanced at Prudence. "Like you both, all I want is to end this war, so the stain of slavery will be done away with forever."

Prudence believed him. One could not fake that type of passion.

"What is the plan?" Prudence asked. "I will help however I can."

After leaving Cynthia and Austin, Prudence took Moses home. Jason, reluctant to let her participate in the evening's activity, had finally relented after she promised to only do her part and then return home. She must not stay and find out what happened. Prudence had agreed. She had no need to find out the resolution. It was in God's hands.

The fall sky was streaked with color as she trekked to the inn to check on the little ones. Jason and Moses had appreciated her chicken pot pie and cider, and she had enjoyed making a meal for her family, cleaning up afterwards, talking with them. She cherished the simple moments, knowing she led her "other life"—the dangerous one that involved after-dark rendezvous with spies—so other parents could experience those same moments. Moments everyone had a right to experience.

She entered through the front door and headed to the secret rooms. Reaching the room where the twins were hiding, she paused, expecting to hear their innocent voices, but it was silent. She angled the door open. Elizabeth sat in the chair, and both the children's sweet faces rested in sleep on the cot. They were sucking their thumbs and clinging to the rag dolls Prudence had made them. Her heart melted at the sight of these precious children, made in God's image.

"They were worn out," Elizabeth said with a smile. "After dinner, they fell fast asleep. Are they not lovely?"

"Indeed, they are," Prudence said. "Any word on transport for this cargo?"

A broad smile appeared on Elizabeth's face. "Yes, while you were gone, we got word that a package was coming tonight who would be willing to adopt these two. A family from Canada, just across the border, with two of their own. It is surely an answer to prayer."

"It is." Prudence silently thanked the Lord for this. "When do they leave?"

"Tonight."

"Oh my." Much activity was happening tonight. She gazed at the children. Much was at stake.

"A conductor will meet you at midnight to pick up the children," Elizabeth said. "At the usual spot."

"Yes, of course." Prudence prayed her other mission would be successful. For the sake of these little ones, she would give her life if she had to in order make sure it was.

With Dahlia sitting next to her, LuAnn began the eight-minute drive to the historical society. After a few minutes of small talk, she brought up the topic most on her mind. "I'm so glad you're willing to talk to Roy," she said.

Dahlia sighed. "I am too, I think. I was pretty upset at first, but I've calmed down and had time to think about it. I'd like to hear him out, at least."

"I'm happy to hear that," LuAnn said. "I think you'll be glad you did."

Dahlia inhaled and let out a shaky breath. Something else was on her mind.

"Are you all right?"

"To be honest, there are some things I haven't told you."

"That's okay," LuAnn said. "You don't owe me any explanations." She turned onto the street of the historical society.

"I feel like I do," Dahlia answered. "The truth is, I didn't have the best motives coming here to see my aunt. In fact, it was me who—"

Before she could finish, they pulled into the historical society's parking lot, and LuAnn's attention was turned to the door. "Do you see that?"

"The door's open," Dahlia said. "How'd that happen?"

"I don't know." LuAnn parked and turned off the engine. "We better go check it out."

They approached the half-opened door.

"Whoever opened it could still be around," LuAnn said. "We need to be careful. Do you want to wait in the car?"

"No way."

LuAnn peeked inside. Everything was dark except the light to the stairway leading to Margaret's office. LuAnn's heart raced. "Hello!" she called. "Is someone here?"

No answer came, so she stepped inside, leaving the door ajar, as it had been.

"Hello?" she called again as she and Dahlia headed toward the stairs. "Is someone down there?"

They moved down the stairs. LuAnn heard no sound except their footsteps. What was going on down there? Why was the light on?

Finally reaching the bottom, she still saw nothing. "Hello?"

She and Dahlia glanced at each other.

"I guess whoever was here left," Dahlia said.

"I guess so." LuAnn relaxed and moved into the office. A bin lay open on the table and a chair next to it had been pushed back. "I wonder—"

Before she could finish, Dahlia screamed.

Chapter Twenty-Two

LuAnn jumped at Dahlia's scream. "What's wrong?"

Dahlia had wandered down the middle aisle of shelving, where she now stood about halfway down. She was staring into one of the smaller aisles of shelves, her hand over her heart. "He's dead! I think he's dead!"

LuAnn rushed to her side. A man lay facedown on the floor. LuAnn hesitantly moved to him. The man faced away from her, but she could tell by his hair and build that it was Roy.

"Is he dead?" Dahlia's voice trembled.

As LuAnn got closer, she touched his back and could feel his body move as he breathed.

"I'm not dead," his rough voice said.

"Oh my goodness!" Dahlia released a breath.

Roy moved his head to face LuAnn. "Just thought I'd take a nap."

LuAnn then noticed that his jacket was wadded up as a pillow beneath his head.

"Roy," LuAnn said. "You scared us."

He shifted his weight to his hands and slowly sat up with a few moans and groans for effect, LuAnn expected. "Hey, now.

I didn't tell you to come down here and wake me up." He winked at LuAnn, and she smiled.

"You left the front door open!" Dahlia's voice was sharp. "Why would you do that?"

Roy worked his way to his feet. "I'm sorry. I don't know. I must not have been careful to latch it."

"That was very irresponsible," Dahlia said.

"That reminds me." LuAnn rushed back up the stairs and latched the door, then returned. By the time she got back, Roy and Dahlia were sitting at the table. Dahlia's stern look had relaxed, but she still seemed frustrated.

"Well," Roy started. "What brings you two here?"

LuAnn gazed at the shelves. "I'm trying to find some information." She moved her gaze to him. "But I'm concerned about you. Are you well enough to be out and about?"

Roy sighed. "I was tired of sitting at home. Needed to get back to learning about history, about Marietta, about Margaret, and . . ." He shook his head. "I just needed to get busy."

"You need to be more careful." Dahlia's gaze found his. "Roy, I'm sorry I was so angry before. I want to get to know you, if it's okay with you."

Roy grinned from ear to ear. "I would like that very much." He sobered. "And you don't have anything to be sorry about. I'm the one who's sorry. So very sorry."

"Last time, I didn't let you finish your story," Dahlia said. "I'd like to hear the rest."

"There's not that much left to tell. Your mom and I loved each other very much, but when she got pregnant, her family rejected her, including your great-aunt Margaret."

"I know about that," Dahlia said in a small voice.

Roy continued. "We ran off together despite her family's disapproval. We were happy for a while, but money was tight—really tight. That made us both act in ways we weren't proud of. I said things out of frustration I never should have said. And so did she, to be honest. I don't blame her. The pressure was unbearable. Finally, I found the job on the fishing boat. I loved escaping the stress of marriage and...well"—he looked at Dahlia—"the responsibility."

"You mean me," Dahlia said.

"A baby was way more responsibility than I realized. I was immature and stupid. At first I sent money to you and your mom faithfully, but then I started spending it on booze, on playing with my friends, acting like child. I was a child, in many ways." He gazed at his large rough hands, then back at Dahlia. "After about a year of being gone most of the time, I was served with divorce papers. I never saw your mom or you again."

How could this ever be made right? LuAnn wondered. Reconciliation seemed impossible. Forgiveness? Yet, here Roy and Dahlia were. They were together. That was a step. LuAnn held her breath and prayed.

"The only thing I have to say to you is I'm sorry. I will say it with my last breath if I have to. I regret leaving her. I regret leaving you. I wish I could be a father to you. I don't blame you if you never want to see me again."

Dahlia wiped a tear from her eye and took a deep breath. "I've hated you my whole life," she said. "I hated your facelessness. Your absentness. Your willingness to abandon us. And I also hated my great-aunt."

"Margaret?" Roy asked.

"Yes. That's why I came here. To find her. To hurt her." She glanced at LuAnn. "My mother told me how Aunt Maggie judged her. How she scorned her for being pregnant out of wedlock. Margaret had been the only mother my mom knew, and then to be rejected and judged by her—my mom never recovered from that rejection.

"When my mom died, it seemed so unfair that she never had a chance to show Margaret the truth. She had made a life for herself and me without Margaret. She had succeeded in life regardless of her rejection. She was the best mom. She worked so hard, she played and laughed and loved me. Never thinking of herself." Tears rolled down Dahlia's cheeks. "I decided to find Margaret. Hurt her somehow."

"What are you saying?" LuAnn asked. "Did you...?"

"Hate her? Yes." She shook her head. "But when I came here, the first thing she did—the very first thing—was sit me down and tell me everything. She admitted how she had judged my mom. She apologized. She said she'd spent years regretting what she'd done. She'd even looked for us. But my mom changed her name, and she couldn't find us. Aunt Maggie was thrilled that we finally connected. She showed me kindness day after day. Still, I didn't know if I believed her. I'd spent my whole life hating her, but I was starting to trust her, to believe her. I wanted to, you know. I want to have family. Doesn't everyone?" She looked at Roy. "And then she was kidnapped, and I lost my chance."

"I still think we're going to find her," LuAnn said. "Don't give up hope. You'll have your chance to get to know her."

Dahlia clenched her hands together. "I hope so." She looked at Roy. "There's something I don't understand. Why did you want to find Aunt Maggie? She was cruel to you. Why go to the trouble to find her?"

Roy bowed his head. "When I was diagnosed with cancer, I knew I had to find you and your mom. I couldn't track you down, but I found Margaret. I thought maybe she would lead me to you." He smiled. "And she did."

"Did she know who you were?"

"No. I don't think she recognized me after all these years. And I didn't know if she would still hate me. I needed to find out what kind of person she was now. She was my only hope of finding you."

"Does she know who you are now? Did you ever tell her?"

He shook his head. "I haven't. But I will. I definitely will."

Dahlia took his hand in hers. "We can tell her together."

Roy's eyes flooded with tears as he placed his other hand over hers.

"We'll be together from now on, okay?" Dahlia said. "I won't leave."

"Neither will I." Roy smiled. "I promise."

At that moment, LuAnn's phone buzzed, breaking the intensity. She wiped a tear then peeked at it. It was Winnie, asking her if she could pick up some extra paper plates for the Taste of Marietta. LuAnn texted her back, then looked at Roy and Dahlia.

"So," she said. "Not to break the mood, but I have an idea, and I need to know if there was ever a submarine in the Ohio River during the Civil War." She peered at Roy. "You've been researching this town. Have you seen anything about that?"

Roy tapped his fingers on the table. "Submarines—I know there was one in the Revolutionary War—the *Turtle*."

"Right, but—"

"Actually, I may have seen something." He stood, and LuAnn followed him as he wandered to the boxes of history magazines like the ones he had in his house. "I just love this magazine." He flipped through the file. "It's all about the intricate details of US history. I think I might have read something about subs being used by the South." He pulled out an issue. "Here." He handed LuAnn a copy of the magazine.

On the front was a black-and-white photograph of a submarine. She opened it to the article and skimmed it, then hurried the others upstairs and out of the museum. She needed to get to the Taste of Marietta to tell her friends they were right about the secret message.

A few minutes later, LuAnn, Dahlia, and Roy were parking in the vendor section of the Taste of Marietta with extra plates ready to go. A pang of guilt hit LuAnn when she looked around at all the booths set up. She knew the inn's booth would be set up and looking welcoming, professional, and inviting. And she knew her friends would understand why she wasn't there. Still, she would have liked to help.

She turned a corner and there it was, just as she expected. A gorgeous booth, and she could smell the cinnamon rolls and coffee from where she stood. She also saw Winnie and Janice chatting and smiling as they applied the final touches. Tess was probably back at the inn, along with Taylor.

She approached the booth, and as good as everything smelled, she hankered even more to tell them about the submarine.

"Hey there," Janice said as LuAnn moved behind the front table. "How'd it go at the historical society?" She glanced at Roy and Dahlia. "Hi!"

"Well, hello, Miss Janice," Roy said. "Good to see you."

Janice gave him a hug. "Are you supposed to be out and about?"

Roy smiled. "I'm doing a lot better today. I wouldn't miss this." He held Dahlia's hand.

"I have something to tell you," LuAnn said. "I think I know what happened to the gold coins." She whispered "gold coins." They still didn't know who was after them, so she wanted to be careful.

"Really?" Janice said. "Tell me."

"Remember how we found the word *submarine*?"

Janice nodded.

"I think that's how the coins were delivered here."

Janice put a hand to her mouth. "That's incredible."

"It is. But think about it. Sub Muskingum. It wasn't south of the Muskingum at all. It was saying there's a sunken submarine in the Muskingum."

"And you think that's where the gold coins are? Why?"

"Well, remember we found out from the second article at the historical society that there was a Confederate sympathizer in the North who sent the coins to Camp Putnam. The South sent a submarine up the river to get the coins. It makes sense. There were outposts around the rivers, so any boat would have been spotted. But they wouldn't have seen a submarine. Although, I don't think it was the famous Confederate sub, the Hunley. I don't know that that one was ever in a river. The South made about twenty other submarines that would have had a better chance of making it through the Ohio. They couldn't totally submerge the smokestack or their breathing tube, but it would still be less visible than a boat, especially at night. I don't know why, but the submarine sank before they could get the gold from it."

"Maybe the teacher spy found out about the plot and stopped it somehow," Janice suggested. "With Prudence's help!"

"Maybe. I don't know."

"This is all so interesting, but we still don't know who was after the gold coins. Or do you think..." Janice paused. "Seth said he was here for information about his family, but his wife said something about him coming here for a dive job that would get him a lot of money." Janice's eyes widened.

LuAnn's mind spun around the events of the last few days, her thoughts circling toward the answer. Before she had a chance to answer Janice, one of the baristas from Jeremiah's Coffee House walked up.

"Hey," the young woman said. "How's it going for you guys? We've been pretty busy."

LuAnn struggled to focus on what their visitor was saying. "Yeah, we've, uh, been busy too."

"Hey." The barista's voice softened. "Have you heard anything about Margaret? We've all been praying she'll be found. She's a regular at Jeremiah's."

LuAnn focused her thoughts on what the young woman said. "She is?"

"Yeah, she loves our coffee and raspberry scones." She chuckled. "Gets the same thing every day."

LuAnn's mind raced. "She hasn't been found yet," she said to the barista. "I'm sorry. I have to go."

The young woman smiled awkwardly, but thankfully Winnie stepped in and served her.

As she stepped away, LuAnn pulled Janice's arm. "We have to go."

"What?" Janice said. "What are you talking about?"

"I'll tell you on the way. But we have to go right now." She turned to Winnie. "I'm so sorry to do this to you, Winnie. But we have to go. I know where Margaret is."

"You go then," Winnie urged. "I've got this."

"Wait!" Dahlia and Roy had returned, and Dahlia must have overheard LuAnn. "You know where Margaret is?"

"You do?" Roy asked.

"I think so," LuAnn said. "But we have to go."

Dahlia looked at Roy, who nodded.

"We're going with you," Roy said.

"Okay then. Come on!" LuAnn said. They all rushed to LuAnn's car and got in, Janice in the passenger seat and Dahlia and Roy in the back.

"Are you going to tell me what's going on?" Janice asked as she buckled.

LuAnn was too focused on driving to talk. "Trust me. It'll all make sense in a few minutes. Call Randy, okay? Have him meet us at the Castle."

"The Castle?" Dahlia asked.

"You'll see why." LuAnn broke a few speed limits as she made her way down the streets. All she could think about was Margaret, locked up in a cold room, afraid, wanting to go to her cozy home with her bird, and especially to her treasured historical society. She was probably worried about it.

She pulled onto Fourth Street and parked. Glancing over the grounds, she saw a truck. "That's Seth's truck," LuAnn said. "He's here."

Janice's eyes widened. "Seth's here?"

LuAnn and Janice ran to the front door. Dahlia hung back with Roy, who was unable to run. The door was locked. LuAnn pounded on it and rang the doorbell. "Are you here? Open up!"

LuAnn heard footsteps inside and then from the side, a door open and slam.

"The kitchen door," LuAnn said. "Come on."

Sirens sounded in the distance as she and Janice ran to the far side of the building with Dahlia and Roy following behind.

"Where is he?" Janice asked as they ran.

"We're not looking for Seth…" As LuAnn answered she spotted Ashley racing across the grass to a garden shed.

"Ashley!" LuAnn called. "I know you kidnapped Margaret! Let her go!"

A gardener's truck was parked next to the shed, and Ashley jumped in. She started the truck and began to drive. The only way out was down a driveway that led to Fourth Street where LuAnn was parked. LuAnn raced to the sidewalk where two trash cans were waiting to be emptied and shoved one of them into the driveway, spilling the trash and making Ashley have to back up and work her way around it.

"Ashley! Stop this. Talk to me!"

Ashley hesitated, and Janice followed LuAnn's lead, shoving the other trash can down and kicking it in front of the truck. Ashley pushed on the gas, and Janice scampered out of the way, barely missing getting hit by the truck.

Ashley honked, and her brakes screeched. "Get out of the way! You're going to get hurt!"

"Ashley!" LuAnn yelled. "Please! Stop this!"

"I can't!" Ashley yelled from inside the truck. "Let me go!"

But it was too late. Randy arrived and parked his patrol car, blocking her only way out. Ashley turned off the truck and hung her head.

LuAnn reached the truck before Randy did. "Ashley," she said, "I don't know why you did this. I don't care right now. Please, tell us where Margaret is."

Dahlia and Roy reached the scene as Ashley dug into her pocket and pulled out a key. "She's upstairs." She glanced at the Castle. "In the highest room." She pointed to the tower overlooking the town. The windows were still covered with tarps because of the renovation.

At Ashley's words, Dahlia rushed to the truck. "You kidnapped her? How could you? What kind of person are you?"

"I'm so sorry." Ashley shook her head. "I'm a fool."

As she spoke, Randy came up to the truck. "What's going on here?"

LuAnn pointed toward the truck. "This is my friend Ashley. She's the one who kidnapped Margaret Ashworth."

Randy's eyes widened. "You have proof of this?"

"It's true." Ashley began to cry. "It's true."

Chapter Twenty-Three

After Randy questioned Ashley, he grabbed the keys from her, handcuffed her, and allowed her to lead them back to the Castle. He unlocked the door, and LuAnn felt a chill from the old place. White powder dusted the entryway.

The group climbed the stairs in silence. Upon reaching the top, even Randy seemed a touch winded. They came to a glossy mahogany door, and Randy inserted the key. LuAnn held her breath as the door opened.

Peeking in, she saw Margaret lying on the bed with her back turned to the door, the afghan Margaret's sister made covering her. On the bedside table sat two prescription bottles.

"You broke into Margaret's house and got her pills?" Dahlia asked Ashley.

Ashley nodded. "I was following your posts on that site, so I knew she needed them. I didn't want to hurt her."

They spoke in hushed tones—the room seemed to call for it. Margaret remained on her side.

LuAnn stepped closer, then looked back when Margaret still didn't move.

"Is she okay?" Dahlia asked. She scooted in front of LuAnn and placed a hand on Margaret's back.

"She hasn't felt well for a few days," Ashley said. "I was going to let her go today, no matter what happened with—"

"She's been sick?" Dahlia glared at Ashley. "Aunt Maggie." She leaned over. "It's Dahlia. We found you. You can go home now." She rolled Margaret over, so she was now lying on her back, very still. Dahlia placed a hand on her own chest. "Aunt Maggie." She looked at LuAnn. "She's not…?"

LuAnn stepped closer and picked up Margaret's hand. The older woman's skin was dry but warm. "Margaret?" she said gently.

Randy moved next to the bed. "Ma'am!" His voice boomed. "Mrs. Ashworth. Are you okay?"

Margaret's forehead scrunched, and her eyes finally opened. "Why so loud?" she grumped. "What on earth would make a person yell like that?" Waking up, she suddenly gasped and held the covers to her chest. Her eyes widened as she gazed around the room, until they found Ashley, standing in handcuffs. Then they narrowed angrily.

"You!" Margaret said. "Ha! They caught you, you crazy woman."

At that, Dahlia burst into tears and hugged her aunt. "I was so worried."

LuAnn thought she spotted a tear on Margaret's cheek too. "Dahlia, dear. Now, now. I'm all right." She patted her back as Dahlia clung to her.

September 22, 1863

The only hitch when dropping off the children at midnight was that the conductor was thirty minutes late—that and the heartbreak of saying goodbye to such sweet darlings. Prudence prayed unceasingly as she rushed to the designated meeting place outside the camp. She would meet Austin, who would give her the go-ahead or not for the mission. It was Prudence's responsibility to deliver the message to Cynthia, who waited on a hill. Cynthia would send a lantern signal to the waiting Union ship.

Prudence was thankful for the simplicity of the plan. She was merely a messenger. She could do that. And as soon as she delivered the message to Cynthia, she'd hike home to Jason's waiting arms.

Dampness seeped into Prudence's leather boots as she walked through the grass to the meeting place. Other than a half moon, it was completely dark outside, and the lantern she carried only lit a few feet in front of her. She could not tell if Austin waited in the shadows or not. Willing her eyes to adjust, she hesitantly walked toward the meeting spot.

"Austin?"

"Shh," Austin said. "Go."

Suddenly Prudence doubted. "Is it really thee?" she whispered and stepped closer. Finally, her lantern lit his face. She exhaled. It was him. "I am sorry, I just had to be sure."

Austin's face was stern. "Go."

Prudence did not say another word but took off toward the hill where she was to meet Cynthia. She paced through the darkness until she spotted Cynthia's frame silhouetted against the moon. At least she thought that was her. She sped up. "Is that thee?" When she got closer, she was sure it was her friend. "It is a go. Two flashes. It is a go."

She stepped closer but then a scream halted her.

"Go back! We've been compromised!" Cynthia screamed again, and then a shot rang out. Cynthia crumpled to the ground.

"Thank you for letting me see her," LuAnn said a few days later to Randy as he let her into a small room at the city jail.

"You only have a few minutes, okay?" he said.

"I understand."

Randy left the room, but through the window in the door, LuAnn could see he waited just outside.

Ashley was seated at a table in the middle of the room. She stared at her hands, not looking up as LuAnn sat down.

"I found out about Dustin," LuAnn started. "I thought you'd want to know how he's doing."

Ashley finally looked up. "Is he okay?"

"Paul said he's doing the same. He's still in Florida, but he'll get home soon. Paul's not going to tell him about what happened until he gets back."

Ashley relaxed. "I'm so glad. I was worried it would ruin his trip."

"Ashley, I have so many questions. You and Paul are divorced?"

She nodded.

"I don't have much time," LuAnn continued, "but please, explain why you did this."

Ashley inhaled deeply. "You deserve to know—and Margaret and her niece deserve to know. You'll explain it to them?"

"I will. I promise."

"It's my Dustin. I told you he has cancer. The only treatment is in France. France! I didn't have the money to send him."

"But I thought—"

"You thought a Princeton professor would make a good income? I did, but we made some bad investments and lost all of our savings. Then when we divorced, I fell apart. I lost my job. I have nothing, LuAnn. That's why my car was repossessed."

"What?" LuAnn gasped. "That's what happened? How did they know you were here?"

"They are clever. I gave the post office a forwarding address to the Castle." Ashley shook her head. "It's so humiliating."

"Oh, Ashley. We all go through hard times." LuAnn folded her hands on the table. "I still don't understand why you kidnapped Margaret."

"I did it for the gold coins," she said. "When I did my preliminary research on the Castle, I learned about them." She closed her eyes. "I also had a former student whose family had history in Marietta."

"Seth?"

"Right. He was my student when I taught at the community college, before I ever started at Princeton. We had chatted about our mutual interest in Marietta. I remembered that he had some relics from that time period."

"The *McGuffey Reader* and the cipher?"

"That's right," she said. "They were handed down from his ancestors, a schoolteacher and Union soldier at the time the gold coins were lost. We don't know why she and whoever she worked with put the clues in that format. Maybe they didn't want to search for the coins until the war was over and then weren't able to. Maybe they thought they would leave the coins for their progeny. We don't know. Anyway, I found out in an obscure document I uncovered in my research that the coins were transferred to a Confederate submarine before it was sunk by a Union Navy ship. No one has been able to find the coins because no one else had the reader and the cipher, and no one knew about the submarine, but—"

"But it didn't work." LuAnn gazed at her. "You were missing the key word."

"Right. I thought if anyone could find it, it would be Margaret Ashworth from the historical society. I talked to her over the phone, but she said she didn't want to help me find those coins. She said I didn't have any claim to them, and if they were found they should be donated to her historical society."

"That sounds like her."

"So I came."

"And Seth came too."

"He wanted to make sure I didn't skip out with the coins."

"I see."

"When I confronted Margaret, she wouldn't help me find the key word. I was desperate for the money to save my son, so I came up with a plan. I knew you and your friends had solved several mysteries, so I thought maybe you could figure out where the coins are."

LuAnn looked at her friend. "Why didn't you ask us for help?"

"I couldn't, LuAnn. I just told you why. I'm divorced. Fired from Princeton. Broke. A failure in every way. The shame was overpowering."

LuAnn touched her hand. "Shame is so powerful, but it's a lie. There's nothing shameful about falling on hard times. It's how you react to them—"

"I know, I guess...but I couldn't face you. So, I planted the reader in your jacket the afternoon of the lecture and the cipher at the inn, hoping you would find them and be intrigued."

"I definitely was. We all were."

"How did you find the key word?"

"Prudence," LuAnn said. "A woman who helped with the Underground Railroad. It was in her journal."

"Well, then. I guess I was right. I never would have found the coins without you."

"They haven't been found," LuAnn said, shaking her head. "You were right, they were in a Confederate submarine that was attacked by the Union. We did find the key word and were able to decipher the message. It said 'sixty feet dock.'" She sighed. "Whether that means the sub was sunk sixty feet from a dock, or it was sunk near a dock that was sixty feet long, your guess is as good as mine. No matter what it means, any dock it's talking about is long gone, and there's no way of telling, after a hundred and fifty years, where it might have been."

Ashley rubbed her temples. "It was foolish. I don't know if you realized it, but I never told you what to do with the coins once you found them. I couldn't think of a way to get them without getting caught." She dropped her head in her hands. "I'm a fool."

"You were desperate to help your son," LuAnn said gently. "There is something you didn't know though. One of Dustin's friends set up a crowdfunding account to raise money for him to go to France for the treatment. They've raised almost nine thousand dollars. That's the goodness and generosity of people, Ashley."

Tears flowed down Ashley's cheeks. "I really am sorry."

"I know," LuAnn said.

September 22, 1863

Holding up her lantern, Prudence saw a man tumble next to Cynthia. He gazed at her, holding the side of his face. "Thee!" Prudence yelled. It was Reynolds, the one who had taken the firewood. Apparently, the gun had recoiled and struck his face, pushing him over. As fast as she could, as Reynolds struggled to his feet, Prudence raced the last few feet to the top of the hill. She raised the lantern, then lowered it behind her back, then raised it again. She counted to ten, then repeated the sequence.

"What do you think you're doing?" Reynolds's voice sounded behind her, making Prudence freeze. Did he still have the gun? Would he strike her? Before she could decide how to respond she heard a loud smack and then a tumbling sound.

"Prudence, are you all right?" It was Austin. "I heard the shot and was worried about…you both."

"I am fine," Prudence said. "But Cynthia." She ran back to Cynthia and held up the lantern, revealing her friend lying on the grass.

Austin knelt next to her. "Can you hear me, Cynthia?" He smoothed the hair from her forehead. "Cynthia?"

Cynthia moaned and grabbed her shoulder. Prudence noticed a rip in her dress and a wound beneath it.

"The bullet only skimmed her shoulder," Prudence said after examining it. "If we get her to my home, she will be all right. I will care for her." She ripped her petticoat and applied pressure to the wound.

"Oh, thank God," Austin said, taking over holding the wound. "You're going to be all right." He picked her up.

"So you really are on our side?" Cynthia asked, gazing into his eyes.

"I am. Mostly, I'm for you."

"Autumn is in the air," LuAnn said as she arrived back at the inn after her meeting with Ashley.

"You're back," Janice said.

Brad scooted over, making room for her to sit next to him in front of the fireplace. "How'd it go?"

LuAnn smiled. "It went well, I suppose. Her biggest concern is her son, of course, and hearing about the crowdfunding drive lifted her spirits. I wish she would have taken a route like that in the first place."

"Yeah," Tess said. "Grief and desperation can mess with a person's thinking."

"It can," Janice agreed. "Do you know if Margaret's going to press charges?"

LuAnn let out a breath. "I think she is, actually. I don't blame her. And, honestly, even if she doesn't, the prosecutor could still charge Ashley. She committed a felony."

"That word is so ominous." Tess shuddered.

"It's her first offense though," LuAnn said. "And there were extenuating circumstances. Randy couldn't really give his opinion, but he hinted that he thought the judge might take that into consideration." She let out a breath. "But she's still facing years of prison time."

"I feel so bad for her," Janice said. "And for her family."

"I do too," Tess agreed, then perked up in her seat. "Are you all ready for our visit to Margaret?"

Janice stood. "We are. Winnie, Robin, and Taylor are all set to cover for us. We shouldn't be gone long though."

"I'll grab some scones to share," LuAnn said.

About ten minutes later, they sat in Margaret's living room, barraged by LaFayette's grumblings. Occasionally she screamed, "Get out!"

Roy and Dahlia sat in chairs on either side of Margaret, who lay on the couch.

"It's good to see you all," LuAnn said as she set the box of scones on the coffee table.

"It's good to be home," Margaret said. "But I don't think I need to be lying down. For goodness' sake, I'm fine." She scooted up on the sofa, then tipped over a bit.

Dahlia patted her arm. "The doctor said you were dehydrated and exhausted—thankfully that was all. But you need to listen to your body and rest."

"Fine then." Margaret grabbed a scone from the plate and took a bite, then settled back down. "These scones aren't as good as Jeremiah's though."

LuAnn, Tess, and Janice eyed each other.

"Better not let Winnie hear you say that," LuAnn said.

"Nothing but the truth," Margaret said, then returned her gaze to Dahlia. "Anyway, I was doing better until you went and shocked me with the news of that man being your father." She pointed at Roy. "My niece's long-lost husband."

Dahlia sent Roy a loving glance. "It took a bit of getting used to for me too, but now I'm so glad we found each other." She looked at Margaret. "And I'm glad you know the truth."

Margaret nodded. "I am too, I admit." She reached for Roy's hand. "I treated you something awful back then. I am sorry."

"As am I, sweet Miss Margaret." Roy patted her hand. "It's behind us now. I'm so thankful to be with you both during this... time."

"Yes." Margaret's eyes glistened. "We'll spend as much time as we can together."

"As much as we can," Dahlia repeated.

LuAnn gazed at her friends. "We should give you some of that time."

Tess, Janice, and Brad took the hint and together stood to go.

Soon they were back at the inn, standing around the island in the kitchen.

"So, are you going to do the writing class?" Janice asked as she moved to start some coffee.

"Cole asked me about that too." Brad smiled. "I think he was sincere about the writing. Who knew?"

LuAnn glanced at Brad. "I'm so happy you're keeping in touch with him. He needs a friend."

"So you are doing the class, then?" Tess asked.

LuAnn tapped her pen on the island. "I don't think so," she answered hesitantly. "I like teaching, but my real passion, at least right now, is something else."

Janice sat up. "Writing! You're going to write that book, aren't you?"

"Is she right?" Tess asked.

Joy sprang inside at the thought. "I think I will." LuAnn smiled at her friends. "But not the wounded soldier one. This one will be about Marietta. Maybe some old friends who buy a hotel from Civil War times and make it into a quaint, warm, and friendly inn. Do you think anyone would read it?"

Tess and Janice clapped in approval. "Absolutely!"

Dear Reader,

Recently I reached a milestone birthday. As this day approached, I asked myself if I've accomplished enough in my life so far. I still have many goals to pursue, many books to write, many ways I long to serve. In *Submerged Secrets*, LuAnn has achieved valuable accomplishments in her life, yet she too wonders if she should have pursued her long-ago dream. For her it was writing a novel. What is it for you?

I also sometimes wonder if it's too late to pursue my goals. Is my period of productivity, creativity, and accomplishment over? Perhaps this is a common question for those of us gaining in years. The Inn Crowd fights this tendency with their mantra—"We will never be boring or bored, and we will never act our age." The ladies of Wayfarers Inn remind me that it's never too late to embrace life.

As I ponder this, I'm also reminded that another anniversary is coming up in a few weeks—the anniversary of a death and rebirth event I suffered eight years ago when my heart stopped. As you can imagine, my sudden cardiac arrest stalled all my plans for that year. I realized then, and I try to remind myself every day, that my goals are in God's hands.

Like LuAnn, Tess, and Janice, it's not too late for any of us. As long as our hearts beat, we can serve. And each passing year only brings more productivity—sometimes not in ways we planned but always in ways directed by our Father who loves us.

God bless,
Ocieanna Fleiss

About the Author

Ocieanna Fleiss's passion is sharing God's truth through fiction. She has authored several novels. However, she veered from her novel-writing path briefly, when a cardiac arrest interrupted her plans. *Love Like There's No Tomorrow* is the story of her death-to-life experience and how it changed her life. She also enjoys speaking at churches, parenting groups, and writers conferences and especially teaching a Bible class to homeschooled junior high students. She's been featured on several local television and radio stations as well as in *US News and World Report.* Ocieanna makes her home in Seattle, Washington, with her husband and four kids, where they enjoy hiking, swimming, and reading good books on the many rainy days. Connect with Ocieanna at ocieanna.com.

The Turtle

Many are familiar with the *Turtle,* the small ball-shaped submarine used in the American War of Independence. The *Turtle* was a one-man vessel, powered by the pilot's leg muscles—not unlike a bicycle. Its goal was to come alongside an enemy ship and drill holes in its hull, causing it to sink. Although the *Turtle* never succeeded militarily, it set the groundwork for future submarines—including ones developed in the Civil War.

No evidence exists that a submarine ever cruised the Ohio river during the Civil War (that part is fiction), but we know at least one submarine actually sunk a ship. That sub was nicknamed "Fish Boat," "Fish Torpedo Boat," and "Porpoise," but was officially known as the *W. L. Hunley.* It was forty feet long, just the right size for an eight-man crew—seven to pedal and one to steer. It was built privately by its namesake and then commandeered by the Confederate Navy.

The navy hired Hunley to continue his work on the sub, which turned out to be his downfall. The *Hunley* sank three times. The first was on a test run. Five crew members died, but the navy raised the *Hunley* and refurbished it. The next time, Mr. Hunley himself was aboard. Sadly, it sunk again, and Mr. Hunley, along with the entire crew, drowned. Yet again, the navy raised it. This time they decided to employ it against a Union ship. The *Hunley* successfully sank the ship, but something malfunctioned and the sub never emerged. It was lost for over 150 years until in 1995 the wreckage of the *Hunley* was finally discovered. In 2000 it was raised and has been the object of study ever since. You can visit it at the Historic Hunley Submarine and Interactive Museum in South Carolina.

So even though a submarine probably did not glide through the murky depths of the Ohio River during the Civil War, we can enjoy imagining that one could have been employed... and sunk.

Unfortunately, no gold coins were found in the *Hunley*'s remains.

Something Delicious from our Wayfarers Inn Friends

Tess's Chicken Divan

Ingredients

- 3 cups fresh, chopped broccoli or one 16 oz package frozen, chopped broccoli
- 4 cups cooked, chopped chicken
- 1 can cream of chicken soup
- ½ cup mayonnaise
- ¾ cup grated parmesan cheese, divided
- ¼ cup lemon juice
- 1 tablespoon curry powder
- 2 teaspoons garlic powder
- Buttered egg noodles

Directions

Spray a 13×9×2-inch casserole dish with cooking spray. Spread broccoli over bottom of dish. Mix chicken, soup, mayonnaise, ½ cup parmesan cheese, lemon juice, curry, and garlic powder in medium bowl. Spread chicken mixture over broccoli. Sprinkle remaining parmesan cheese over the top. Bake covered in preheated 350-degree oven for 40 minutes. Serve over buttered egg noodles.

Read on for a sneak peek of another exciting book
in the Secrets of Wayfarers Inn series!

Hushed October
by Becky Melby

"Too tight." Tess Wallace's strangled whisper matched the reddening of her face reflected in her antique vanity mirror.

Janice Eastman, one of her two best friends and business partners, tugged at the back of the vintage-styled dress. "Only one more button. Suck in."

"I am." Tess could only mouth the words as Janice forced the last button through its hole.

"There." Janice fingered a pagoda sleeve on the rust, brown, and sage-green plaid dress. "Perfect colors for your hair." She picked up the hairpiece Tess would pin to the back of her head to give the illusion of an 1850s hairstyle—long tresses braided and twisted into a bun. The swirl of faux hair glinted copper in a shaft of morning sun streaming through the fourth-floor window. "You'll look positively Scarlett O'Hara-ish."

"A sixty-four-year-old Scarlett would have gotten over herself and wouldn't be vain enough to wear something she couldn't breathe in." Tess gripped the side of her dresser. "Unbutton it before I pass out."

Thankfully, the tiny pearl buttons slid out much easier than they'd slid in. "I could let it out a bit," Janice said, but Tess heard the doubt in her voice. Tess had already checked the seams. Not much extra fabric for "letting out."

When she was finally set free, Tess gasped, "No more cinnamon rolls." She collapsed on the bed. "I have to drop a couple of pounds before the Heritage Tour."

"We can do that if we really put our minds to it."

"We?"

Janice nodded as she patted the space just above her waist. "Unless I want to spend the day strapped into a corset, I have to lose an inch or two." They'd ordered the dresses from an online seamstress two months ago, not taking into consideration the allure of the goodies produced by Wayfarers Inn Bed & Breakfast and Soup Café's extraordinary cook, Winnie Washington. Including the big-as-a-man's-hand pumpkin cinnamon roll Tess had devoured a few minutes ago.

"Bet LuAnn's dress fits perfect." Tess didn't bother disguising her envy. The third member of the Inn Crowd, as the owners of Wayfarers Inn called themselves, had been blessed with a naturally trim figure. Well, to be fair, LuAnn Sherill possessed something else neither Janice nor Tess excelled at when it came to healthy living...self-discipline.

"It probably does. And speaking of bet, wanna make one?"

Tess sat up. Holding the bodice of the plaid dress to her chest, she fanned her face with her other hand. "Why, Miz Eastman, what are you proposin'?" She gave her best Scarlett impression. "Fine-bred Christian ladies do not bet."

Janice feigned a look of remorse. "A contest then. Nothin' wrong with a little friendly competition. We agree on a goal, then whoever doesn't make it has to donate to the Moore House fund."

"I like it." Tess stood and scooped up her much more comfortable twenty-first century outfit—non-skinny jeans and a sweater with a pumpkin embroidered on the front. "How much?"

"It has to be painful enough to motivate us. How about—"

LuAnn's entrance interrupted whatever Janice was about to suggest.

"Are you guys talking about me again?" LuAnn tucked sleek silver hair behind one ear. Without waiting for an answer to her question, she beckoned with one hand toward the door that led to the hallway of their fourth-floor living quarters. "Come downstairs. Elliott wants to show us what he found out back."

"Elliott…the metal detecting guy?" Tess asked. Five new guests had checked in this morning, and she hadn't had time to attach names to faces yet.

"Yep." LuAnn smiled. "You'll be proud of me. I restrained my history-loving self and said I couldn't look at any of it until you two are there." She took a step back and pivoted. "So you'd better hurry."

Janice followed LuAnn, leaving Tess alone to get dressed. As she ran fingers through her short spikey hair, she scanned a row of framed pictures hanging above her dresser. There were six of them, and they formed a timeline of the phases of her life. The first was taken when she was nine, on a weekend getaway with her parents the day Cedar Point amusement park opened Blue Streak, a seventy-eight-foot roller coaster. Next, a wedding picture of her and Jeffrey standing on the church steps, oblivious to anyone in the world but each other. Number three was taken the day they adopted Lizzie. Five-year-old Jeff, Jr. sat in the middle, grinning as he held his new baby sister. The next picture of her and Jeffrey alone never failed to tug at her heartstrings. Their re-honeymoon trip, he'd called it. California redwoods formed the backdrop. She leaned on his shoulder, his head rested on hers. Two years later a stroke took his life.

She'd thought, for a while, there would be no more smiling photographs, but the next two pictures were proof her joy had dimmed but not disappeared. One showed Tess with three giggly toddlers on her lap. *Three.* The thought still shocked her at times. She remembered the day Lizzie and Michael arrived at her house after the ultrasound. "Three, Mom. *Three*," Lizzie had stammered over and over. Henry, Harper, and Liam had turned four in April. The last picture was only a few months old. Tess and LuAnn and Janice standing on the stairway, proud new owners of Wayfarers Inn. "Thank You, Lord," Tess whispered as she shut the door to her apartment then descended three flights of stairs to the café where LuAnn and Janice waited with Elliott MacIntosh.

It only took a moment for Tess to catalog Elliott as one of the inn's most colorful visitors to date. Larger than life in more ways than one. The many-pocketed Scotch-plaid vest he wore with equally pocketed cargo pants broke all the rules of clothing that camouflages an ample waistline. With a swoop of his arm, Elliott gestured toward a white cloth that covered one of the square tables. "Are you ready for the reveal, ladies?" Bushy red-streaked-with-white eyebrows wiggled, independent of each other.

Tess pointed at the drab-green zippered pouch Elliott held. "Tell me you found something that will pay off our mortgage."

"Sadly, no. But I guarantee you will be richer in historical knowledge." He winked, then gave a jovial laugh, his belly jiggling like a Scotch-plaid Santa. He pulled out a rectangular object about two inches wide. "I'm guessing this belt buckle is Civil War era."

LuAnn gushed over the piece of tarnished metal. Having taught history for more than three decades, she had a genuine passion for rusty artifacts. Tess tried to appear interested but couldn't hide her disappointment as Elliott pulled out two wheat pennies, a suspender clasp, and a bent-up lamp sconce.

"And now"—Elliott tapped out a drum roll on the table—"the *pièce de résistance*." He reached into his bag. "This Art Deco piece is from the early twentieth century. You could probably get a hundred and fifty dollars for it, but I'm guessing you'll want it right over there on your front desk." Slowly, he pulled his hand out, then carefully set something on the palm of his other hand, revealing a reception desk bell with a decorative brass base and "Wayfarers Inn" etched in the brass dome.

"Whoa..." Janice and LuAnn echoed each other, and Tess found herself mouthing the same word. They gave Elliott the honor of placing it on the front desk. The ornately carved desk had once been used as a bar and had sat below the massive mirror that still hung at the back of the café.

"The inn used to be called the Riverfront House," LuAnn said. "It was renamed Wayfarers Inn around the time of World War I."

Elliott lightly tapped the bell. "Maybe this was a grand reopening gift."

"Maybe..." LuAnn looked thoughtful, and Tess knew she was daydreaming back to a time when Woodrow Wilson was president and women's hemlines crept daringly above the ankle.

"Where to next?" Elliott looked at Tess. "I'm here on business, but I'm setting my own schedule. Today, I've got all the time in Ohio." He laughed. "Do you know anyone who wouldn't mind me detecting on their property? I'm meticulous about covering my tracks, and anything I find goes to the property owner. All I want is pictures and the right to share my finds online. Not in this to get rich...except in historical knowledge." He winked again, at no one in particular.

Tess glanced at the clock. "I need to be at our booth at the farmers market in about an hour. If we leave right away I can take you to the Moore House site." She looked to LuAnn and Janice for confirmation. The sparkle in two pairs of eyes was all she needed to continue. "We found a journal belonging to a woman who once worked here at the inn back in the 1800s and was also a conductor on the Underground Railroad. The tract of land along the Muskingum River where she and her family lived belongs to the city, and the city council recently sold an acre of it to a foster family. The father is a paraplegic, and they want to take in children with disabilities. They broke ground last week and found what they assume is part of a foundation wall for a barn. I'm pretty sure Jerry Moore will be there this morning."

"Perfect!" Elliott gave a three-finger salute. "Yesterday's rain made the ground just right for digging. Lead the way!"

A Note from the Editors

We hope you enjoy Secrets of Wayfarers Inn, created by the Books and Inspirational Media Division of Guideposts, a nonprofit organization that touches millions of lives every day through products and services that inspire, encourage, help you grow in your faith, and celebrate God's love in every aspect of your daily life.

Thank you for making a difference with your purchase of this book, which helps fund our many outreach programs to military personnel, prisons, hospitals, nursing homes, and educational institutions. To learn more, visit Guideposts Foundation.org.

We also maintain many useful and uplifting online resources. Visit Guideposts.org to read true stories of hope and inspiration, access OurPrayer network, sign up for free newsletters, download free e-books, join our Facebook community, and follow our stimulating blogs.

To learn about other Guideposts publications, including the best-selling devotional *Daily Guideposts*, go to ShopGuideposts .org, call (800) 932-2145, or write to Guideposts, PO Box 5815, Harlan, Iowa 51593.